Isabelle the Navigator

"Isabelle Airly is a triumph of Davies' poetic imagination...prose that tempts you to laugh and cry at the same time, but has you gasping with delight instead."
—*The Age*

"...a stunningly beautiful narrative."
—*The Bulletin*

Totem

"Davies is unquestionably our greatest love poet ever; anyone who cares about verse cannot afford to ignore him."
—*The Age*

"Terrific, sustained, ebullient and buoyant...I think 'Totem Poem' will come to be recognized along with Slessor's 'Five Bells' as the great Australian long poem, and one of those rare poems that praise and celebrate..."
—Judith Beveridge

Interferon Psalms

"It is a brave and bracing book and everyone should read it."
—Peter Craven, *The Australian*

"A tour-de-force...Davies doesn't so much write his psalms as pray them."
—*The Conversation*

GOD OF SPEED

Luke Davies

A Novel

A Barnacle Book | Rare Bird Books
Los Angeles, Calif.

A Barnacle Book | Rare Bird Books
453 South Spring Street, Suite 531
Los Angeles, CA 90013
abarnaclebook.com
rarebirdbooks.com

Printed in Canada
Set in Goudy Old Style
Distributed in the US by Publishers Group West

Publisher's Cataloging-in-Publication data

Davies, Luke, 1962-
    God of speed : a novel / by Luke Davies.
    p. cm.
    ISBN 978-1-940207-27-8
    Includes bibliographical references.

1. Hughes, Howard, 1905-1976—Fiction. 2. Billionaires—United
States—Fiction. 3. Drug addiction—Fiction. 4. Obsessive-compulsive
disorder—Fiction. 5. Airplanes—Fiction. I. Title.

PR9619.3.D29 G69 2014
823/.914—dc23

Also by Luke Davies

Poetry

Four Plots For Magnets
Absolute Event Horizon
Running With Light
The Entire History of Architecture...and other love poems
Totem
Feral Aphorisms
Interferon Psalms

Novels

Candy
Isabelle the Navigator

INN ON THE PARK
LONDON, JUNE 9, 1973

. . . EVENING . . .

THE EMPIRE OF MY BED

FUCKING, AND FLYING, WERE the best, the most solid, of all the things I did.

It's been so many years. I have lost track of almost everything.

But fucking and flying: I was like a god. There were sparks coming off me.

I will fly again. And very soon. It is cleaner than fucking and involves less people.

It is time to branch out, or else what would I say to myself: that in the end I did nothing?

I've called Jack Real to London, a fighter ace, a Lockheed man. In the fifties we flew together, talked endlessly of airplanes. It is always good to find someone as obsessed with aviation as oneself. But my trusted servants, my clean, reliable men the Mormons, don't care for him. They see him as an intrusion into our "situation." He says, Howard, you can regain some control over your life. I believe him.

He is sleeping one floor below. He is a little tired from the flight, Los Angeles to New York and across the Atlantic here to London, my new tax-exempt home. When he wakes there is so much I have to tell him. What I had. Where it all went; time, most of all. I have seen no one but the Mormons for more than a decade. But Jack Real was like a friend.

I have been reading once again, and with great pleasure, all the aviation magazines. Airplanes are so extraordinarily improbable. I am enamored all over again, of horsepower and wingspan, pitch and roll and yaw rate, thrust and range and endurance and ceiling, maximum payload, manifold pressure, density altitude, glide-path angle. And so much circuitry holding it all together! There's been so much advancement this decade and a half. What a glory of sleekness was this war in Vietnam, and how lovely, how exquisite is industry, from the simplest turning of the lathe to the most gargantuan of turbines.

From a distance, from a great height, the whole damned country hums.

What will I say to Jack when he wakes? I've been incommunicado for too long. I talk too much inside my head. Sometimes I forget whether I spoke it or thought it. It will be good to get the words out. It will be good to talk, long hours of talk, something a little more complex than the Mormon instructions, bark bark bark, solid men but we don't, we don't, we don't...hit it off. At that level. Jack Real, on the other hand.

On the phone last week we were tossing up, Jack and I, between the Hawker Siddeley 748, a beautiful turboprop, and the new De Havilland 125. All the information at hand, spread before me on the empire of my bed. Color photography—now there's something else, how lovely, how exquisite, what a glory of sleekness. Even the printing; even the smell of the brochures.

On the phone I said, Jack, I'm excited.

He said, Howard, it will be wonderful to see you again.

We are old men now. This afternoon he sat by the bed and drank a scotch on the rocks. I broke with habit; instead of bottled water at room temperature, I ordered from the Mormons an iced lemonade. Lash out, I thought. It disturbed me, the way the droplets of condensation beaded and pooled on the bedside table as we sat and talked. But not so much that I did anything about it. His very presence was a liberation!

The Mormons are very stiff with Jack. I winked at him: let them be. If they had it their way, I'd never move from this bed. A while back, we were in Vancouver, before the tax deadline ran out, and I tried to open the blinds. They thought I'd gone mad, but I just wanted to see the sky.

We all ready for the morning then? he said, late this afternoon.

You bet your bottom dollar we are, I said.

The bottom dollar. What a funny concept!

He drained the scotch and swirled the ice. I knew I would have to let him go to bed. He was almost nodding off in his chair.

Any time you wake, I'll be awake, I said. I've given the men instructions to let you in.

I'll keep it in mind, he said. And if not, I'll see you in the morning.

Bright and early. We've an awful lot of catching up to do.

Of course we do. And I look forward to it.

When he left I felt a bursting sensation, simply too much anticipation. I slid open the bedside drawer, took out my medicine tin—a bright red cross on its lid, always easy to recognize—and prepared an injection, to slow down the pressure, to separate the concepts.

The ritual of it all. So bare, so methodical, so unadorned. The pulling back of the plunger, the spurt of blood into the liquid, the plunge forward, the meticulous control of the fingers, the withdrawal, the dabbing of the droplet, the flushing of the syringe in the glass of water. Once long ago, in the production hangar at the Culver City plant, I could pull apart a carburetor so effortlessly, in my business suit, with my sleeves rolled up, just one of the team. I could talk with the men. Some point or other I was trying to make. The noise of industry all around me, but my focus so pure, each task laid out. To be so absolutely present, so undistracted. So I slow down the pressure and separate the concepts, and find a vein.

It is so very good to breathe.

Eventually I drift to sleep. I call it sleep. My dreams are of the sky, a blinding blue, and the towering cumulus I could never locate for the aerial shots in *Hell's Angels*. Without clouds the viewer has no sense of the movement of an aircraft: the shots remain static, the plane seems motionless.

In dreams, too, a clear blue sky devoid of clouds can mean only death. Once I was obsessed with numbers and statistics. Once I knew the average weight of all the clouds around the world in all the skies at any given time. (Sixteen million tons.) Then for a long time I knew nothing.

Technology. Now there's another thing.

It will be nice, with Jack, the number of times we will get to begin with, remember. Remember when. Remember this. Because I don't talk to the Mormons like that. Jack Real, on the other hand. Did I say that already?

I

...as if everything in America had wings...
—Berryman, *The Dream Songs*

I WAS NO FRED Astaire, but on July 9, 1938, the night before I took off to fly all the way around the globe, I danced with Katharine Hepburn at the Starlight Roof of the Waldorf-Astoria. So there's seven or eight minutes of my life accounted for already. No Fred Astaire, and she no Ginger Rogers, but I loved nothing more than the feeling of my hand placed flat on the smooth skin between her shoulder blades as we ebbed and flowed among the other dancers. The utter simplicity of it, the peace I felt. I had the sense that my hand itself, rather than my mind, was soaking up a memory and storing it away for future use. That turns out in a way to be the case, for it is the coolness of her skin that I am remembering now. I have, of course, other memories of more intimate parts of her than that smooth cleft of back between two shoulder straps, but just at that moment, on that glamorous and distant night, the delicate pressure of my fingertips on her skin was what it meant to be a couple. It seemed that my future was contained there in my present.

Now, thirty-five years later—and on the night before another significant flight, God bless us both, Jack—my mind goes back to that time when my limbs were more supple. It would do us not one whit of good to be able to predict the future, for nothing turned out the way I expected, and yet here I am, my bruises and scars intact.

Kate would be an old woman now. I was never one for old women, so I don't imagine we would have gotten this far together, not with all the will in the world. That is irrelevant to the specifics of 1938, when it was entirely sufficient to believe in the eternal. Her perfume was like a promise of the oasis that lay ahead of us that night. We were out and about in the admiring crowd. The next day I'd be flying off to glory.

Tomorrow, a more private kind of glory. No one here with whom to share it, no one but the unperfumed Mormons, or Jack Real, for whom I have much affection, but whose bare back I would not wish to touch. But I am dealing with my circumstances. And trying, at last, of course, to move beyond them.

We spoke of so much, in bed the next morning, July 10, 1938, the sky so blue through the hotel window. How extraordinarily beautiful was Kate, even stripped of all make-up, even emerging bleary-eyed from her Howard-entangled sleep. I had never seen a greenness so transparent: it was as if the light reflecting off her irises illuminated the faint freckles on her nose. I thought she was in love with me. The very idea seems preposterous now.

I'll miss you, Kate, I said.

She smiled and kissed me on the forehead. You be safe up there. I want you to be safe. And warm!

Yes, yes, I laughed. I've packed your scarf.

And I want you to contact me...any which way. Telephone from Timbuktu. Cablegram from Cairo.

I'll find a way, I said.

And do come back in one piece. Because I don't want to be picking up the pieces.

What it meant to be a couple: it was like being *breathed* upon. It meant that later in the day, among the thousands of well-wishers seeing me off from Floyd Bennett Field, it was Kate, at home in Connecticut by then, who was more present to me than anyone else. It meant that she was with me as I flew, because I knew that all was right with us, and that I would be flying in a vast circle just to see her again.

I stood proudly by my plane, the so eloquently named *New York World's Fair, 1939*. The press asked me many questions. It is nonsense, the idea of "news," Jack. But oh, to be a hero.

VERY MANAGEABLE CONTROLS

I KNOW I AM awake because my head is nodding rhythmically; I am agreeing with all the wondrous notions that have ever been put to me or are slowly dawning on me or will one day arrive. Another way of putting this is that here I am, merrily merrily merrily merrily, in the heartfelt embrace of inert splendor.

It is so very good to breathe. Unhindered by the obstacles. A Mormon brings a glass of water and holds it to my lips. I take the glass and drink, a great gulp. Then a second. I place the glass on the bedside table while he packs away the medicine tin. The red cross will now disappear from view for a while.

I sit up for some time in the half-dark, in the silence, listening to the universe vibrate. I hope I can find it within me to tell Jack everything that happened.

It certainly may be possible. And tomorrow we will fly.

But I shouldn't be getting ahead of myself. It's Saturday night, not Sunday morning. A long while yet before I'm sitting in the cockpit. I need to come back to where I am, so as not to get too excited or confused.

To where this single bedside lamp illuminates the entire room. Heavy drapes, taped tight over the windows, block out all possibility of exterior light entering. But even in the gloom I can see just what a stylish suite it is. Abundance of space. An antique desk, unused on the far side of the room. Framed prints of fox-hunting scenes on the walls. I think it is foxes, it is hard to make out from here. On the far side of this bed, along the wall, a bank of file boxes, ten wide and five high, neatly stacked and labeled by date: my memos, which come with me wherever I go. Perhaps I will show Jack my memos. Some, at any rate. Wouldn't want to drown the man. Enough so that he gets an idea of just how much I have to deal with.

I'm trying my best to imagine how a newcomer might see me. I am naked as always, propped up on pillows, beneath a single white sheet. No doubt my eyes are sunk deep in the shadow cast by the lamp, but that is just the way lamps are. Perhaps, yes, my body is like a gnarled twig on this grand expanse of bed, the sheet barely altering in its undulations as it flows across my unassuming thighs, my bare muscleless arms covered with scarring, the scars following the blue translucent veins beneath this lamp-white skin. Perhaps. But it is all irrelevant.

I know I've lost some weight in fifteen years. I know I'm a little unkempt. Really nothing that a haircut and a touch of sunlight wouldn't fix. Well, I'm getting there! I will have to explain to Jack that the medicine situation is not half as bad as it looks to one inexperienced in the ways of syringes. I'm not going to hide it from him, of course, or send him out from the room each time. He's a decorated war hero, for God's sake, and he didn't get those medals for being squeamish.

No, all that will look after itself. I must simply begin to remember the things I have to talk about. Beyond that I have no cause for anxiety. Let me see. I will have to thank him for helping get my pilot's license renewal rushed through from the States. There's something nice and practical: a little thank you.

I will have to get it all in sequence, everything I'm going to tell him. I'm searching for a starting point but my mind keeps jumping forward; I can't stop thinking about tomorrow. The Hawker Siddeley is an elegant plane with very manageable controls. Nothing too much for an old man, I said, earlier. (Jack put himself in this category, too!)

But that was earlier. Where was I just now?

I was thinking about Katie, her elegant shoulders, her grand green eyes, about the morning of my departure from Floyd Bennett Field, and the lost, lamented luxury of waking in the arms of a lover. But I have the feeling that would be skipping forward somewhat, and no way at all to give Jack the picture. I need to go back, while I'm lying here smoothly, while the obstacles are not in a hindering mood, I need to go back to the beginning.

The maid is in the kitchen, where the oat-and-molasses cookies bake. I'm way out the back, over the hedge, among the butterflies.

It is summer in Texas. I am everything there is.

In the soft soil of the morning glory patch I am lying with my tin toys mottled by the sun and the swaying of the leaves. I am outside myself with happiness. I'm drifting in the shadows of my glade, beyond my locked-awayness. Here I can see how the sun exposes everything; fifteen feet away I can see the butterflies hovering over the dandelions. Not anybody in the world knows I am here. Further away there's the house, then there's Houston, then the whole of Texas, then other parts of the world. I've seen them in my atlas.

Mother said Father would be home soon. But Father loved to be away, all those years of building the business. (What Mother loved was to sniff his collars for distant traces of perfume. She could smell a perfume molecule at a hundred yards.) I, too, longed to be away, though mostly I had to fight to be alone, even out the back among the butterflies.

Because eventually dusk would come. And with it the bath-time rituals, the pleasure peppered with anxiety, the rough shock of the towel-drying, the running of her fingers through my hair. And every night, for as long as I can remember, the inspecting of the testicles. I would stand, dry now, still pink and warm from the bath. She would bend down, lean in close, and take each testicle gently, one at a time, in her delicate fingers, looking for telltale lumps. She would take her time, her head tilted, like a doctor with a stethoscope, and very gently, almost imperceptibly, prod and massage those tiny globes. Then she would pat me down with talc and help me into my pajamas.

Oh, how diligent she was. She viewed my stool before I flushed. Or no, perhaps I won't tell Jack that part. We'll see what happens. Perhaps I will.

Also, sometimes it is very pleasant to mix up two hundred milligrams of Valium and Librium in a single shot. Then you blend softness with stamina, and distance is immense, and it is easier to think comfortably.

Father says, Sonny, what are you reading there?

I'm looking, Papa, I say. I'm looking at the world.

Where was I, Jack? This was last week, I mean the week before the butterflies. In the parlor with the atlas, such blueprints of promise, and every page a world.

AIRPLANES IN HEAVEN

THEN EVERYTHING STARTED TO fly. I have been trying to catch my breath ever since. I have attempted to remain steadfast, for the most part, in the face of both glory and catastrophe.

My first accident was with Dudley when our billy-cart flipped down the steep drive at the end of the street. I had imagined, sitting on that wooden tray, holding tight to the leather reins while Dudley held tight around my waist, only rapid acceleration and the possibility of rising up on two wheels as we turned hard onto the road, hollering with joy. I had imagined that the propulsion afforded by the steepness of the driveway might last us several streets. (I was only seven years old.) I had not imagined the terror of our ignominious end, of our becoming unintentionally airborne as our bodies continued blithely on their way when the billy-cart overturned. I ran home crying to Mother, in need of her comfort and at the same time terrified of trouble.

I don't know if speed was the desire for danger or if already I simply needed to slip from my mother's embrace; what's clear is that she liked the air very still and the curtains drawn, while I liked the wind in my hair and no curtains at all. Sixty years later, of course, I worry that I've become my mother, on that score at least. Except that I'd have no interest in picking the gravel from a small boy's bloodied knees, God bless her anxious heart.

At twelve I invented a motorized bicycle by welding to the frame a two-cylinder Triton motor, connecting the drive shaft to the chain, and removing the pedals. They put my photo in the Houston paper. See, I had broken the bonds of childhood already. Danger or no, what I wanted was speed. When the tiny Triton built up revs, I flew. At times I was so excited it was an effort to remember to breathe. On Yoakum Boulevard the whole bike shuddered the faster I took it and my wrist muscles quivered as I wrestled the handlebars, and suddenly I gasped and heaved for air. The idea of a boundary should in no small way have been comforting but it was always seamlessness that interested me. I could hallucinate myself into wind.

It all made it hard to relate to the other children. There was so little one had in common. But Dudley was my friend at least, and I thought he would be forever.

At Camp Teedyuskung, by the fire. Away from Mother, the world was in fact not as menacing as one had been led to believe. The Pocono Mountains all around you, a glorious dark presence. You burst with such love for Dudley...how the hell to express it? There is so much fear that goes unnamed. When the night owl hoots and the embers crackle and the songs die down, there is a sleep down deep beneath the blood. You wake up smiling so broadly from that kind! You know you'll never get to where you've just been, except in such exhausted sleep again, and none of it matters, no knowledge, no body, not the passage of life itself, since the fact alone of it has been so exquisite.

Do you think there'll be airplanes in heaven, Jack? Should I ask him a question like that?

These days I drift more and more, even hours after an injection. I wonder, in fact, could I give it up? It would surprise them all. On the other hand, I could inject an Empirin and think about it for a while. Since every act is merely a rearrangement of all the other acts that have gone before and will come after, then whether I continue or give up would amount, in effect, to the same event. And also, I'm an old man now. My vertebrae are fused. There's not a great deal left, of bravery. Because we were brave boys, back then. We were Teedyuskung Braves. Oh for that war whoop now, the tremulous terror of fleeing, the hysteria of games, the softness of Pennsylvania in summer, where the swallows reeled with pleasure.

At Dan Beard's Outdoor School at Camp Teedyuskung I swam one summer's day in a creek whose water was at first so cold my balls ached and my scrotum was tight with contracted pores. We swung out from a rope hanging from a tree branch and dropped like pencils into the murky brown. Later this would be called a Tarzan rope because the century— and I helped create it—would open itself to cinema like a woman on her wedding night. But in 1917 we called it a tree swing. Dudley lay on a boulder, soaking up its radiant heat. I floated in the shallow water in a shaft of sunlight, sifting my fingers through the mud by the shore. The reeds seemed far away. The current bent the stalks. Low to the water, a dragonfly plotted out the odd angularities of its course like a draftsman charting constellations. The dark water was a bowl of night. A horsefly bit me on the shoulder; I wrote proudly of the welt to Mother.

Who one week later yanked me from the camp. I was devastated. There was only one week to go before I received my Buckskin Man badge. I could pitch a tent. I had mastered the canoe. I knew all the knots. I could start a fire without matches. I *had cooked my own bacon and flapjacks.*

For five weeks at Camp Teedyuskung I had become friendly with the world and all its forces, and now Mother came to take it all away. It wasn't because of the welt after all; she'd heard of the polio sweeping across the land. I cried and cried in the back seat of the car. The windows were so high and far away. Misery in the leather. You'll see Dudley soon enough back home, she cooed, missing the point entirely.

You don't understand. Mother, you don't understand. He will be a Buckskin Man and I'll still be a Boy. He will have the badge and I will not.

I had something. I had something going. It was mine. We called it Scoutcraft. I knew the names of all the birds.

I KNEW THE NAMES OF ALL THE BIRDS

I KNEW SO MANY things, Jack. And for so long. And now? I can barely keep it all straight. Which thing came first? Since there's no first on a circle. Only the ecstasy, before it all starts to go too fast. Scoutcraft? Carole Lombard knew how to build a mean fire. She arrived one summer afternoon in 1940, disguised, riding a motorcycle, and took me away. Twelve years earlier we'd had a brief affair after she had auditioned for *Hell's Angels*. I was not one for revisiting situations, but Carole made everything easy, and I never felt she wanted anything in return. She yelled up at me from the street; preoccupied with a script, I was taken by surprise. I looked out the window. A red scarf bunched around her neck and chin, its tails flung behind her. Her hair trailed out from the sides of an open helmet. I could barely recognize her behind the aviator's goggles she wore—goggles which, in fact, I had given her—but I had no trouble recognizing her husky strong voice.

Howard! Howard!

I walked out to the porch.

Come for a ride!

I did not feel comfortable entrusting myself to a woman, but she handled the machine (an Indian) superbly. I leaned into the corners and held her around the waist, though I can't say I could feel the contours of her belly beneath the bulk of her leather jacket.

The glorious mess that she called her bedroom was huge, and hung with silks. The bed itself seemed enormous, too; colored draperies of gauze and chiffon were nailed to the beams on the ceiling and I felt I had entered a harem girl's retreat. She flung her clothes off. The goggles left pressure lines in a wide horizontal eight around her eyes, the sign of infinity. I had only taken my shoes off. I was always embarrassed by my body—the damned length of the thing, its obstinate elongatedness—and never entirely comfortable with being naked in daylight, diaphanous hangings or a long, handsome cock notwithstanding. She climbed onto the bed beside me and dragged off my trousers. She took me in her mouth. I swept her hair aside and watched. She looked like a raccoon, with her white eye patches. The absurdity of Carole Lombard carrying on her face the mathematical symbol for infinity, of its moving backwards and forwards in a narrow field of depth in front of my pelvis as she bobbed on my prick, in-out, in-out, was made all the more poignant in that moment of understanding that Carole was no more infinite than any of us.

Symbols notwithstanding.

Afterwards I dozed or caught my breath and she left the room for a short while. Soon she came back, leaned in across the bed, took my hand and said, Come. She dragged me across the cool stone floors and out across the back patio. She lived in a hacienda with a deep high-walled backyard that afforded complete privacy. The disheveled verdure and spillage of jasmine and vines down the side walls suggested that one might be in a decaying Bolivian estate seventy years earlier. In the center of the yard stood a bathtub, claw-footed and apparently unconnected to any plumbing. Beneath it was a small fire. By now it was dusk and a pink sky streaked with blue-tinged clouds curved above us, emptying its celestial beneficence over all of Hollywood. The fire was neat and well constructed and reminded me of those I had been taught to build at Camp Teedyuskung.

Naked, her breasts jangling slightly, Carole dragged a garden hose over to the bathtub and started topping it up. I leaned smiling against a pillar. Venus with hose.

You hold this, she motioned. I'll do the fire.

The water gurgled into the tub. Carole moved onto the patio and leaned down to a soda crate full of kindling twigs. All my attention focused on the curve of her buttocks and the way the dark swathe of her sex was like an irresistible shadow—one was powerless but to be drawn to it, to fall toward it like a parachutist, like a magnetized ion—where the lines at the center of the W met. When she stood up I imagined slipping my hand between her legs, at that point of join, and my fingers into that dark hot wet web of space.

She walked back to me now with her small bundle nestled in her arms. Twigs made tiny dimples on her breasts. She crouched down and tended to the fire. She looked up and flicked my testicles, gently, languidly, as if to test their specific gravity.

You look nice from down here.

I flinched and involuntarily covered myself with my hands.

Get in, she said.

We lowered ourselves into the water.

It's a little cold, I said.

The fire will warm it, she said. It'll only get better.

Indeed I could feel the warmth radiating through the enamel floor of the tub and into my buttocks. We sank into that water and looked at each other. She smiled and blew a spluttering of bubbles, like the wake from a propeller. My nose and ears rested just above the water line. Far below me, like the distant pops of redwoods exploding in a forest fire, twigs crackled as they burned.

Carole Lombard's backyard was the cornucopia and Lombard naked in it the very Flesh of the Fruit. There is a certain time of year when the jacaranda blooms. Then when dusk descends and colors are leached from the atmosphere, the final color that remains in any given backyard is that astonishing mauve, the jacaranda's resistance to annihilation. But in the bathtub that dusk, it was the blue of Carole Lombard's eyes that held fast against the coming of the night.

In the end her features fuzzed; her eyes were a darker darkness than her face. But until our backsides got too hot it was a lush long time of drifting.

STATISTICS ARE VERY HELPFUL

OUT IN THE WORKSHOP that Father had had built for me, I put together my own wireless, a Zeigler crystal set. I was a member of the Radio Relay League, and I communicated with the other operators around the world. Jack, I spent happy years out there as an eleven-, twelve-, and thirteen-year-old; the whole of Houston, surrounding me, was sweet; the very air was sweet. You organize everything inside your head, you track it and chart it. Statistics are very helpful. Tables and graphs make a lot of sense. You begin to see patterns emerging.

All I ever wanted was to be elsewhere. Or at least connected to it. I taught myself morse code. It was easy to stay home from school. It wasn't as if I had to plead. The mere mention of a fever or a cough was sufficient for Mother to close the blinds and puff up the pillows and stroke my brow. So I lay in bed all day and read the manual, my pulse racing with anticipation. From the dits and dahs of Continuous Wave Transmission a whole language grew, a binary deliciousness, complexity beyond imagining.

There are ships in the Gulf of Mexico, great steel vessels plowing through the night. When the house lay asleep I crept down the stairs and out the back to the workshop. Lost inside my headphones, I would sit for hours and listen to the world come in, pulsing through the darkness. At times I picked up signals so weak they might merely have been exotic distortions faintly registered in the ionosphere as the waves crossed the equator or bounced over the pole. I pounded the brass. There was lightning in my fingertips. I sent my thoughts back out the other way.

At the workbench I twisted the dial. Sounds looped into that hollow space as if from another reality. I felt that every other boy in Houston was fast asleep, while I was exploring not only the cosmos but the beaker in which it was fused. I talked to ships from Ecuador and France. My name is Howard Hughes. I am eleven years old. I live on Yoakum Boulevard in Houston. Where are you going? What are you carrying? How many crew?

It's funny how at night I could feel myself to be entirely weightless. But every morning I felt pressed in by the world of *things*. Little by little I wanted them: the workshop, the wireless, the best of all bicycles, everything shiny, everything full of heft. At some point the piston of desire smashed a jagged hole through the master cylinder, and I wound up wanting the entire world, the great tangle of it all.

I'm getting a little ahead of myself. Because first, in the workshop, we were all just communicating, and nobody owned a thing. We were so liquid. What is the opposite of that? Arthritic. Because now there is a power of arthritis in my life and the only reason I am kept from the worst of its excesses is that the medicine holds it all back. That eleven-year-old boy by the crystal set in the dark of night wanted nothing more than the great flood, forever and ever. Little Sonny Hughes. But at some point, things changed—at some point, catastrophe became a definite possibility. And then, for a long time, self-protection seemed to be everything. Because you have to be careful. And it was easier to number it all if you owned it all first.

Now, so many decades later, I like the flooding again, that sense of being liquid inside all this dryness, which is only *apparent* dryness, of course. The way Empirin glides, and flows. The way at times, after an injection, I could swear not that I am in but that I have in fact become a stream, rippling over the pebbles as I flow. Or the way Valium dulls the roaring of the sky, and makes the vultures pigeons.

HOW EACH THING FITS

IT DOESN'T TAKE FOCUS to be born into wealth. I'm the first to admit it. But it takes an awful lot of focus to turn a moderate fortune into vast billions. And I had it for as long as I can remember. At fourteen I convinced Father to buy me a brand new Stutz Bearcat, for the sole purpose of taking it apart, then putting it back together. That is a very big undertaking, but not too big for me. I had the garage space (an area around the car four times its own size) in the enormous workshop, and I had the will, the conviction, and the determination to understand how each thing fit. Out of fourteen thousand eight hundred and forty possible actions, possible paths wrongly chosen, I broke only a single object—a backseat latch I too roughly jiggled out. (I was still learning patience back then.)

A Bearcat, completely dismantled, completely revealed, spread out across the workshop floor, ready to be reassembled in reverse. Such left-right, up-down symmetry. Such meticulous attention to detail. Every bolt, every washer, every wing nut in its proper place and order.

It was easier to control it if you understood it. It was easier to understand it if you numbered it all first. Mother would call me in to dinner. I found even dinner an intrusion. I had to get the measure of the engine of the world.

Memo, 1958: No matter what

No matter how extreme the emergency, no matter how unusual the circumstances may be, no matter what may have arisen, it is extremely important to me that nobody ever goes into any room, closet, cabinet, drawer, bathroom or any other area used to store any of the things which are for me—either food, equipment, magazines, paper supplies, Kleenex—no matter what. It is equally important to me that nobody ever opens any door or opening to any room, cabinet or closet or anything used to store any of my things, even for one-thousandth of an inch, for one-thousandth of a second. I don't want the possibility of dust or insects or anything of that nature entering.

THE FERROUS ORIGINS OF DESIRE

I WOUND UP IN THE air, without a doubt. But it started in the earth. My daddy said there were many things under the ground, most of them good. After he patented his drill, he came up with the bright idea of never ever selling it. The drill could only ever be leased, one per well, all around the globe, at thirty thousand dollars per lease; when oil was struck the drill would be returned.

Years later, after the empire had passed on to me, a reporter asked, Mr. Hughes, is it true that the Hughes Drill Bit is a monopoly?

Of course not, I said. People who want to drill for oil and *not* use the Hughes Drill Bit can always use a pick and shovel.

Many things, most of them good. My daddy dropped out of Harvard, where everything was abstract, in 1893, and for ten years wandered the West, where all things were present, he said; albeit submerged. He mined silver in the mountains of Colorado, zinc in the wilds of Indian Territory, lead in southwestern Missouri. He struggled, until the drill bit, and even then he struggled some more. The final prototype, the one that was to make all the money, was not ready until 1908. The point was actually not what lay beneath; the point was the piercing, and the access. My father designed the best drill bit in the world. Does Jack know that? By 1912 there were forty thousand wells around the world, each one leasing a drill bit from Father.

He was like a sleeper, waking from a dream of light, to find, in fact, that light was everywhere.

What do you want? he whispered, a glint in his eye, reading me a bedtime story by electric lamp.

Dig for it, dig for it.

A DIFFERENT SORT OF PRESSURE IN THE GROIN

THEY GROW UP SO fast, Jack! I'm speaking about myself, of course. When I was fourteen, Father sent me to Fessenden School in Boston. The summer before, I had become very ill and thought I might die. I could not move from bed for many weeks. My parents paid for Dr. Chickering to move from New York and into our house in Houston. I did not like this cold, hard man. He tried to get me into a wheelchair and out of doors, for the fresh air. I merely wanted delirium in the bed by the window, overlooking the birch trees.

Eventually he told my father, in secret—that is to say, away from my mother—that I was suffering from hysterical paralysis. In fact I wasn't entirely paralyzed and was far from being hysterical. I was quite still. I was stoical in my suffering. But could there have been something to that? Hysterical paralysis, I mean? I'm open now, of course, to the psychological hocus-pocus, because I'm trying to get a better grip on things. Father spent so many years all over the Southwest as he built his, my, business, that there was, for as long as I could remember, a...strangeness between him and Mother. *Dining in the dining car, with ladies fine or otherwise. Oh yes.* She would screech it so that it pierced my eardrum even from downstairs, and I would wake up to the sound of crockery breaking. *You'll wake the boy, you'll wake the boy,* that deep tone weary with whiskey. Perhaps there were times I became ill simply to stop them from fighting.

So Dr. Chickering dragged Mother and me to Michigan, to escape the putrid humidity of Houston. Up there the nights were cold, and at dusk the air was murderous with gnats.

Mother would tuck me into bed and read to me from *Uncle Tom's Cabin.* Those Houston vowels are the loveliest in the nation. But in Michigan I felt bored rather than sick, and she did not fit into my tiny bed there. In any case, I desperately wanted to be alone, for Dudley had entrusted me with a satchel full of Sunday funnies, more than a year's worth.

Momma.

Sonny?

Can we find another book?

She shut the book. Well, if that's how you feel—

No, I mean. You can read some more tomorrow, Momma.

Michigan seemed like eternity, but not in a good way.

Back in Houston as fall approached, Father said, My goodness, young man, you're as tall as a tree. It must have been around this time Mother stopped inspecting my testicles for lumps. I became at last self-monitoring at the duty.

I think that Father tried to send me far from Mother, to make more of a man of me. So Fessenden was an escape. But then I needed to escape Fessenden.

The first time you leave the earth can mark you forever.

It happened that Father was free one week, and took the train to Boston from business in Chicago. He picked me up from school. We drove to New London, to the Harvard-Yale Boat Race on the Thames. Father promised me if Harvard won I could have anything I wanted. There was only one thing on my mind. In Boston Harbor a Curtiss seaplane was moored. Rides were five dollars each. It was not what he had in mind. I cajoled, I cried, I pleaded.

The plane bounced along the water as if it were solid ground. We picked up speed and the ripples began to blur. The engine roared louder and louder. We reached full throttle. Suddenly—it didn't feel quite right but there you have it—we were lurching through air, about six feet above the water, skewing slightly in left and right flutters as if at any moment we might turn ninety degrees in one direction or another. Then we strained steeply upwards and the plane seemed to funnel all its focus forward. I felt a pressure in my groin that I would come to know many thousands of times. We looped out over Boston. The dockside terminals became little boxes. Father stood down there somewhere, 1920 on the Massachusetts earth, watching me soar away. The tiny cars made tiny turns at tiny intersections. The world so very oddly wrought. The fields were merely containers for color. The cows did nothing but mark out space. The wind attacked the wing struts in its roaring. The noise was deafening. The pilot, with limited swivel in his cramped seat in front of me, tried to point out landmarks, but his hand-signals seemed overly general. The whole world was down there, and me up above it.

KATHARINE ON THE WING

IN HOUSTON ALL THOSE oil baron boys had called me a sissy. At Fessenden they were eastern preppies and things were a bit more subtle. In Texas they hurt you openly. You copped a beating. In Boston they did it ever so politely, and with a smile. It was much, much worse. You could smell it in the air. When Father enrolled me at Thacher School in California I felt my world open out somewhat. I was fifteen when I went there in August and sixteen when I left about a year later; in that time I'd begun to have a sense of myself in my own body.

The Thacher boys were not in fact that much different from those at Fessenden, it's just that in California one was freer to be left alone. At Thacher I felt myself to be my own man. Father sent me money to buy a horse, the status symbol du jour at the school. It was not like the motorized bike back in Houston: it was not just a matter of speed. On a horse there was smell, and muscle, and thighs on a saddle, and a sense, merely, deliciously, of being here.

Thacher was like paradise on earth—or microparadise, at least. Often in later years I would fly over the Ojai Valley, banking over all the contours of the hills, out over the orange orchards and the peach trees in blossom, remembering such simplicity down there two decades earlier, when for a moment no gap had existed between life as I experienced it and life as I wished to experience it. I would dip down the pine gulches, watching the shadow of my plane race across the land; remembering those days when I was happy.

Sometimes, remembering that time when I was happy, I was happy in my remembering, too. Loop-the-loops of happiness. Kate Hepburn, fearless, full of laughter, looking up from a crossword puzzle in the co-pilot's seat.

That's where I went to school, down there.

Oh you poor lost lamb, she said. Saint Howard of the Desert.

Katharine was so beautiful it would scare a man. Beautiful and hardly even tried. For a while I loved that freckled girl, though her strength and independence made me nervy. Nonetheless, one way or another I was in her life and she in mine for a year or two, of which I would count at least several glorious weeks, a month or two perhaps, as burning more brightly than usual, flame and flight and fucking everywhere.

She was wonderfully supportive. When things were just beginning, when everything was still just chase and consummation, it was she to whom I first laid out my plans to fly around the world, and she who said, Do it all, grab it all, eat it all.

In 1937 we flew all summer long, mostly in the Sikorsky S-43, that lovely big amphibian. We landed wherever we pleased. The days seemed to bristle then burst with heat. In the middle of the lagoon on Santa Catalina Island we sunbaked on the Sikorsky wing as a giant turtle rose nearby to float and watch, with implacable curiosity, ourselves and our strange craft. On the other side of the continent, one day high above Long Island Sound, Katharine stripped and stood beside me in the cockpit, her cunt all but in my face. She had the knack of making me laugh, somewhat nervously, from time to time.

I'm ready for a skinny dip! she said.

We landed smoothly on the sound. We dived off the wing (she was clothed now, in a yellow bathing suit) and swam a circle around the plane. There was a time in my life when all this wetness mattered. There was a time, lying side by side on that warm port wing and drying off, when droplets of water clung to the backs of her thighs and when my fingertip could prod and test the heft of a single droplet's elasticity, viscosity, until that drop's potential energy burst forth into the kinetic and ran in a tiny rivulet down between her legs. I traced my fingers down there, too. She shifted her weight, imperceptibly, spread her legs an imperceptible distance wider. I stroked her inner thighs. My knuckles pressed (and all this imperceptibility was growing less imperceptible by degrees) against the soft plumpness of her sex. She arched her backside (quite perceptibly) into the air, and pushed a little harder against my knuckles. There was a time when summer actually loosened me up, as I gather it can from time to time for most of the rest of the world.

Hmmm, Howard, she murmured, face hidden beneath a sun hat and buried in her arms, stretched out on that membrane of sunstruck wing. Do take me inside and fuck me when you've half a mind.

There was a time my life was so filled with potential.

THE HORSE WHO LIVES ON IN THE STABLES OF THE INFINITE

I WAS UNSADDLING MY horse in the Thacher School stables when a junior boy came to tell me there was a message waiting for me. Mr. Sherman Day Thacher himself came out from his office. I knew immediately something was wrong. It's from your father, he said, handing me a cablegram. I opened it and read: *Mother is ill. Rupert will bring you home to Houston. Love Howard R. Hughes.* I went a little blank just then. On the train to Los Angeles I tried to imagine all the ways in which life would be different if Mother were dead, at the same time trying to override such thoughts with a constant stream of prayer: for Mother to be all right. I had no idea of anything that could be wrong; there was no specific sickness I knew of. But the mind of a sixteen-year-old is infinite in its potential for self-pity. It was not consciousness of my mother as a separate being that I felt, but rather sorrow for myself. The train passed through endless fields, but even agriculture seemed part of the overladen, the rather irrelevant, weight of existence. Tractors trundled distantly, dragging behind them splayed plumes of dust, which appeared almost static in the flat midday light.

I traveled through the oranges that day, every orange glowing, all of California brightly glowing. Every sphere suspended.

I was lost, becoming free, sixteen years old and rolling through the dark heart of those fields of fruit, the secret blackness of the Golden State.

Uncle Rupert was there to pick me up. I searched his eyes. He looked away. He wrote for the moving pictures but was not much used to real life impinging.

How is she?

She's very ill, he said.

Less than ten minutes later, he turned to me in the limousine. All right, he said. You have to know. I don't think it can wait until Houston. Sonny, your mother is dead.

It is difficult to jam memory into just such a moment. She stroked me through all the illness called childhood. Through late nights when I wheezed and wheezed her soft hands massaged camphor oil into my chest. She slept in the same room with me until I was eleven years old. Father slept in the study upstairs. How many sleeps till Santa Claus, Mother? Three more sleeps, Howard. You must be patient. Two more sleeps. One more sleep. In the morning when you wake, it'll be no more sleeps, and Santa will have filled your stocking. We can go through all the presents together. Hush now, hush now.

The point is, Jack, that sometimes I was the anxious one, and she calmed me. Surely you'll understand if I tell you that. But she had great fear about impending illness, and taught me how to fear it all myself. I had watched for many years as she scrubbed and scoured the pots and pans, relentlessly, as the maids rolled their eyes. I had watched her triple-sink system, for dipping and scalding and disinfecting the amoeba-swarming vegetables. Not even the lowliest carrot escaped her attentions. Her vigilance was the last defense.

In the parlor at Yoakum Boulevard my mother lay in her coffin, just thirty-nine years old. It is really very difficult to see the physical lineaments of a face, of clasped hands and the bulge of feet, and try and separate from that irrevocable stillness the one who thought, who lived and breathed, who smothered me with kisses. All right, she went a little too far, perhaps. But I have never been loved like that. She would have laid down her life for me. She would have suffered every germ and every calamity.

For a minute or two I stood alone at the coffin. I felt, forlornly there, a searing thinness and a desperate panic, as if the oxygen had been sucked out of my body. I bit my lip. I tried to focus on her face through brimming tears. I had never known her to wear her make-up in that way. Or so much of it, at least. On the one hand it seemed an affront to her dear memory. On the other hand it hardly seemed to matter now, and numbness seemed an appropriate response. The lid would be closed in an hour or two. I ran my fingers along the polished grain of the coffin rim; fingers that had once touched that hair and those lips.

The rest was rather a blur. There were many relatives, much somber darkness in the grand old Yoakum house, all cedar and velvet curtains. It was decided that Aunt Annette would move into the house, to look after me while I was there. Which wasn't to be long. Clearly it would be best for me to return to the patterns of school life at Thacher.

They treated me kindly on my return. I liked it there; I liked getting away from the sadness. At Thacher I quite literally smelled the future. I sensed the closeness of the adult world that waited. I felt a sudden lightness, too, as if a mother is not just pure, weightless love, but a measurable mass, strapped invisibly to the shoulders, making every step heavier. When mine died I felt for the first time connected very deeply to every plant and every insect. The blazing beauty of the world rang out like a bell.

On my first day back at school after the funeral, I rode my horse out through the sagebrush and the scrub oak, far away from school as the sun began to set. Deep shadow filled the gulches and ravines. We cantered through soft soil. The crickets had all stilled. When I was low in a gulch the sun went down behind the ridge. But when I came back up it rose again. I sat astride my horse and watched it set a second time. The horse whinnied softly. It seemed somehow I'd gained a day.

Memo, 1951: Coats

I want all coats that need to be cleaned to be cleaned and hung together some place. I want the same thing done with the trousers and hung together away from the coats at least five feet. This may be in the same closet, but only if large enough to accommodate the insulation provided by the indicated space. I want all shirts and everything else laundered and put in a container of some kind. A white cardboard box is preferable to wood. It is not good to leave these in the laundry boxes, however, because there are other items in there, too. All pockets should be emptied. This means pockets in shirts, coats and overcoats. You may consider that all coats and trousers which are hanging in the closet are empty. But any coat or trousers that you pick up from a chair or anywhere else should be searched. Whatever you take out of the pockets should be placed in the proper category. I want you to think like me and be on your guard about contamination. I want to thank you for thinking ahead about this.

VISTA DEL ARROYO, 1923

I NEVER GRADUATED FROM Thacher; in the end it never mattered. I was beginning to see the way in which money changes one's interactions with the other human beings. I was torn between staying and moving closer to this life I knew awaited me: Los Angeles, the oasis. But what surprised me most of all was seeing Father weak and insecure after Mother's death. In letters he was lonely and bewildered. He'd never been effusive in telling me he missed me.

I can't get a grip on myself, he wrote.

I'm terribly lonely without you, he wrote.

I miss your mother terribly, he wrote.

I hope you are all right, I wrote back.

I passed my arithmetic, I wrote back.

One day, about a month after Mother died, Mr. Sherman Day Thacher called me to his office once again. Father wanted to pull me out of school. There were only two months left until graduation. Thacher thought it would be best if I were to remain there on equal footing with all the other boys. If I were not to receive any special treatment. For I was, after all, doing well. I was gaining in confidence. I was enjoying my time there. I could hardly disagree with him.

Come back to Houston, Father wrote. Your Auntie Annette misses you terribly, too. You can start working in the business.

I wrote that I thought it best if I first finished what I had begun.

He wrote back and suggested we all move in together to the Vista del Arroyo, the retreat in Pasadena where we had occasionally holidayed. It was quite a different matter from Houston. It was hard to resist the thought of all that sumptuous pleasantness. Or the additional lure that my cousin Kitty would come across from Texas and stay with us, keep me company over summer. Or the allowance Father promised me, of five thousand dollars a month.

So we moved west with Auntie Annette and Cousin Kitty into the Vista del Arroyo. There were long Pasadena days so aflame with bougainvillea that I had trouble finding reason to leave the bench in the terracotta courtyard, where the gurgling of the birdbath rang deep behind my eyes. One day a great white bird flew high overhead: I imagined him happy as a lark. The momentum of stasis could sustain itself till hunger or discomfort came along. Of course now, with the Empirin and all these vast spaces, I am better with the stasis and can hold off far longer on the hunger and discomfort. But back then I was sixteen; you could hear my bones crackling as they grew, like acorns popping open on the hot summer days.

Houston was a swamp; pretty Kitty was dazzled by the sharpness of Pasadena County. It wasn't just that creaking of the bones; all sorts of highways were unfolding in my blood, and spending time with Kitty near drove me crazy. Every minute was delicious. We strained against the tides of propriety. We never said a word. We didn't have the language. By the pool we lay wet on the warm concrete. My eye closest to the sky was closed, but the one against the concrete I could open in secrecy. For some time, contented, I watched the downy

hairs on Cousin Kitty's kneecap. They were, quite
literally, transparent in the sun. On certain nights I may
have spilled my seed in bed, extrapolating from single
hairs and concrete-dappled thighs the sublime surrender
of the flesh. At times ever since the whole world has
opened up in this unexpected transparency.

Auntie Annette watched over us at the Vista
del Arroyo. Father was mostly away on Hughes drill
business. Or spending the proceeds throwing parties
on some yacht. I chaperoned Kitty to many movies.
There is something very stimulating about sitting in
the dark theater with all sorts of tensions, explicit or
implicit, in the smoke-filled air. Cousins. That bright
projected beam and the mayhem of sex on the screen.
Everything was just beginning then. The way everything
would turn out, I mean. The movie business, the *show*
business, was so new, no one really had any idea of
what would happen next. But I had a growing sense I
wanted to be there in the middle of it. It was all just
possibility: superheated blood, cool theaters, Kitty at
my side while summer afternoons blazed white outside.
And yet I knew I was witnessing something simply ready
to burst.

Sometimes I just had to get out of there. The driver
might enquire if I was planning to go to college that day.
(A carefully placed donation from Father meant that I
was allowed to attend classes at Caltech, though since I
hadn't actually graduated from Thacher School I wasn't
officially enrolled.) I enjoyed spending time in the metal

shops, but the truth was I spent less time at Caltech than Father would have liked to believe. On the other hand, I made good use of the Duesenberg he put at my disposal. I drove and drove, some days leaving the driver at home with nothing to do. You could take the ridge line of the mountains through the Ten and the Sixty-Two all the way to Joshua Tree. In winter you could be driving through snow in forty minutes. Back then there were still mountain lions, to whom all of Los Angeles, glowing and sparkling down there in its bowl, must have been nothing more than a fabulous flitting dream of light on the periphery of their prowling.

The century was waiting. From Father's drill bit, money rained upon me. And three times a week, from out on Haber Field, I took my flying lessons. I loved being among the aviators, those Christs flying heavenwards faster than rockets.

Father was unenthusiastic, but I wanted to be a pilot. In the open cockpit of a Sopwith Pup I felt so much power coursing through my biceps and fingertips that no speed seemed improbable and no glory unobtainable. Los Angeles spread below me like the original garden, everything contained therein. In one vast Sopwith circle I could pass above every climate and microclimate. Dry gulches east of Lucerne Valley, the canyons slicing the Hollywood Hills like ripples, snow up north in the Tehachapi Mountains, valleys of orchid and fern, creepers cooling the stucco walls of the Los Feliz mansions, dust rolling over the land past Victorville—

everywhere coolness and deep shadow offset violently by a burning nakedness of light, so that luminosity and infinite space were a kind of prison in themselves. And beside it all, deeply and monstrously elegant, lay the ocean, blinding airmen with the ruffling and flashing of its diamond-crusted surface.

Then, in January of '24, Father's heart burst wildly, and he died.

His last great act had been to increase my allowance from five thousand a month to five thousand a week. He was a man whose sense of priorities I loved.

Leaving childhood was like pushing through a semi-transparent membrane. There was a long slow elasticity, a give and a resistance, before the pop of maximum tension and the tearing of the fabric. And all the world was hymen then.

VEINS

PERHAPS A MORE POLITE way of looking at it would be to say that for a very long time, for a lifetime in fact, I had been pinioned between the overattention my mother paid to me and that which my father paid to himself. Then they both died; I shot out from between them like a cannon. So in the summer of 1924 I went to Europe with Dudley Sharp, my Teedyuskung Brave, American dandies the both of us, eighteen years old.

Europe is an old-fashioned kind of place. Its people are peculiar. Mother had died less than two years earlier; Father less than six months. I was gathering breath before returning to Houston for a showdown with my grandparents and uncle and other family members, who thought a European tour just the antidote to a young man's pain and grieving. I saw Big Ben. Saw breasts at the Moulin Rouge. Bought a mohair coat on the Boulevard St. Germain. Went boating off the Amalfi coast. Could not get a good steak anywhere.

Dudley had been, I suppose, my only friend. His father had been a partner in my father's drill bit company until he'd died in 1915. My father had been generous with Dudley and his mother in the buyout. Dudley had helped me with homework. (I was not the academic type.) He lied for me when I brained Charlie Post with a rock lobbed from our opposing hummock. We had been playing soldiers: Charlie and his friends were the Huns and the rock was a hand-grenade. I thought no further excuse was needed. But Dudley lied the proper way, by denying I actually did it. He was a boy whose words carried weight. Then for a few years I was at Fessenden and Thacher while Dudley stayed in Houston. We would see each other in the holidays. But the drift was beginning. By eighteen it seemed more like a rupture, pleasantness of Europe aside. Because at some point you need to strike out and make your own way. And there are too many habits, there is too much intimacy from childhood. We knew each other's weaknesses. He knew so well how all those years earlier the other boys had picked on me, the momma's boy. One likes to supersede the remaining forensic evidence, to clear the way for the future. Dudley was my last tie with the past.

So Europe with Dudley was tinged, for me, with that sense of a predeveloped nostalgia looming for future loss. Nonetheless, boating off Sorrento was a splendid experience. We were men now. There were awkward but still romantic assignations in Rome. Language-wise, we all got by on a minimal diet. There was a sickly smell of sweat masked by too much perfume. It was hard to work out the exchange rate.

Back in Houston I had a legal battle to fight, the first of many that would scatter themselves through my life. Everyone was out to plunder my father's company and good work. I didn't want to wait until I was twenty-one to inherit the seventy-five percent share that awaited me. I wanted to own it all, now. Complete autonomy is the only way to make one's vision pay. Texas civil code allowed me to be declared an adult if I could convince the court I could handle my own affairs. This I did, to the consternation of my relatives, in front of Judge Walter Montieth (my father's friend) on my nineteenth birthday. Then I mortgaged Yoakum Boulevard and borrowed on the tool company's assets and bought out all the relatives for one-third of a million dollars.

And it was that simple. I was free.

Emptying the coffers was a radical form of starting from scratch, but at nineteen that looks and feels about right. And I could do it. There were more than fifty thousand wells in operation at any given time, all around the world, at thirty thousand dollars per lease, drilling through crust and rock, into the underflow. Veins, veins. Everything is either flowing toward the heart or away from the heart, but everything is flowing. I wanted the tool company to run itself. I knew precisely where I wanted to be: back in Los Angeles, making movies, and learning to fly. But Auntie Annette pushed me into the marriage with Ella first. Not one of us is not burdened at some point with the foolish mentalities of youth, where one simply goes with the flow of momentum. Thus, Do you take... Do you take...and I said, I do; though, of course, I didn't.

THE ELLA-BONE IS CONNECTED TO THE BILLIE-BONE

YOU NEVER MET ELLA, I'll say to Jack. She was gone before your time. Where we came from, money married money. I was only nineteen. A ridiculous age to be hitched. How it lasted four years I'll never know. Mostly I kept her in Houston out of harm's way. Her endless cablegrams drove me crazy. The whinier she became the more I froze up. I couldn't stand the thought I was being manipulated. The marriage never really got off the ground, Jack.

We tried to make a go of it; instead we made a hash of it.

Toward the end I put her out into a house on 211 Muirfield Road in Hancock Park, Los Angeles. I'd started seeing other women by now. It was all rather close quarters. I was gaining in confidence. Hollywood was hotting up. I drove a crimson Rolls. There was a desperation in the air already then. We were all of us desperate. And there were so many women willing to compromise themselves.

Ella wanted to like Los Angeles. She tried.

In March '29 she threw a big party at Muirfield Road, hoping to bring the two worlds together: her high-society people, all those moneyed Texas morons, and my Hollywood friends, fun people, really a lot of fun. I arrived late (I had been fucking Jean Harlow in the broom closet at the Cocoanut Grove), but the tension was already well established and an awkward divide remained between the two groups.

I was never one for small talk. Well, I think you know that already, Jack.

Soon after this Ella moved out of my life for good. I was relieved to be relieved of a big part of what was annoying me. She was like a mosquito. No, she was like a tenant living rent-free inside my head.

Clutter is so bad for your health. Billie Dove, on the other hand, was the certificate of well-being. In 1929 I was twenty-three, she was twenty-four, I was nothing (nothing yet), she was Hollywood, I was scared of my own shadow, she was pure light. I had seen her in darkened theaters for six years already by now; in fact I had first seen her in the flesh across a crowded room at one of Uncle Rupert's parties in 1923, when he was writing screenplays for Sam Goldwyn and I stood in quiet corners, seventeen years old and gangly as all hell, staring at the starlets.

I saw *The Black Pirate*, a silent film, in 1926. Douglas Fairbanks' father dies in his arms, the victim of a pirate attack, and Fairbanks, secretly vowing revenge, joins the pirate ship, bides his time, and kills the old captain. They board a merchant ship and in the plundering find Billie Dove hidden in a hold. The pirates are about to rape her when Fairbanks sees by the emblem on her necklace that Billie Dove is a princess. He tricks the other pirates into letting her go. He rows away with Billie.

She says, You risk your life for me.

Fairbanks replies, I would do more—and give it.

They go to kiss. In movie houses I had studied the kiss for years, I had dreamed of perfecting the art. But I never believed I would one day be kissing her.

Because eventually we were introduced, at Victor Hugo's Garden Room, and then one night there we were, on the beach at Malibu, kissing. She dug her fingernails into my scalp. Somehow one expects the lips of the famous to feel different. But they are not so different after all. And do you remember those little button lips, that little heart-shaped pout, Jack, that was the fashion on the actresses in the silent films? She had nicer lips than that in real life.

She had a real body. She had real eyes. Her fingers were chubby. Her dark hair gleamed. It was quite an odd experience. I could cup and squeeze her buttocks in my hands. Years later it would come to mean nothing. Not nothing, Jack. I'm trying to say I got used to it. I'd see a beauty on the screen, and some months, or weeks, later, I'd be lying with her in the flesh.

They're all gone now, of course, and I get to watch them on the screen again. But Billie was the first like that.

We sailed across to Santa Catalina Island. We were so naked on those crisp sheets: coming, I was astonished by the glory of my cock.

I was waking up, to myself and to the world and to me there in it.

When you thrust into Billie at just the same moment that the hull thrusts into a dip between rolls of swell, you are effectively weightless, pushing into nothing. There is nothing to resist you. Nothing. Even then I began to know that all of this, this life, this everything, was filled with zeros; look deep into their heart and the real world appears.

After that trip I bought her an eighty-foot yacht, named it *Rodeo* (after her character Rodeo West in *The Painted Angel*), and it became our love nest, a term very much gaining vogue in those days. I had to pay her husband $325,000 for an uncontested divorce. Jiminy and Gee Whiz.

JEAN HARLOW HAD THE KNOWLEDGE

HE YEAR 1929 WAS the last time I let technology take
me by surprise. I was $3.9 million into my first
film, *Hell's Angels*, by the time I realized that sound was
not just a novelty after all: the talkies were here to stay.
We'd wasted more than a year of shooting, but there was
nothing we could do about it. For the movie to survive
and compete we would need to completely rebuild and
re-shoot it (another two million). Greta Nissen was
wonderful to look at but had a thick Scandinavian
accent and a voice like a hacksaw. We had to find a new
girl who spoke English.

The very rich man can get the star, though riches on
their own are not always enough. The movie-maker, on
the other hand, can make the star, decide who the star
will be. I very much enjoyed being a movie-maker. In
the cattle calls I discovered Carole Lombard, and for a
couple of weeks, until Jean Harlow turned up, it looked
like she had the role. It is unbelievable just how long you
can fuck for, blood, head and body that hallucinatory
trilogy, amphetamines coursing through you like a river
in flood. By this time I was getting better. Sex with Ella
had never been great, but Billie Dove had taught me a
lot, though I was still something of a skittish colt, all
bones and angles and too much self-consciousness. And

now with Carole, we'd make love all night. I don't mean many different times, I mean the one fuck seemed to go on forever. Years later, when she picked me up on a motorcycle and ran a bath in her backyard, things had slowed down, that being a period of relative peace, before the difficulties descended and the drugs went up a notch. Of course, I was off my noggin back in '29, Jack, but that's more the benefit of hindsight. In any case it was all a tremendous boost to my confidence. More to the point it was something of a test-run in relation to Jean Harlow.

I didn't think much of poor Jean the day she first walked into a casting session. I thought she looked too cheap. She had beady eyes and a too-sharp chin, a beacon of white hair so bright it clashed with rather than complemented her pale lemon dress, and eyebrows as ungenerous as her lips. And yet when she grinned crookedly, such promise of mischief was released. Still, I didn't think she had the sophistication to portray the girl in love with my two flying aces. But her agent, Art Landau, convinced me that in fact she was just the kind of girl who would put out for airmen, selflessly, knowing they might soon die, whereas in fact Carole Lombard might come across a little too virginal and clean in this regard.

It wasn't easy breaking the news to Carole, and there were tears, of course, of the sweet, distressed kind. Carole, forlorn and disheveled, saying, Am I not good enough? But one simply had to move through tough decisions. Besides, the more I watched Jean in the test

rushes, the more I saw there was, as Landau had pointed
out, something about her: a golden slut of sorts. The girl
who said, If you would like to fuck me I have absolutely
no problem with that, I don't need to know your motives,
I don't need to know the future or the past. Whatever
happens, I don't mind. I am completely open, completely
pliant, to all your wishes, Mr. Hughes. Jean Harlow
was like a night of roaring winds and waterfalls, and a
clinging, a desperation soft and sweet beyond imagining.
Carole, okay, of course, you can imagine. She went on
to do great things. You've seen the movies, we all have.
But there was something unbelievable with my blonde,
my blow-job queen. Jean gave that extra something. Jean
went that extra mile. My first great star creation, too, I'm
proud to say. Jean literally elasticized one's sense of time
until the bed was nothing but the expansion of space in
the compression of a heartbeat; nothing but swirling.
Because Jean had the Knowledge. Knew what to do with
every fingertip, every stroke of the palm of her hand on
the nape of your neck or the small of your back, every
shifting of hips; every hot-breathed kiss. Two in every
hundred women have it deeply, instinctively. The rest
work at acquiring skill with greater or lesser diligence.
Jean had it all. She was only nineteen. But I gathered
she'd been spreading wide for a good long time by then.

And I was sailing. I was soaring. There wasn't a call
sheet invented yet that I couldn't deal with. Sleep was for
the other humans. I could shoot all day from six, I could
eat at Saltieri's or Maxim's or the Oasis, go out to all the

clubs, the Montmartre or the Cocoanut Grove, till dawn. And somewhere in there fuck little Jean all night.

Of course, I was still officially "with" Billie Dove at this point, a little ball of energy, you could almost hold her in the palm of your hand. And I was most in love with her. I had helped her through her divorce with Irvin Willat. She had helped me through mine with Ella. I really did intend to spend my life with her. Billie was my first love; Ella was more like an arranged marriage. And all those other girls: spur-of-the-moment situations, with a sprinkling of momentum thrown in. Also, clearly for a man it is quite difficult to have sex just the once. First you have to get the awkwardness and newness out of the way. Twice is much better. Three times is better than twice. I am talking about occasions, full nights, nights bleeding into days, sequences of events, rather than single fucks. A couple of weeks' worth is best of all. You just get on a roll. You owe it to yourself to explore all the way to the end of the river, as long as the river stays interesting enough. Jean was never really my type. It was never going to be more than a quick and dirty fling. Sometimes that's exactly what makes it so damned good: the fact of the necessity of imminent cessation. We really shouldn't be doing this. It's like a chorus down through the ages, like bells ringing out some secret history of infidelity.

I never felt a moment's guilt, not a second, not a microsecond, about Billie. Not in the middle of the swirl with Jean, at least. Nor about Ella, in relation to Billie. Guilt had a habit of coming later. But wait a minute.

Should I say all this to Jack? He is, after all, a family
man. But I did what I did, for better or for worse. Even
now, more than forty years later, I feel my blood stir,
codeine-sluggish though it is, even now, thinking about
Jean, through the endless savannahs of the Empirin.
Her life was one grand game. When Billie was filming
up in Oakland one time, and Ella gone by now, Jean
arrived in LA at the house on Muirfield, chauffeur-
driven, naked beneath a mink fur coat, on a day when if
you stood outside the dust blew fiercely and grit found
its way between your teeth, crunch crunch. Yet inside the
house there was only smoothness, and so much juice to
be gobbled up.

THE TENDENCY OF GRAVITY

I DIDN'T ALWAYS KNOW what I was doing—behind the
camera or behind the controls—but I didn't think
it really mattered. I had so much money and so much
energy, no mistake was beyond fixing. We had to shoot
the big dogfight scene with forty-five airplanes. Nothing
like this had ever been done before. There were many
contingencies bubbling. There were weather delays,
mechanical difficulties. Production costs were running
at twenty-five thousand dollars a day.

It was my first movie, Jack. In truth, I was feeling
more than a little stress. I was perfectly aware the eyes of

the world were upon me as the hayseed from Houston with too much damned money. But the amphetamines helped me to understand that all would unfold correctly and in sequence and that indeed correctness was the deep state of the world. My decisions emerged from my throat with the ease and authority of a god, and I marveled at their majesty. Do this, do that. Cancel this, buy that. In any event, my first plane crash was not as bad as a couple of the later ones.

A blue-sky winter day over Inglewood, early '28. Paul Mantz was my head flyer, a decorated war ace and a fine pilot but an obstinate man and a stickler for the rules. He refused to allow any of the stunt pilots to perform a strafing dive in which I wanted a plane to come in steep and get as low as two hundred feet above the runway; he said a thousand was the bottom safety limit. Men without vision!

Ten years earlier all these aviators had been to hell and back, to Poitiers, Ypres, Cantigny. Everything they knew they knew from their own hands; their continuing existence was the proof. Others less fortunate had nosedived into Flanders or the English Channel, patient and abiding. These guys, princes among men, had made it back to their fiefdom, Los Angeles. Things could only get better. I suppose they wanted to live long lives.

But I was cranky. I said I'd do it myself. I had set up a camera tower, eleven cameras stacked vertically to catch the action. I wanted the plane to describe the low arc of its parabola as close to the tower as possible. I knew the ins and outs of the Thomas Morse Scout, a simple enough plane. Maybe the lesson I should have learned that day was more about not flying in anger than any mastery of technology. I had mastered the goddamned technology! I radioed *Action!* and began my dive, feeling that glorious tug in the groin and contemplating oddly enough the fact that if something did go wrong, it, and I, would be immortalized on film.

At fifteen hundred feet I knew the dive was out of control. I tried to pull out but the plane merely maintained its path like a bullet. I felt, if there is an adequate way of describing it, serenely panicked. The horizontal earth, as harmless as a map from up there, flew vertically upwards, and very fast, to meet me. The engine strained and whined. The wings rocked and shuddered as if ready to detach themselves and leave me sitting in this streamlined cylinder gaining speed. The controls seemed only ornaments by now. I dropped down through one thousand feet as in a dream. Seven hundred and fifty feet was already a distant memory. I felt perhaps I was underwater, one only among a species, giant manta rays drifting free through the stately oceans. Five hundred feet. The wind fed through my nostrils and my skull. My eardrums popped, preparing for silence. I pulled one more time, without hope, at the controls. The Scout pulled ever so slightly into a curve. I banked, ready for impact, thinking to spin the plane sideways. Then an eruption of noise and wing and cockpit. I thought I might come apart.

Then I remember my head hurt very much, though the blood in my ears and eyes was comfortably warm. I looked out over the red tarmac to the distant red figures running through the red smoke and dust.

I stood somehow, though my back ached tremendously. Then I thought I was walking in a garden, perhaps the Zoological Garden, the Houston Zoo, on a cool fall day, and I was a giraffe, a giraffe made of air, swaying gently, stretching, stretching, to eat more sky. My head felt cool up there. Then I found myself bending at the knees. Then in fact I fell to one knee. Down there, crouched like a quarterback in the huddle, a little dizzy, I had time to look at the beautiful tarmac, just a little local sliver of it, as it became wet, as dark oil seemed to pool and grow and spread, and I thought, An engine somewhere is leaking, we must tell the foreman, where is the foreman, where is the head mechanic, where has everybody gone? I tried to follow the source of the oil but it seemed to be growing from inside its circle of spread. I touched my fingers to its darkness but they came up inexplicably red. Then I seemed to be leaning against some very solid structure. I looked up around me. I was standing alone in a vast hall, somewhat like an empty aircraft hangar. Outside in the red daylight was a plane, a Thomas Morse, apparently recently crashed, crumpled and in pieces. Smoke rose from the wreck as from a pyre. I felt very peaceful by now; the dizziness had gone. Perhaps in fact it was not after all the remains of an airplane but the sand traps and hump leading up to the seventeenth green. To where I was strolling at that very moment. A chip shot, and things were looking good.

But then I recognized these red men, Paul Mantz and Roscoe Turner, running toward me like figures from a nightmare, and I was a little confused because they were my pilots and not my golf partners, and then I felt very tired and wanted to lie down a moment.

I had a short nap and when I woke up I had been in a coma in the hospital for three days, and the light was very bright. Noah, my accountant, my friend, was by my bed with others. Harold, he said, you are a very lucky man. There must be some mistake, I said, my name is Howard not Harold. The doctor shone a torch into my eyes and said, Mr. Hughes, you are somewhat concussed and you have suffered under the yoke of a terrible accident. This was all the approximate sequence of words and events from that day three days later. Everybody was greatly relieved.

THE LUXURY OF A COHERENT REALITY

I RECOVERED QUICKLY, BUT IT took a hell of a lot longer to finish the movie. At some point I broke the record for the longest film shoot in history—but I was always breaking records. I sent aerial photography crews far afield, to Oakland, Sacramento, San Diego, to get the right damned clouds, which were never there when you wanted them. Months would pass like this. Cablegrams and weather reports. The continuity of the light. It mattered to me to get it right.

That stab of annoyance in the edit room, when the cutaways did not exactly match up. Nonetheless there comes at last a time when everything is in alignment, even our limousines all in convoy at the *Hell's Angels* premiere at Grauman's Chinese Theater on June 30, 1930. Jean Harlow, our new star in the firmament, traveled in the car in front of us. Billie Dove sat beside me holding my hand, but all my yearning was funneled forward into that Daimler thirty feet ahead. Jean's smooth legs, the gymnastics of her abandon. Billie suspected nothing at this point and Jean behaved herself all night, in public.

We finally made it, I said to Jean, referring to the movie, smiling for the flashing bulbs. I squeezed her elbow tight for an instant. Most everything has a multiplicity of meaning, and everything stands for something else, but sometimes, as in that brief squeeze, metaphor and intent fuse, and one enjoys the luxury of a coherent reality.

Still, I stayed with Billie Dove a while longer. Things could never have lasted with Jean, as I said. There was an enticing tang to her imbecility but the long-term prospect was for boredom, and in any case her own frail self was not to last long. Goodbye Jean. In the summer of 1930 I took a European tour with Billie. Europeans didn't *think* the same as Americans, and did things, most things, more dumbly. It is simply not an efficient continent. In addition they make very little effort to get their English right. But in July we sailed on the *Europa* from New York.

Leaving the harbor and all those buildings and all that heat behind, I felt the sweat cool on the back of my neck. When choices are reduced you can perhaps really love someone, and I thought I might love Billie after all. Concentrate on her, at least. Too much choice and you can go into meltdown. But when America recedes, you can make love in the *Europa*'s Presidential Suite, slowly, deliberately, and then suddenly there does not seem too much heat in the world after all. Liberty. Liberty. The ship trundles across the Atlantic, the cabin itself is a river, the bed a ship of flowering. You are drenched for days.

We took out the light bulb in a narrow powder room at a party in Paris. We had lurched, laughing, to the far end of the house. We were trying to be quick. But the door swung open the moment we'd stopped caring, and a pale red-haired woman gasped, *Oh, pardonnez-moi!* as the slat of light revealed perhaps a glimpse of cock, or Billie Dove's pale thighs hoicked to mine, her dimpled buttocks pressed to the marble sink, or her stockings dangling helplessly from her toes.

We visited the Arc de Triomphe. From the Eiffel Tower there is a very pleasant view.

RICOCHET

BUT THE FIRST TIME I ever experienced a clearly identifiable stammer in the monologue of life was

1930. Amphetamines helped me get through those long days trying to keep *Hell's Angels* together. I liked the energy modern pharmaceuticals supplied; I liked how fully Here and Now the world became; I liked the way 1930 was surely the most present of all presents the world had ever passed through.

The amphetamines smoothed me out, and yet after a while they were just so inconsistent. One night in bed in the house on Muirfield I was a little angry to think there were stonemasons nearby sawing through granite—what the hell were they doing what the hell were they doing up at this time of night—and at one point called the police, but we couldn't identify the source of the noise, couldn't get a fix on the direction. The police in fact claimed they couldn't actually hear anything.

I was quite embarrassed several nights later when I realized it had only been the grinding of my teeth.

At other times I got somewhat exhausted and *needed* noise to deafen the clatter in my brain, some kind of override device (I wouldn't discover morphine for another sixteen years). After shooting for twelve hours and then viewing the dailies I would come home late at night not knowing what to do with myself, not knowing even how to properly sit on a couch. I would pace the house, dread chewing at my stomach. The very stillness seemed menacing. So in the basement at Muirfield I let fly for a few seconds with a Thompson submachine gun I'd taken from the movie set. It was as if the machine gun were pleading, then and there, for its purpose on the planet to be fulfilled.

Exposing myself to the danger from ricochet in that confined cellar was probably a sign that things were not well. But the noise was magnificent, and took me for a moment away from my own sense of exhaustion and into a still and silent place, warm and welcoming. So that I was rather calm when Noah rushed over, alerted by one very worried maid.

He said, Do you want to talk?

I didn't have the energy to answer.

We stood in silence, both leaning against the cool stone walls. I had taken him on as my chief accountant; he would be with me for many years, until his welcome wore out, as they do. But for a while, a couple of decades, we would be close. Smoke wisped lazily up from the barrel of the gun. I had a sudden sense that above me the whole of the world burned too brightly and it was better to live in the darkness here, in a cooler place, nearer to the tendrils of the orchids reaching down, nearer to all these labyrinths in the soil, than that world up there of Each Bright Object Too Clearly Encased In Itself. I also had a sense that although we were close, Noah and myself, friendship was hard. It was hard enough just concentrating on the women.

After a while Noah took me by the arm and said, leading me up the stairs, I'll put you into bed. He was like a father to me. He was a wonderful accountant, too.

COOL ARE THE FAIRWAYS AT NIGHT

SOMETIMES WHEN THE MOON was bright I would leave the house on Muirfield, climb the back fence, and roam completely free on the empty golf course, free of Billie Dove, of Jean Harlow, of the complications of how to interact. It soothed my head to wander. The shadows of animals, squirrels or rabbits perhaps, moved tentatively across the fairways. Sometimes I would take my clothes off and lie down on my back on the seventh green, arms and legs spread wide. Daylight is merely like an electric lamp; when it is switched off you can see out the window to what lies outside. And this is what night is: the eyes adjusting to the things outside of here. Sometimes I saw my place in the world, and felt precisely the right size.

THE BILLIE-BONE IS CONNECTED TO THE WORLD-BONE

BILLIE LEFT IN '31. Howard, she said in the end, you're frightfully young in the head. Howard, she'd said in Paris, when I couldn't hide my boredom in the Notre Dame cathedral, can't you just feel the beauty?

We were all just rattling our cages, Jack, for quite a few years back then. And yes, Billie, of course I felt the beauty. For nine hundred years that stone had held its shape, which is better than any of us can say for ourselves.

Late at night, in one of the screening rooms at Goldwyn Studios, I would run reels from *Cock of the Air* and *The Age for Love*. Just to once again watch her face in silence on the screen. Well, she was better off up there.

The rest is the blink of an eye. Billie left me but it didn't matter. There were no hard feelings when we crossed paths at Maxim's. The world was full of color.

We had spent much time together on the *Rodeo*, but it was time for change. So I bought the *Rover*, the fifth largest private yacht in the world, and renamed it the *Southern Cross*. The refit included crystal chandeliers, teak floorboards from Siam, pink marble in the bathrooms, and wolf skins for the master bed, a great circular expanse. My thought was that it would impress the debutantes and starlets.

And indeed, it's as if their underwear fell to the deck the minute they stepped on board.

For years then I tumbled through urgency, each new woman, it was so exciting, I mean she was so exciting, I mean the whole situation: how would she smell, how would she look naked, how would she make love, how would she taste, what heat would leak from her lips and tongue? We would strut through the clubs, me and Pat de Cicco, Johnny Maschio, Alex D'Arcy. We thought if they want it they give it up. There was simply no strain in the whole of the world. In any one life it may be a narrow epoch, when the women's legs go weak and the handsome young men come to bark at the moon. But in Los Angeles it is always summer.

THE HANDSOME YOUNG MEN

CARY GRANT HAS BEEN leaving messages this week. He's in London—did I tell you? I'd like to see old Cary but it is damned hard to conceive of how it might be done. I feel ashamed, Jack. I know I look different. It's a long time since the thirties, my friend. Bodies entering a room are so dense with intrusion. Got to keep it all to a minimum. It took me an awful lot of effort just to get you here. You're the first outsider in ten years. It's a big decision to let someone in. There are so many possible disasters. Maybe I'll never see Cary again. It might well be better that way.

He was the gentlest of men. And how the women loved him—far more than they ever loved me. We met in 1935. After he divorced Virginia Cherrill he was spending a lot of time with Randolph Scott, who was spending a lot of time on golf courses, in nightclubs, with me. When Cary Grant walked into a room it was just as if the doors had opened wide on spring, on all its breezes and the smell of fern. It was just as if the God of Charm had filled the space around you. I felt that I had learned my manners, all my ways of being, in public. How to hold a fork. How to ask a lady for a dance. It all came with effort. In Hollywood, one way or another, everyone was watching you. But you'd swear that Cary Grant was born with every skill already there.

So the Latter Day Saints have told me that Cary has been in contact. He'd very much love to see me. We talked on the phone a few years back, in '69. He's a very private man, more so than me, and was reluctant to go to the Academy Awards that year to collect his special Oscar. A lifetime achievement, perhaps. I told him he should go, to share in the collective goodwill, to accept his due, to shower them with his love. He said, I'll go if you go, Howard. We laughed. Well, nothing came of that, of course.

And now he has called again. It breaks my heart that he's still so willing to try. It's just that I am rather ill, and I don't think I look so well, and it's terribly embarrassing to be like this, and surely one visitor is enough for the week, or the month, or the decade. I need to get better again. For Cary. That's no offense to you, Jack. It's just... it's different worlds. You were one of my most trusted executives. I need you for the planning of this flight. But it goes back so much deeper with him.

When you come to think of it, I've had so few friends, really. So few voices other than my own. Lots of employees, of course. Some who fared better than others. And some who didn't fare so well at all. Dick Felt, Ceco Cline. But does Lake Mead even have to be mentioned? Why spoil a good evening? Things go wrong, from time to time. I risked no one's life more than my own. I was luckier, that's all. Let's talk about you, Jack, when you wake up. I'll try not to talk about myself too much. I'll ask you how your wife is. How is the weather in California? Let's talk about California.

Latter Day Saint! Syringe!

The problem is, we have these walls set up here, the Mormons and me, and it's so hard to imagine them breached. Even by Cary Grant. We have a system in place, carefully built up, layer by layer, over the years. The whole point of systems is to fine-tune them, not to introduce random new elements into the modulated lineaments of their precision. But Cary. But Cary. If I really could get better...then maybe next year, I could have him over. What do you think, Jack? I'd be living in a different place by then. A real house, perhaps. And perhaps California is not such a bad idea after all. We could go for a stroll, just me and Cary. Perhaps even a round of golf. We could sit in the garden and watch the sun go down over the Wilshire Country Club, as we did once at Muirfield Road. In summer the gnats would hover like a holy gauze above the greens.

THE END OF HISTORY

I WILL NEED TO TELL him, more than almost anything, about the injections. Because that's just something that can't be hidden. What Jack perhaps won't realize is that the more I take the clearer it all gets. He needs to understand, this is not something I do just for fun. This is about putting myself in the position I need to be in to make everything function. It's not just about me. It's about everything that surrounds me. If I've got enough of the appropriate medicine in me everything is flat, perfect. A levelness to existence is what you want to aim for. This is all made more difficult by the fact that the world is so full of things without any intrinsic meaning. Well, I mean to say, chock-a-block. Mothers with babies in prams. All children, everywhere. The poor and the nigger. The past. The other side of the planet. Joy. Suffering. Grocery lists. National parks walking trails. Football. Religion. Road crews. Ironing boards. Antique collections. Books. Telephones. The stock exchange. Hope.

Clearly you take more medicine to extinguish all the tensions.

Inside the syringe, Jack, think of how safe that place must be. And yet, from the dose's point of view, there is nothing to grip. Inside the barrel there is nothing but endless curvature, and a point to which everything drains, and a needle so narrow the atoms must pass through in single file.

I can half-inject the Empirin and lie so still that the needle remains docked in the vein, and a while later, with serene balance, I can push the plunger the rest of its merry way. Every object in the world is journeying.

And the Mormons. Clean men. For clean medical procedures. But mostly I still like to inject myself. In a good glass-barreled syringe you don't need to jack back to find blood in order to confirm the puncturing of the vein. Instead when you hit a vein the plunger slides backward effortlessly—something to do with the vacuum, which is apparently more abundant than we think.

In any case a syringe is like a drill bit, if you really think about it. It pierces through the rock of the flesh to the oil of the blood.

What's more, sometimes I'm of the opinion that the only purposeful and pure direction, now and forever—1973 so clearly being the end of history—is a gliding that takes place in the thirty seconds after the plunger's rubber tip meets the barrel's far wall, at which point everything has been squeezed through the steel of the needle, and meets with my body, which is all that there is and the essence of all that is welcoming.

And only after some time, though time is rather an elastic concept here, does the blander warmth of being able to watch television take place.

The by-product is that one remains, like all good monks, closer to the eternal. I have been fearless at times in my life. Okay, maybe not so much of late. But these years have not been so much a retreat as a purifying. And tomorrow I'll be entirely fearless and fly again. Or is it already today? Completely naked, should the fancy take me. Because everything is cleaner, high in the air.

Also, quite obviously I have an empire to run.

FLUSH RIVETING

IN 1934, WORKING ON the prototype of my H-1, the *Silver Bullet*, I had a moment of great clarity, let's call it an aerodynamic epiphany. I had all thirty thousand round-headed rivets bored out of the fuselage of the plane, and replaced with thirty thousand flush-head rivets.

Flush riveting? I invented it, Jack. Every knob, every protuberance, every obstacle to progress: *Begone*, I said.

You never saw Jean Harlow's Venusian mound after that time she clear-felled the bracken with my razor, but let's just say she would have met no wind resistance either.

Because everything that gets in the way of the wind, or of anything else, is expendable.

TRANSCONTINENTAL RECORD, JANUARY 14, 1936

W HAT I WANTED TO say, after all the noise died down, was simple, and easy, and pure.

That the world's magnificence was enriched by a new beauty: the beauty of speed. And I played no small part in that.

In September '35, in my beautiful H-1, I had already broken the land speed record. But everything just kept getting faster, for a long, long time. There are two types of people in this world. You have to know what you want and focus on getting it. Or not, as the case may be. If your head were on fire, how urgently would you sprint to that nearby body of water? That is what I mean by focus. The *Silver Bullet* was a long time coming: I spent long days and nights through '34 and '35 out at the wind tunnel at Caltech, my alma mater, so to speak. There was so much to learn, peering through that small window, watching the vapor move over the polished hardwood surfaces of the model. There was so much to modify. You shave off every second you can find. This was the first land aircraft to use hydraulically retractable landing gear, and when retracted, it was difficult to even see the seams, so perfect was the fit. We are all moving toward the speed of light.

For the transcontinental attempt at such we grafted a 925-horsepower Wright Cyclone engine, still being tested for the army, onto a Northrop Gamma, the result being a monstrously powerful beast. Also I realized that by climbing up to eighteen thousand feet I could immerse myself in the westerly jet stream and greatly reduce my flight time. From the moment I took off from Burbank, there was a sublime humming in my bones. I arrived in Newark at 12:42 a.m. I had crossed the continent in nine hours and twenty-seven minutes. *Cyclone* seemed a barely adequate name for the vehicle of my conquest.

What I wanted to say was simple: that I liked speed a lot.

You see, I'll say, I knew all about the future, Jack. I saw it coming. I rode on it, I crested it, rode in on it. In an ocean the waves have water to ride on, and sound waves fight their way through air. But light is the medium itself! On the RKO logo, there is a tower on top of the planet, emitting pulses of pure information. My dream was to girdle the globe. My dream was the Empire of Light. The RKO tower was knowledge. But scattered all through the transparent air were those invisible packets of information, resplendent, resplendent. I could make everything happen at once. Every morning I was young again.

And yet now, my old voice whining *cheep-cheep-cheep*, my wings withered to parchment, I am still here, and there is nothing, nothing at all in the world anymore, that could possibly surprise me.

Luckily, there is an incredible aerodynamic twinship between the jet and the syringe, a point worth making despite and not because of its obviousness, since in jet and syringe the flow of time is pierced.

Also I was very much enamored of women. I felt myself courageous in their presence. And sometimes, I simply relaxed.

FUNDAMENTALS OF OXYGEN

A T OTHER TIMES IT didn't pay to completely relax, and one did one's best to fight the drifting snows of sleep. In order to still be here at all. On January 18, 1937, at 3:45 a.m., twenty thousand feet above Arizona, heading east at 330 mph, the oxygen suddenly, inexplicably, cut out. At first I felt no panic. I toggled the switch but to no avail. I noted that my breathing was becoming more rapid, but at exactly the same time

I was overcome by the very lovely sensation—a kind of flooding—that everything, all flight, all of the world and the atmosphere around it, was playing itself out exactly as it should and must. And yet a certain sharpness was gripping my forehead. You have a headache, the happy part of me was telling the other part, I forget which part. And yet a deep and pleasant sleepiness was descending. I could see nothing at the edges of my vision. Oh, how beautiful the world is as a circle, I thought. This little world in front of me, these my knees, these my distant hands. This little lit gauge, these beautiful numbers, so significant in their whiteness, so stark, so self-important: what on earth could they mean? But my eyes felt too big for their sockets, and I blinked. I reached for the emergency supply switch. Nothing changed. My mind swooped into slowness, a grand expanse. There were thoughts taking pleasure in their new stately pace. There were planets being born. There were other thoughts, more distant, and more panicked. The fast thoughts were very annoying to the slow thoughts. The fast thoughts said, You are starting to feel the effects of oxygen deprivation. But what I was feeling, in fact, was something very neutral, and clean: I am my own garden; the sun bears down; a single leaf divides the false and true. Then I discovered I could not even raise my hand to my face. Then I discovered I could not even feel my fingers. My legs were also apparently paralyzed. The glow of the control panel seemed to mean something, but beyond that was absolute blackness, a funnel coming at me, not at the speed of light but at 330 mph, which is fast enough in the dark night, with the fuselage vibrating all around you. Bubbles of nitrogen fizzed distantly in my toes, but up here I was wallowing in my own carbon monoxide, a kind of fog of lassitude. I looked across to my notepad, that pencil dangling like a plumbline on its string. The roaring of the engines suddenly seemed unbearably loud, but the rest of my senses were now far away. My mind was split entirely in two. I was gripped with the sweet hopeless feeling that within a few minutes I would doze off to sleep. Just a little nap would surely see me through. And then I knew I was dying.

Pushing my arms forward from the shoulders, I nosed the plane downwards with all my remaining strength. I needed to get down to where the oxygen was thicker. The danger was I would relax once more and sleep through all that hurtling. It would be a pleasant enough dream of momentum. But I dropped fifteen thousand feet, and gradually my mind returned, at the proper speed, and my body came back together, in this world of broken vessels, and I leveled out the plane from its descent. My heart flared wildly then, and a hot adrenaline burned through my shoulder blades. I held my head, relieved at the simple pleasure of being alarmed. Below me was the Painted Desert, insofar as anything had substance, or even surface, at night, in or from a cockpit. I strained to look upwards, for a glimpse of star or a sliver of moon through clouds. But already it was only distant memory, half-sensed, half-lost: that I had been up there, afloat through the constellations, chewing down hydrogen and argon, gnawing on ether, endlessly unsated, and happy, too.

I HIT THE GROUND RUNNING

M Y NEW YEAR'S RESOLUTIONS for 1938 were: marry Katharine Hepburn, be the first to fly non-stop around the world, and turn Hughes Aircraft into an aviation giant.

It had been a very busy couple of decades. Whenever I looked back I couldn't find the gap that divided events one from the other. I couldn't decode the punctuation that gave one a sense of the way things unfolded. I couldn't put a pattern on the screeching onslaught of time. I had gone to school at Fessenden and then Thacher, and Mother and Father had died in rather quick succession. I had married Ella, basically to keep everybody else happy. Have I spoken about her already, Jack? It is not easy, keeping the events in one's mind. Money married money, like I said. I had fought my relatives and taken control of Hughes Tool, my rightful and eventual inheritance, after all. I had liked the look of the movie game and I'd liked the fine dry heat out west. Los Angeles seemed to me the dawn of everything. I hit the ground running.

The years had passed. I hit the ground running and eventually ran straight into Katharine Hepburn, whose green eyes sparkled. Then I felt I was not the only person on the planet. Even Los Angeles was growing up. And Katharine, as always, brooked no nonsense. I gave her a little help in obtaining the rights to *The Philadelphia Story*, not because I expected anything from her but because of the delighted certainty with which she propounded its imminent, or eventual, success, whichever came first. The only thing not in doubt was that she would thrive, and one always felt somehow blessed in the presence of a thriver.

We ate apple fritters on a cold fall day at the Farmers Market.

I'm astonished that I've even met you, I said. (It had been my experience that unsurprise was what made up the bulk of my days.)

She smiled through a mouthful of apple and batter.

I've a vision for today, she said, and you're included in it.

Well, I'm happy about that.

I see a winding road. I see the ocean.

Sounds like we're going to Malibu! I said.

I see us walking barefoot on the beach.

Even back then I was not a great fan of such close contact with nature—the terrible intimacy, the whiteness of the soles, the loose sand underfoot, the lack of inherent order—but she made all things seem possible for a while, and two hours later I duly rolled up my trousers to the knees.

I had always been exhausted but I was fifteen years or more exhausted when I thought that love, or Katie, would slow things down. Looking back now I see that all things move slowly if at all, that zero is the number toward which all things cluster, that stasis is the condition, that it is only the mind that screens it all so fast and runs the frames together, and that events cascaded, yes of course, it goes without saying, but that the inside of myself somehow consistently eluded me. Meaning I had no sense of space.

And now it matters to me. I mean, everything which is gone forever: which is everything. Because sometimes, Jack, I can't *move* in here, I tell you. And all there is left to do is to tell you what's been lost.

$$\mathrm{I\!I}$$

Speed is simply the rite that initiates us into emptiness.
–Baudrillard, *America*

ROUND-THE-WORLD RECORD, 1938

IN 1938 I CIRCLED the globe. The Lockheed Cyclone, most reliable of airplanes. I flew around the world in an endless arc; my end was my beginning. I was the image of glory, to which the whole world turned. My power was immense. Floyd Bennett Field changed only in time while I reeled away. Everything was still there. I taxied the Cyclone into the same hangar. The same wheel blocks in the same place. I was the master of Time. Tom, Dick, Harry, and Ed—my four-man crew—were the minions of Time.

There we were, in the flow and the smoothness of power and speed. There were no angles on this record-breaking flight. I flew a straight line, nothing but a straight line through curved space. More or less. We left New York at 7:19 p.m. and flew all night and fought fierce winds.

I stared for hours; you would think the horizon doesn't change. But I moved east, across the Atlantic, away from the sun, with the spin of the planet, so darkness falls early, a grand migration into newness.

And I knew that with daylight would come Paris.

And they would be waiting, with bulbs flashing, to connect me back to the world of light. Then I would be me again. I was Howard. Howard Hughes. Desired by all.

The planet spun, the night rolled into dawn. I ate a stale sandwich, drank some water, pissed. The horizon began to glow pink. Above and below that line of light the sky and the ocean seemed equally dark. After about twenty minutes I could begin to make out the soft shapes of clouds in the distance.

In Texas as a boy I had known solitude in the woods with my tin toys. Then airplanes allowed me to take my solitude into the air, into space, encased in the freedom my money could buy, that dazzling horizon always unfolding, beyond which could be anything: good, evil, anything.

Finally the sun began to emerge, scattering light through every scratch and fragment on the windshield. I was shivering by now. The sun was welcome. The cockpit glowed a warm orange. I closed my eyes. I hadn't slept in nearly twenty-four hours. I must have dozed for a minute or two.

I woke with a start, thinking the Lockheed was engulfed in flames. Just the sun. Ed Lund was beside me, smiling, refreshed. I saw an ocean liner far below. I woke Dick Stoddart, the radio man. He sent a cablegram via the liner to Katharine Hepburn.

The morning took shape and there in the distance was the coast of Ireland. Soon we'd cross England, then the English Channel, then track inland to Paris. I stamped, stretched, yawned, cracked my knuckles, drank some coffee, swallowed another amphetamine.

Some hours from then I would land, like an angel of glamor. Howard Hughes, descending from the clouds, arrayed in silver. Light wrapped itself around the world.

Le Bourget airfield. The outskirts of Paris at last. I lowered the flaps, dropped toward the field.

The Lockheed bumped to a halt amid the cheering throng. I could feel my body vibrate as I climbed down from the cockpit. God's pitchfork, Howard Hughes, the biggest, and the first. The clear sound of the future. He has come through the ether like a light wave.

Félicitations, Monsieur Hughes.

All of France welcomes you!

You are tired, sir?

My ears rang as the propellers died. The bulbs snapped. I was blind among my subjects.

The afternoon was hot. Through all the human activity I could hear the whole field thick with the buzzing of insects. Perhaps the whole of Paris that day, July 11, 1938, was a hive of nectar and pistil and stamen and flowering, of all the bees sucking the life from the buds. A juicy kind of day. Perhaps the whole of France was awash with the drone of cicadas.

I walked toward the hangar. It seems to me now there could not possibly have been a single stray thought in my flight-weary brain. I whispered in an official's ear.

Mr. Hughes will have two hours' rest, he said.

OASIS OF BLOSSOM AND LIGHT

SOME GIRLS WOULD GET all weak-kneed, but not in a good way, about planes. It was not like it's become by now, with the big 707s and the rise of the airlines ferrying passengers all over the globe; in the thirties all this was only just moving into the possible. (And I helped make it happen.) To some women planes were frightening and powerful at the same time, which seemed to work as a kind of aphrodisiac. There were women who got very nervous about my coming in to land. Well, it's not like parking a car. Implicit in that balancing act, that aligning of Dunlop with tarmac, was the notion of disintegration, flayed skin and crumpled steel, annihilation and exploding flame. There's a lot of power involved. You don't slow it down to twenty knots and come in soft. And from the windshield you can't fully see what you're doing. Women sense this. In the co-pilot's seat it will either give them heart palpitations and dry their throat in a rush of constricted fear or it will flood them with adrenaline and desire. Someone like little Faith Domergue, I knew she never really liked it, those trips out to the airfield, the taxiing and take-off and landing, and I knew especially that the fucking in the air was something of a duty to her, no more than the expected thing. While Katharine Hepburn loved nothing more than a good fuck before or after take-off.

We were like two bony whippets going at it. I created my own early version of autopilot by jamming a hammer and wire into the joystick, level with the horizon, cruising speed, cruising altitude, all systems go, we had liftoff, we had landing, plump clouds in the distance, the whole vulvic extravaganza, bagpipes playing in the engine's drone, flight approval, the works. I did more than almost anyone to put the cock into cockpit. I was a leader among leaders.

One time we flew all night in the Sikorsky, LA to Salt Lake City, Salt Lake City to Lincoln, Lincoln to Chicago and on to New York by dawn, to refuel yet again and head up the coast to Connecticut, to Fenwick, the Hepburns' summer home. Kate curled up and slept on the daybed. I'd had the seats removed. It was like our little apartment in the sky. For a while I forgot about her. Blackness was everything; or the vague suggestion of horizon. I was there with my dials and controls. The great Midwest rolled under us, milk and honey and the restless cattle in the dark fields, the high schools asleep, the children asleep, the soft breathing of millions. The hours passed. The city lights like diamond glints or clusters of algae phosphorescent in some deep ocean. There's always about an hour when you expect to see the faint pink smudge of dawn appear and when you think you're beginning to see it, but you are not. You imagine it all. It is the longest time of night. And finally it really does start to come, that longed-for hint of sun. An hour or more before the sun itself, a blue glow lightening slowly away from darkest blue, to pale mauve. To pink. Suddenly (I mean eventually, I mean the two things came at once) there were hands over my eyes. Boo! Guess who? She ran her fingers down my chest, down into my groin. I stirred, half-turned, her shirt hung open, her dart-like breasts protruding. Her silk underclothes fell effortlessly to the floor, six thousand feet above the earth. She was red, red, red, her freckles, her fiery bush, her hair set free, the bands of flushing up her neck that overcame her whenever sex was close. I was ramjet-ready, Lord yes. I sprawled out from the seat, my long legs spread. She sat astride, she smothered me with slippery kisses. Oh, to be straddled by a star in a high, thin atmosphere. Oh, the vibrating of the pilot's seat. She ground and groaned, smearing my thigh with her wetness. We kissed a good long while as the light seeped in and the objects reappeared. Joystick. Altimeter. Ignition. Intercom. She docked at last. I slid into Katharine Hepburn like Joy into a burrow, if Joy were a rabbit, heading for home. I held her bony ass in the palms of my hands. Beyond her flaming tresses the sky was turning pink. This was way past purple, I think I need to stress. And of course there is that Other, that Ultimate pink, in there, down there, where I am, where I am in, where I am in and out, where I am in and out, where I am in and out, where I am watching with such wonder, watching the edges of her pink, her pinkness, her pinkocity, almost hidden, almost exposed, enveloping, regularly, pretty much, my dick. I am in and out of there, more often in, more often in, it is in that really matters. The sky is beginning to flare pink behind her. Goodness I seem to have changed tense in all the excitement. The sky was beginning to flare pink behind her. We slowed it down. I held her buttocks in place with the controls. We gently rocked. The plane swayed, tracing a path of sine waves through the air. Katharine, Katie. I watched the first edge of the sun split the sky. Then I looked down at our genitals so happily enmeshed. Then back up at the sun. It's like a dialogue with the host star of your system: *Are you watching this? Are you watching this?* And I looked into Kate's green eyes. And perhaps, turned inwards to the fuselage of that plane, turned away from that fluorescently expanding display of light, she saw that sun come up on the horizon of my pupils. Who ever knows such things? You would think all that angularity meant a certain coldness. On the contrary, she comported herself, she faced the world, she did her thing, demanded her demands, methodical and businesslike...and then she let go. And she was gone. I passed much happy goneness with that girl.

Later, returning from the east, the Grand Canyon opened beneath us, a giant gash, astonishment made geological. Lake Mead passed. The Mojave desert was like a wreck, a great ruin, the lone and level sands stretching far away, coming into that oasis of blossom and light, Los Angeles.

There was a time my life was so filled with potential.

LESSENING THE RISK OF FAILURE

BUT POTENTIAL HAS A way of going sideways. I was always moving from woman to woman, but they were in motion, too—it could get confusing. Everybody leading their own separate lives. What a concept.

After Katharine, I distracted myself with the delicious Fay Wray, whose whole body tensed when she finally came, whose very lungs contracted and forced out of her that mournful whimper. There were moments with Fay when I felt a kind of balance, afterwards; so completely opened out was she, in her sweetness, when she sighed, and sweetly smiled, and slept. Memory is a funny thing. Time can be sped up or slowed down according to your means. But mostly we had trouble ever catching up with our breath, and I sweated a lot, and it dripped from my chin into Fay Wray's eyes. She had a tiny potbelly that bulged when she pushed. We fumbled for each other, we grappled; it seemed, while it lasted, there was no struggle ever so sublime and serene.

But then I was getting bored already, and at any rate was back in contact with Ginger Rogers by now, the post-Hepburn consolation chase. One fading, one active, and one to pursue: always a good system to keep rolling over. The very last time I saw Fay she'd covered the entire bed with gardenia petals, an act more imaginative in the symbolism than the reality, though the smell, admittedly, was exquisite. They are very soft to lie upon, at first. Three days later I was still fishing fragments of mulch from between my buttocks.

I was a mystery even to myself, Jack. To be perfectly frank, after Kate Hepburn, just as after Billie Dove, I suppose one could say I went off the rails again, sexually speaking. A lot of Ginger Rogers, a little Bette Davis. It was all too much. Katie, Carole, Fay. Even the greatest

prize was not enough. Did I say too much then not
enough? It was a very long time ago. I pissed everybody
off. I remember one time trying to make Hepburn jealous
by being very public over on the east coast with Rogers.
At the same time I was chasing (and fucking) Olivia de
Havilland, bad manners enough from Ginger's (and
Kate's) points of view. Then I was chasing (but not, alas,
fucking) Olivia's sister, Joan Fontaine. Absolute idiocy,
and I wasn't thinking on my feet, and I did not account
for sisterly loyalty. That about ruined it for everyone.

And none of it actually meant anything; the simple
fact was I couldn't stop myself. I acted on the spur of
the moment. Often I didn't know what I was going to
do five minutes before I did it. There's no explanation
for anything. I was driven. Because it was there. Because
you either respond to the Instructions or you don't. And
you only live once. It was just who was who at the time.
Olivia was riding on *Gone With the Wind*, Joan heading
into *Rebecca*. It's not that I actually was a shallow person,
Jack, more that existence itself is nothing but a laminate.
I went with the flow of my power.

But I knew that change would find me, eventually,
regardless of whether I sought it first. So as a preliminary
step I spring-cleaned the Muirfield house in 1939: there
was ten years or more of junk there stretching back to
Billie Dove, back even to Ella. I packed it all up, all the
silverware, all the crystal goblets, sent it all off to the
storehouse, 7000 Romaine, where it could gather dust
and dream deep inanimate dreams for the decades to

come. I wanted to be alone. I wanted some space. Well, I wanted to be relatively alone.

In a crate in the cellar I found the propeller from the Thomas Morse Scout that I'd crashed in 1928 when I was shooting the stunt for *Hell's Angels*. I dragged it clunking up the stairs and laid it in the corner of the dining room, like a display in a museum. Damned thing had stalked me, nearly taken my head off as the plane collected the runway and shattered like glass. And now, eleven years later, what a busy eleven years it had been. How quickly all the women came and went, Jack.

So I kept that deformed propeller on display. Cary Grant came for dinner one night and sputtered, Howard, what the hell is that?

My reminder, I told him, that death is only ever an instant away. I didn't really believe it at the time, but I liked the theatricality.

For weeks I brooded up at Muirfield, missing them all. Ginger, the lot of them. Ginger especially, who had once told me she'd slept with a lot of men, she knew a lot about them, and that she had insight that I was fundamentally damaged in my relationships with women.

How many men? I'd interrupted.   ·

That's a typical man's question, she'd replied.

No, but how many?

Howard, please don't sidetrack the conversation.

No, but it seems a reasonable—

—four hundred and seventy-nine.

Now you're just being facetious.

My point, if you'll let me continue—

Four hundred and seventy-nine. Now *that's* some damage.

She shook her head and sighed. It's like you're not really there.

I'm always here. Look, here I am.

You don't open yourself, Howard.

There was a long silence then, longer than the kind I would ever allow in my movies.

I'm completely open, I said. I'm just not good at talking about it.

Then she smiled warmly, or rather, sadly, and said, Howard.

Spending time with Ginger had always made me feel good. I respected her bluntness. She didn't seem as desperate or flighty as most of the others. It seemed that for Ginger sex was like laughter. Like oxygen perhaps: it seemed she was saying, We none of us need bother be very aware of our breathing. As for me, I merely thought the fun would go on forever. At all times back then, with everyone, mind you.

Yet I hated the uncertainty of Ginger's affections, and I hated her nonchalance. She acted as if she could take me or leave me! It put a panic in my throat. I always found the best thing in these circumstances—in most circumstances, if I'm truly honest—was to sleep with other women, to lessen the risk of failure by spreading it around.

What was I to make of her insight? I'm sure we're all damaged, when you think about it, Jack. I'm sure we've all got something we don't want to feel. Like feelings, for instance! I don't see how that's relevant to how we...well, how we brace ourselves and move forward. Because that is what we do. We pull up our socks.

Yet on Muirfield Road, sleepless from the amphetamines and endlessly going over everything in my head, what I remembered, time and time again, was that rainy day when the circus all became too much for Ginger, and she ended it. The roads were slick. I had not been concentrating and, coming down La Cienega, had a small car crash, possibly my fault. My head hit the steering wheel. I wound up in the hospital, concussed. Noah was downstairs doing his best to keep the press placated and informed in the waiting room. Then Ginger burst into my hospital room, startling me with the foaming incoherence of her rage. It was most unfair. My head hurt. I told the nurse to leave. Ginger flung the engagement ring at me. Why you, why you, and words to that effect.

And there was nothing I could do. I just thought always that if it's *possible* to fuck all these women then *how the hell could you not?* The simple desire for acquisition: what on earth was wrong with that? There was something fallacious in my logic but I couldn't quite pinpoint the problem.

But the timing was awful. The other women had meant nothing. At the moment I lost Ginger, I understood both her magnificence and my stupidity. I wanted her merely to caress me, to make it all better. But that gold band missed my head entirely and pinged off the bedside lamp and disappeared, perhaps forever or into the pocket of a hospital cleaner, beneath the gurney on the other side of the bed. Ginger stormed out of the room and out of my life.

But think about it, Jack. It was bound to happen. With her "insights" and her mature viewpoint—her dastardly trick of shifting the ground from the pure physicality of bonding to the where-are-we-going-with-this?—Ginger was always trying to goad me into thinking. Yet the problem was precisely that I thought too much. When what I needed to do, at any given time, was brace myself. And move forward.

GORGEOUS GIRLS LOOKING FOR SCREEN BREAKS

AFTER ALL, JACK, THERE was a war going on by now. Why would I bother myself with this girl or that girl, with the goddamned specifics of it? These were momentous times. When the Japanese bombed Pearl Harbor I knew instantly there would be a lot of business coming the way of Hughes Aircraft. I knew it was my duty to rise to the occasion.

You have to make your destiny. I promised the government I would build and deliver five hundred cargo airplanes—my ill-fated flying boat *Hercules*, or the *Spruce Goose* as everyone unkindly called it. So I spent a lot of 1942 preoccupied with research. Then it was stressful work all through '43 and on into '44 and '45, trying to develop *Hercules* at the same time as trying to get Defense to buy the XF-11, a contract worth forty-five million—an awful lot of money back then, Jack. A group of brass came out from Washington, the military board headed by Colonel Elliott Roosevelt, the president's son, making the decision about which airplane contract to award to whom. I got Johnny Meyer to find starlets to spend time with these guys for the next few days—gorgeous girls looking for screen breaks; we called them the Boob Buffet. The flexibility of morality is truly hilarious when a studio contract looms. Likewise for soldiers, in the face of the flesh, in the juice of the fruit. We kept everyone plied and sated, wined, dined and blow-jobbed. You have to make your destiny. It was not my fault that, in relation to the *Hercules*, costs blew out and I couldn't deliver on schedule. I did fly that giant at last, but not until three months after they'd hauled me before the Senate War Investigating Committee for never having got it off the water. It was the largest plane that ever flew, even if only for a few minutes. Sure, I could almost have reached down from the cockpit and scooped up some harbor water with my bare hands. But we flew. I felt I'd proved my point, the point possibly being: better late than never.

I gave it my best. At the Mocambo on Sunset Strip, on a jasmine-soaked Los Angeles night, as the Gene

Krupa Orchestra flailed and pulsed, these men, I tell you, felt, if not like gods, then like kings. Certainly not like soldiers, in any case! And even the kings have a little boy's fascination for airplanes, and movies, and girls.

But as for me, nothing was really new; everything was transparent. Late at night I would drive out to Culver City and haunt the huge hangars at Hughes Aircraft. I would stand in the empty blue darkness staring for hours at the XF-11, the pure potentiality of energy, not knowing then how one day that sleek beast would so badly unravel and scorch me. Not knowing anything bad, for just that moment. I would wander through the research divisions, unrolling the beautiful blueprints of the planes, and run my fingers over those surfaces, so flat, so endlessly deep. I thought of my lonely planes, unused, unflown for years, scattered at all the airports as if in waiting and meditation.

I was so very in love with America!

THRUMMING

N OT TO SAY PATRIOTISM doesn't have its costs. One gives up a great deal for one's country. Everybody was after me. Everybody wanted a piece of me. Not everybody was my friend. Not everybody appreciated what I was doing. There were so many decisions to be made. Everything happened on the run. I was always flailing my arms, keeping the bats at bay. Jack, I'm wearing myself out even thinking about it. Because you see, by now I was very nervous, or exhausted, or suffering perhaps on a regular or semi-regular basis from nervous exhaustion or semi-regular nervous exhaustion.

And I just wanted a woman, a little girl rather, who wouldn't answer back. Hepburn and Rogers had taken their toll; the goddamned war was in full swing. So Faith Domergue seemed just the ticket.

It was all so easy.

I said: I have big plans for you.

I said: Let's forget about the party. Let's spend some time alone.

The way even the mothers would collude! One conversation, assuring Mrs. Domergue of my honorable intentions, was all it took to get her, Mrs. Domergue, to allow me, the wolf in sheep's clothing, to have Faith flown to Palm Springs. And that was all I needed, of course. To have Faith indeed.

I flew her to the Salton Sea. Is this the greatest day in history? We walked out into the lake, the salt gloop rising to our ankles and shins, then our thighs. Her fifteen-year-old behind so pert in her brand new bathing suit (mauve, with hyacinths), her fifteen-year-old head reeling with erotic anxiety, feeding on those dreams, those desires (not desire for Howard Hughes, not really, not specifically, I know, I know, I'm not a total fool, but the greater, more abstract desire to be the focus of everyone else's attention, and myself a kind of bridge to that), her fifteen-year-old breasts holding steady, so engaged with the horizon, her fifteen-year-old thighs glimpsed from the corner of my thirty-six-year-old eyes sending my thirty-six-year-old loins beatifically anticipatory with desire. Oh yes, desire. I neglected to mention my own.

Oh, it is all a thrumming and a throbbing. We lay there suspended on the surface of the water. A world of wetness waiting. Water trickling, the soft murmur of seclusion, sunlight like a balm, Faith so pliant. The Salton Sea was a very still corner of the world; even the ripples were silent. And in the midst of all that salt, Faith Domergue's lips were like honeysuckle. When life was so liquid it flowed through your fingers, that's when it mattered the most. It didn't matter that she was fifteen. One day she'll be a hundred and fifteen. Like the speed of light, age is relative to the observer. Perhaps the whole world is corrupt. Perhaps no one need take responsibility for anything, really.

The sun passed high above, beyond desire. Down here the water trickled in our ears.

It is all about bodies of water, Jack. Our bodies, in fact, are seventy percent water, and one day won't we all simply evaporate from the earth? One day we will evaporate.

FORTY FATHOMS DEEP

EVAPORATE, OR GET SUCKED under. Ceco Cline, my engineer, never came back up for air. Lake Mead was less than three hundred miles from the Salton Sea and less than six months later. That was where the furies caught up with me and gathered for a picnic on May 17, 1943. When I crashed my S-43 into the cold, cold water. Yes, people died. Yes, I was at the controls. But it was not my fault. I was sleep-deprived. I had been up all night fighting with, and fucking, but mostly fighting with Ava Gardner. I had defense contracts to fulfill and a Senate investigation to navigate. The government was breathing down my neck and over both shoulders—there were G-men in the cockpit, for God's sake. My supremacy was being challenged on all fronts. I was simply annoyed. Perhaps I brought it in too fast. Okay, I wanted to shake them up, bump them about. Okay. So I came in too fast.

Too fast onto Lake Mead. What can one do? This happened, that happened. On any given day a lot of things happen. That particular day, I think about it as little as possible. And anyway, I always keep the medicine tin on hand.

To which I will now turn my attention.

FAITH HAD THE RANGE OF THE PALACE

SO THEN. WHERE WAS I? We were talking about Faith Domergue, and a time my life was so filled with horizon. Some said she was rather young. She seemed old

enough to me. Fifteen? Okay. So what? I would need to
see the birth certificate. It certainly wasn't complication
that I was looking for. Our happiness lasted, in its
terrible simplicity, for more than eighteen months.

Hepburn and Rogers and Lombard were long gone
by now. Did I say that already, Jack? Loss was never good,
of course, but there was always some solace and clarity
when things became definitive. During this time with
Faith I also saw on the odd occasion, if memory serves...
Lana Turner. Rita Hayworth. Ava Gardner. Because it was
good to mix some adult company in there with all the
schoolgirl fun. But here's the thing, Jack, man to man.
(I hope I can admit this to him.) By seventeen Faith was
already too feisty for my liking! It's hard to credit. She
intimated she was getting sick of things, of being held on
a rope, of my absences. So, embracing the symbolism of
new beginnings, I finally sold Muirfield and leased a huge
house at 619 Sorbonne Road on a hilltop ledge in Bel-Air.
And Faith had the range of the palace.

But even that didn't satisfy her. She harassed me
relentlessly about this role and that role, this screen
test and that screen test. Complained about this starlet,
that starlet. Said that I kept her out of view and that she
was withering, like a flower without adequate sunlight.
She had a turn of phrase, that one! But for goodness'
sake, she was barely an appropriate age. The whole thing
was a delicate matter. She had so much space up there.
She had voice and drama tutors, a dance instructor,
a chef. A swimming pool. What she lacked, Jack, was

patience. I was grooming her, and grooming was always a very methodical business. She just didn't see the bigger picture. I was older and wiser. I had access to the bigger picture. I knew when the time would be right to make our run. *Her* run, I should say. But she merely complained incessantly of feeling trapped up there.

Well. You'd think a little gratitude would go a long way. But one night in early '43 I was driving with Ava Gardner. From memory I'd just proposed to her at Caraway's on Sunset Strip. Ava had said no, good-humoredly of course. Later that night, on Fairfax heading toward Wilshire, Faith Domergue passed us by in the opposite direction, proving that even Los Angeles is not a big enough town. I saw her head jerk around as she passed. Our eyes locked. Almost at the same instant she was pulling a screeching U-turn.

Oh dear.

Ava turned and said, And who is this?

She's a little angry, I said.

I had told Faith...I have no idea. Perhaps I had told her I was going to the screening room. Perhaps the airfield. Perhaps we had had a fight earlier. It may have been the night she had almost caught me with Rita Hayworth, with whom I was only very occasionally sleeping, so it would have been unfair to have been caught. Faith had arrived home unexpectedly. Rita had slipped out the back way. Rita was not the point here but Faith was not to know that. Rita was non-committal and, more importantly, non-complex, sex. Faith, that simplest of girls, was becoming anxious, and needy. And complex! When complexity abounded one turned to states of being that were pure, that rang through like a bell pealing across snow, like Rita Hayworth tumbling bedwards with abandon, ding-dong.

Hard to believe now, but I had quite the energy for all this then. Why so many women? I needed to know that everything was in place. I needed to put things in order. When I was very little, I counted the telegraph poles as they whooshed past, upside down from the back seat of Father's car on a long drive back to Houston on a distant day when we'd driven to test a new drill in a well. So I had a history of putting things in order. It had been a lovely dinner with Ava. It didn't even matter she said no. (I proposed to her a few other times over the next few years, but I think we both knew it was a gentle kind of game: the game of Howard trying to paint himself in a good light. She was an awfully hard nut to crack!) What really mattered was the texture of night, the hint of nasturtium on a soft breeze, the hint of pink (the light not the flesh) high in a late spring sky, the hint of pink (the flesh not the light) imagined, there, beside me, in the passenger seat, between Ava's exquisite legs, beneath the rustling of the crinoline, imagined as a soon-to-be-uncovered event back in the apartment I'd set her up in. What mattered was the Cadillac as a vehicle of ecstasy. Every movement was a movement toward an ultimate peace. The last thing I'd imagined was to see Faith Domergue out driving alone. Compartments, compartments. How did I ever manage?

She fishtailed out of the U-turn, accelerating to try
and catch us.

Oh dear, I said again.

Faith in her Roadster, a red convertible, came hurtling
closer from behind. I felt suddenly a neutral, alert curiosity.
A great acceptance entered my muscles. She rode the horn
insistently. Ava kept turning around. I watched in the rear-
view mirror as the Roadster loomed too close.

Goodness! said Ava.

Then Faith bumped our car, from behind, hard. Ava
screamed.

Faith accelerated and pulled level on the inside lane.

Faith! I tried to shout. She was glaring at Ava.
She was putting the name to the face. She was driving
dangerously, veering close to our car. I braked and
slowed. She did the same. I accelerated, pulled in front
of her, cut her off.

I swung left, across a gap in the traffic, pulling into
the parking lot of the Farmers Market, tires screeching,
Faith hard on my tail. I braked hard, as did Faith.

And there we all were.

Faith gunning the engine of the car I had bought
her. Anger converted to horsepower.

Howard...I don't like this, said Ava.

Then Faith reversed, giving her some maneuvering
room. She stepped on it and the Roadster roared
toward us. Crashed into us, into the passenger door.
Ava screamed again, fumbling away from the impact
back toward me. Faith reversed, floored it again. I had

a moment of secret admiration but it was effectively overruled by anger. Plus, I always felt quite strongly about the wanton destruction of property. She slammed into us three quick times before I managed to jump from my car, run around the other side, reach in and switch off her engine. I shook her and shook her. She was cold with rage. I had never seen such hatred. Ava was screaming. I held Faith tight. Then she began to cry. To blubber, in fact. It was a flood. She looked very unattractive streaked with all those tears.

But that was it as far as Ava went that night. A bystander drove her home. Placating Faith became the order of the evening. We needed to get out of there before too much attention was attracted. I paraded out the same old promises about making her a star. Her sobbing subsided. Who's not to say that the whole of life is nothing more than a legalized form of prostitution? She was a sweet, sweet girl. But things were effectively over then. I promised her great fame; I didn't deliver. Those were momentous times, after all.

IN·FLIGHT ENTERTAINMENT

B UT ALL TIMES ARE momentous times. What you have to remember, Jack, is that I was always one step ahead of the game. I brought to everyone the future on a golden platter. In-flight movies? Oh yes. I invented them, too. I knew that particular war would end, so I saw the future of passenger transport. I invested great faith in TWA. I knew that one day soon we would begin to move the multitudes vast distances. And I know about the multitudes, how no one can sit with themselves, facing forward, for long. So we spooled up films. To cheat the passage of time. Because you can get lost in a good movie. Although sometimes, during turbulence, the film would jump off its sockets—an unwanted interruption to the lostness, of course. There were many problems to iron out. Headphone technology. State screening taxes in relation to North American airspace. I was a world leader!

And did you know, Jack, that nowadays they've taken to projecting the films on something called video? Have you heard about video? It can't jump off the spools, no matter how big the bumps. And you can rewind it, you can make people reverse, you can make time go backwards. You can look at the bits that you like, again and again. Without having to re-spool. And what you lose in quality, you make up for in accessibility.

IF I TELL YOU I HAD SUCKED ON JANE GREER'S DELICATE NIPPLE

REMEMBER, THERE IS A great problem with the passage of Time, which is supposedly, or on the surface at least, merely the measure of motion with respect to

before and after. Our central tragedy lies therefore in the
logical outcome of this fact: to wit, that every sexual act
(I include here of course the truly marvelous and indeed
the transcendent) happens separately and sequentially.
When I would want it all at once, eternally. Someone
once said Time is merely Nature's Way Of Making Sure
Everything Doesn't Happen At Once. Yet if you had
taken Jane Greer to Ocean Park, the fairgrounds that
ran along the Santa Monica Pier, on that summer night,
pungent with sea-salt, in 1944, and played the carny
games, and shot the ducks, and taken her home and
made love, you would want it all to happen, again and
again, all the time, forever.

Mother had not had much time for carnivals,
which were, she said, so patently unclean. And so it
was astounding to become a child again. After I first
contracted Jane to RKO there was a hiccup, a frosty
false start, when I heard she'd started seeing Rudy
Vallee. (Later she married him, but it didn't last long.)
What right had she to see other men? I made her, I
owned her, for now. I found her in *Life*. I housed
her. I would call her when ready. So I was not happy
to learn she was impatient, had hit the nightspots
without my knowledge, albeit with her mother in
tow. I was not happy with her insubordination. I'm
sure she married Vallee just to get at me. Luckily
she was only one of my many problems; there were
always problems, life was always busy. Otherwise I
might have caused real havoc.

In any case the Vallee vector blipped off the radar very quickly. At around the same time, watching Jane Greer in test rushes, I began to realize just how extraordinarily beautiful she was, and I found myself falling in love. Night after night I would watch her on the screen. Her sleepy, puffy eyes seemed haunted with desire. For a time it was clear I had never seen anyone as beautiful as Bettejane Greer. She became a matter of urgency. I sent her vanloads of flowers. In the ghost train on the midway she shrieked, we laughed, she held me tight, while unseen and unheard—the real horror—the sea fog eroded the boardwalk beneath us, patiently, inexorably, with geological cunning.

For some reason, twenty years after the deaths of my parents, this was a time when my mind was having trouble and the past was flooding back. I was trying to relax. It was very difficult. A lot of the time my head hurt. There was a sharp pain, a throbbing behind my left eye. I was trying to hold it all together. It helped to be methodical. I was finding that lists were an asset. Whatever I wrote, it would get done. A starlet's name on a sheet of yellow paper meant a whole lot of planning and preparation. I was in love with Jane Greer. I was cracking up. I was trying to do things in sequence. There is only so much you can get done in one day.

Arm in arm with Jane at Ocean Park I thought I could feel, enveloping us like that sea mist, tendrils and wisps of contentment. I thought of a future. My mind opened out into sunlight, slants of sunlight in a room filled with baby's toys, Jane happy, the infant happy, myself beside myself with happiness. All things are possible. She was the most beautiful girl I had ever seen, tender and delicate and so filled with yearning. Solicitous and compassionate. She would understand everything there was to understand about me. At Ocean Park I hugged her tight. I forgot for a while my fear of women's greed, my awareness that all understood that with me there came a wealth beyond accountability. We embraced. Her lips grazed my ear. I could grow to love you, she said.

I needed only to remember back to that night several weeks earlier, when we had first made love in my suite at the Town House Hotel. After we swam in the pool I suggested she shower in my room. Chlorine is an undisputed force for good, but who wants it to cling there longer than necessary? We took the lift to the suite, wrapped in the hotel bathrobes. I passed her some towels. She went into the bathroom. The shower started running. I waited by the window. She emerged, toweled torso and head. I went inside and showered. Our bathrobes crumpled together on the floor like soldiers haphazardly fallen. I came out, towel around my waist, ready, if she were already dressed, to go into my dressing room. But Jane sat awkwardly on the edge of the bed, her towels still around her. Her eyes were gray and empty like a Sphinx. I sat beside her, leaned, put my hand to the back of her neck. Her skin was hot and moist. She pulled the towel from her head. Her

damp hair fell free. We kissed. You would need to watch
her closely in *Out of the Past* (with Robert Mitchum) to
know from what I tell you here that I have indeed been
one of the lucky men in history. You would need to get
from that movie an idea of her sublime sadness. Did I
say sadness? I must have meant softness. In her lips was
all the ineffable essence of welcoming. Perhaps, on the
other hand, if you watch that movie it will merely make
you resent me. Not you, specifically, Jack. But the world
is full of Hughes-related resentments. For Mitchum was
play-acting and I, my friend, was not. Her hair fell free
and we kissed. We hoisted ourselves more fully onto the
bed. The towel had barely covered her thighs and now
no longer did. If I tell you I had sucked on Jane Greer's
delicate nipple, if I tell you that at the entrance to her so
precise cunt she had smelled, so neutrally, so abstractly,
of nothing but shower and heat, and that down there
my tongue and my fingers had grazed until I had—within
minutes, miraculously, it seemed—drawn from within
her a more pungent feast, acidic and metallic, tasting
somehow distantly of blood-tinged plum, of honey
and licorice, if I tell you she spread her legs so wide
and arched her back and that her ten sharp nails dug
deliciously into my scalp and that she held me there and
ground me there but not for long since I rose up and
entered her, outside and inside carrying now in such a
flood of urgency only the loosest of meanings, before
she had even once touched with her fingers my cock and
my balls, could you grasp just how beautiful this was?

You could only stumble in the dark. You could bring to bear perhaps your own experience. It would be the most unsatisfactory of analogies.

There is a wheel of glory always turning, and wherever I am, I am tracing out glorious circles.

I was really getting into some troublesome loops, the epoch of Jane and the pier in the mist. I could have grown to love her, too. But I was cracking up around this time. I have the feeling I keep making that point. My thoughts were getting very cluttered. The parts of me that acted were being ordered by the parts of me that directed to do the things that had to get done. There was so much cleaning. There were things that could assail you. Good grief, when I think now of all those moist wet vaginas and what they harbored. How did I ever make it through? Quite clearly I was predestined for the quest. On the other hand, in the midst of Greer's great generosity, clearly there was *absolutely nothing to worry about.* Even the clap (though I didn't expect it, and nor did I get it, from this virginal nineteen-year-old) would have been merely another event in the sequence of events that defined the before, during and after of our days. At least the goddamned days moved on! Otherwise you could be caught there forever: washing your hands, did I get it right, washing your hands, did I get it right, washing your hands, did I get it right, is it gone is it gone is it gone is it gone is it gone. Is it gone now?

BAY OF PLENTY

T HE SEQUENCE BEING, IN 1945 I went a little off kilter.
I thought everyone was out to get me; now I realize,
I admit it, I can see it more clearly, that probably only
half of them were. In any case it pays to be careful, to be
clean. And I was very, very tired. It had been a busy war.
I had military contracts to fulfill. I had delivery dates. It
is not pleasant to have the government bearing down on
you. Because everything had to be perfect. So they had
to wait. Sure, the war was ending, that specific one, but
war was eternal, and there was in fact more money in it
cold. But Dr. Verne Mason diagnosed exhaustion. He
said, Stop and take a vacation or your body will do it
without you. I thought he had a point, that I should get
away for a week or so. To slow down the nervous energy.
Surely that's every citizen's right in a democracy.

So I called up Joe Petrali, one of my pilots. He
prepared the plane.

Plot me a route to Shreveport, I said. Because in
1912 it had been a magical town, the grand magnolias
and the woodbine blooming, the softness of the air, the
whistles and the sirens of the Red River steamboats,
the night sky pulsing huge and crimson from the gas-
lake fires. And Father had taken me with him there on
business, a special treat, we were a team, the sun was
shining, the century was young, I was six years old. So

three decades later I was hoping, I was clenching my jaw
with the yearning, that the Shreveport I had known, or
some fragment of it, was still there. Because nothing is
destroyed or lost. Only the forms of the clusters of atoms
change. And all that is needed is patience.

I went up with Petrali. He asked no questions, a
good and loyal man.

I had tens of thousands of dollars in my suitcase,
and shirts and tennis sneakers and very little else. I
thought I might go away for a week, but a great sadness
was brewing and, behind it, the notion that I might leave
my entire life behind, forever.

The decisions we make in a trough.

We were high over the wilds of south Texas, not far
from Houston. I looked down over that pale landscape,
where once I had been small. It had been a very long
time, life so far I mean. I could feel it running through
my hands. There was so much anxiety. The shoulders
were so tight. Suddenly I slumped in my seat. I do not
know what came over me. We might as well have been
free-falling up there, adrift on the Texas winds. Below
us were dinosaurs turning to tar in the swamps. The
eons passed. The ice caps came and went. There were
owls so asleep you could die of old age in their dreams.
With a great sob I let go of the controls and buried my
head in my hands. The plane lurched wildly. Petrali sat
to attention, took his own controls and wrestled the
plane back on course. It was difficult to cry in front of
another man. But I was beyond protocol. I was weeping

until my neck muscles burned and my lungs were a single lost howl.

Petrali was a good, kind man, who never said a word. I sat immobile in that cockpit, my body weightless, my eyes washed clean from the crying, confused by everything, by the instrument panel, by the clouds, all the way to Louisiana.

At last, in the distance, were the vast blue-black bayou cloud formations, pitted with lightning. We fought malevolent thundershowers as we landed near dark. The tarmac steamed with dusk heat. I trundled off the plane, heavy with, I'm not certain. Heavy with despair, or exhaustion, or relief, I could not get the coordinates right.

At the Jefferson Hotel in Shreveport I stretched out in a star shape on the bed. My limbs were still. Life was suddenly plentiful. I fell into a deep sleep from which I woke some hours later. Petrali had gone to a movie, left a note.

Alone in that hotel room I could finally take stock. Only Petrali knew where I was. I was truly free. The peasants slept by haystacks in the framed print on the wall.

I rapidly drank a glass of water.

I tested the bounce of the bed. Its plainness was magnificent.

These infinite riches in a little room. It seemed, that pulsing Shreveport night, that I awoke from my staleness, into perfume, into colors and flavors. In my waking sleep, in my infinite alertness, God existed in perfect solitude. I was at this point as yet uncreated. And still He called out to me, Am I not your Lord?

I said, Yes, I bear witness to it.

I saw myself distantly, dwelling there already, in glorious isolation on some faraway beach.

In the morning I said to Petrali, You'll be hearing from me. I took a Greyhound bus to Florida. I disappeared for three months. I had military contracts to fulfill. I had delivery dates. It was all running far behind. None of it mattered. I knew I had to actually not care, not just pretend to not care.

The white highways of Florida unfolded. I was sensing some palm at the end of my mind; I would know it when I got there, to the place where I could rest in the shade of that tree. My own reflection in the Greyhound window was drenched in light as the wooden churches and roadside diners flickered past.

* * *

I BECAME THE WANDERER. Not Howard Hughes, but a simple man, with modest needs. I rented a beachfront cottage near Fort Lauderdale, three months' cash up front. I wandered all day, for days, just the wind and the seabirds and the tussocky dunes and the noise of the waves. My skin browned. My hair was stiff with salt. I grew a beard. The ocean was a desert; for ninety days I fasted there. I lived on the sun, and on oranges and Hershey bars. I burned almost all my clothes one night in a bonfire on the beach. I understood simplicity at

last. I slept eleven hours at a stretch, dreamlessly and
still. I spoke to no one for days on end. A family said
Good afternoon. Good afternoon, I nodded back, my
pockets full of seashells. But one night I dreamed of a
gold-feathered bird.

And in the morning I felt a stirring, at last, in my
cock. I had found by the ocean God without and God
within, but now the Appendage God was getting restless.
He snapped my mind back into place. I woke as if from
a holy dream. As if from a stillness in the desert. There
were women! There were all those juicy girls. Where had
I been? It was June by now, June '45, debutante season in
New York. And Faith was in Los Angeles. And Ava, too.
There were others, their names escape me right now, but
that is beside the point. Oh, all the girls so wanted to be
naked, Jack. I had to get back, and fast, to the world of
that nakedness. But I felt very replenished by Florida.
And gave it thanks.

DEBS

BACK IN NEW YORK in June '45 I started sleeping
with the debutantes, like Brenda Frazier and Gloria
Vanderbilt. Sometimes it was a toss-up between the debs
and the starlets. But the debutantes were better in bed,
and besides, they bought their own flowers. I fucked
Gloria Vanderbilt in the cockpit at twelve thousand

feet. Then her aunt, her guardian, Gloria Vanderbilt Whitney, old society indeed, called me and tried to get me to engage in a "conversation." Behind everything she said, I could hear it, I could feel it, she was sneering at the oil money. The old bag squawked at me, You are twenty-five years older than Gloria and your seeing her is scandalous and do you have the intention of marrying her and if so could you make that intention formally known?

Twenty, I said.

What's that?

I'm twenty years older.

What a telephone call.

Her niece had a cunt like a peach! Glorious Gloria, those little half-moans and sighs.

But could I even be bothered to lie?

THE ANSWERING ECHO

OH YES. BOOM. THE war ended. It was effortless. And then, after a while, it wasn't anymore. Perhaps if the Mormons had been around on July 7, 1946, the day I crashed the XF-11—my exquisite reconnaissance prototype, a Defense contract I was testing—well, perhaps things might have turned out differently. If I'd been writing memos, instructions, which they'd then been executing, there would have been less for me to concentrate on. I could have shared the burden of responsibility around among the minions. I could have delegated, Jack. That's what I do these days, it frees me up in here. But the Mormons didn't arrive until a decade after all this disaster. And not a moment too soon.

I still to this day don't know what went wrong on July 7, 1946. I was ironing out the glitches, the plane had minor problems, I was pushing its limits for the army tests, and maybe I was a little sleep-deprived. It was the day after I'd met Jean Peters—silly Jean, who much later would become my second and final wife. (I almost said fatal—they are similar words, don't you think?) It was the first glorious summer after the war had ended. I noticed, at those heady summer parties, love abuzz in the air, in the gentle murmurs of conversations, in the nervous giggling of starlets everywhere.

And Jean Peters was radiant. The Fourth of July parties stretched into the Fifth of July, then the Sixth. Everybody was at Jimmy Cagney's place at Newport Beach, from which yachts were ferrying guests across to Santa Catalina Island. Jean Peters, a pretty slip of a thing, was all over Audie Murphy—war hero groomed for a film career, who certainly couldn't act but apparently could fight. I knew, looking at her (she glanced at me briefly, she knew who I was in that room, she positioned herself), that I would have her eventually.

I offered to fly some of the guests over, meaning Jean and whoever else was necessary to make it all look less calculated. Tactically speaking, this meant Audie Murphy, too, but I got him placed up the back of the plane and managed (Would you like to know how an airplane works?) to have little Jeannie seated beside me, admiring all those shiny controls, pretending she wasn't really sitting beside the richest, most eligible bachelor in the country, albeit a man twice her age.

I didn't drink; the energy that kept me awake and going at parties like this was other people's wildness, the smell of sex, the frenzy of connectedness, or at least yearning for such. Parties. They took away my loneliness. I always felt cut off from the other humans. I wanted autonomy, but of course I hated all that distance. There is no way around these kinds of dilemmas. The whole thing is overshadowed anyway by the presence of death. The most beautiful girl of them all, one day she'll be old and dry. A while later she'll be dust. Even old Howard is no exception. In fact, it's possible that parties, indeed gatherings of any kind, only add to the sum of the world's loneliness.

But on Santa Catalina I watched the dancing, and I chatted here and there, and I put up with the exquisitely boring Audie Murphy and even pretended to sincerely offer him advice (How To Make It In Hollywood), all the while merely viewing him as an obstacle to the acquiring of Jean Peters, that wholesome Ohio girl so ripe for the plucking. Perhaps I slept an hour or two in a bunk on Jimmy Cagney's yacht; at any rate I lay down, and morning came. I didn't pay enough attention to the importance of that test flight.

I flew Jean and Audie and Johnny Meyer back to Hughes Aircraft at Culver City. They disembarked and set themselves up on viewing chairs on the edge of the tarmac. Out from the hangar came the beautiful XF-11, sixty-five feet long, wingspan a hundred and one feet, three thousand horsepower engines, a shining bolt of propulsion. I had to prove it could fly photosurveillance runs from sufficient height and at sufficient speed to outmaneuver enemy ground-to-air action. I had to push that little flyer. And I had to impress this brand-new bony-armed girl.

I took the plane through its paces, from Culver City, looping out over Venice Beach, around through Beverly Hills and back to Culver City. There is not a lot of difference between the front projection techniques I developed in my earliest films (in *Wings*, for example, or *Hell's Angels*) and the view through the windshield of the XF-11. A sense of the unreal, a break with the open perspectives of sight. A screen. I'm talking not just of the rush of the wind, but of speed itself. I've flown in open biplanes. But that's entirely different. In an open cockpit what becomes apparent is an immediate relationship with the massive machineries of flight: an immersion in engine and wind. The great noise of a laborious metallic effort to break the bonds of gravity and land. In the XF-11, surrounded by exquisite technology and a plexiglass curve, you can look at the screen and enjoy the movie.

Several circuits later all seemed well. Everything was smooth at five thousand feet. Then the right wing

suddenly tilted as if I were no longer in air but held in
place in a shuddering aspic, the plane gone violent, the
rivets jarring loose. I fought the joystick. It fought back.
The XF banked into a spiral. For a moment I thought
the wing had gone. I stood and craned; it was still there.
I increased power to the right engine, thinking this
would surge us out of the problem; but the spiral merely
tightened, steepened and sped up. I didn't panic. Panic is
a luxury. I reduced the power. I could control direction,
minimally, but not the hurtling descent. Beneath me the
city blurred by, but bigger and closer. I was losing altitude
rapidly: two thousand five hundred feet over Washington
Boulevard; two thousand feet at Venice; a thousand over
Pico; then Wilshire; five hundred feet over Santa Monica
Boulevard. I was trying to pull a curve out of doom and
the engines were making a terrible racket. Up ahead, the
Los Angeles Country Club seemed the landing zone of
choice, my mind computing that trees were a problem but
far less so than these houses looming closer.

The plane was whining, I could not hear, I could
not hear my thoughts. I thought I would try to land on a
street. I would lose my wings but possibly skid to a halt.
But the thing was so hard to control. And I was gaining
speed. And then it was absolutely too late. I planted my
feet on the instrument panel. I tried to keep the nose
up high to flare the ship and avoid a nose-down crack-
up. I sheared the top of a house like a machete through
balsa wood. I have been here before. It was only three
years since Lake Mead. It all comes round in circles,

in the living, in the telling, the initial scream and the answering echo, the rearing water and the upward rush of asphalt, and the last thing that happened before impact, I turned my head and read, with some curiosity, the street sign North Linden Drive, and finally I felt still and serene as I lazily smashed through telegraph poles, as trees, houses, mailboxes, roads, stood up one after the other to smack me in the nose. North Linden Drive. Those gentle letters on a filigree-edged sign, and the clipped hedges of a quiet neighborhood. Then for just a moment it seemed everything had gone silent, despite the gargantuan whining of the engines, and I could think again. You look at the screen and enjoy the movie. I was struck by the unreality of that view unfolding. But when the windshield shatters you realize how fast you are going. Then the gates of hell broke open. I caught fire. The plane stripped itself of itself, screeching all around me.

It was horrible but magnificent. As I sat on the sidewalk, bewildered, so far removed from pain yet so immersed in it, my clothes were melted into my skin and I yearned for relief from the pain as a man lost in the desert yearns for water. Everything was still all around me. The plane was in pieces, along the street, in yards, in trees. Noise wound down, as if the great industrial world had suddenly decided to no longer be, had switched itself off at the fuse box.

From out of the smoke a man emerged. Lloyd Durkin, visiting friends at 808 Whittier Drive. I have never forgotten his name, Jack, since he was the first man I saw in my new life.

Are you all right? Was he hissing, Lloyd Durkin? His head was stretched, his face did not stay in its skin.

I was alive, but I was no longer invincible. From behind the horrified face which loomed over me the late afternoon sun drilled into my retinas and in slow motion on the open sky the frenzied patterns of my blood vessels danced.

That is how I knew that eventually, that sooner rather than later, I must remove myself from the company of men.

UNCROWDED HORIZONS

A ND THAT WAS THAT. My plane fell apart. I burst into flames. The day went quiet.

Life changing, as they say. I was taken to Good Samaritan Hospital. Crushed chest. Fractures to seven ribs on the left side, two on the right. Fractured left clavicle. Broken nose. Large laceration of the scalp. Extensive second-and third-degree burns on the left hand, a second-degree burn on the lower part of the left chest, cuts, bruises, abrasions, collapsed left lung, damaged right lung, heart pushed to one side of chest cavity; not expected to live through the night.

When I got out of the hospital I took stock of my life. I was completely amazed by its emptiness. But the good thing about emptiness is just how much space there is. So I made a decision to protect myself within that space. By participating in the world to the fullest I had somehow ensured that I would withdraw to a like extreme. Of course, I didn't entirely realize it at the time.

Dr. Mason, a very kind man, gave me lots of morphine.

Memo, 1958: Delivering film
canisters to the bungalow

Park one foot from the curb on Crescent near the place where the sidewalk dead-ends into the curb. Get out of the car on the traffic side. Do not at any time be on the side of the car between the car and the curb. When unloading film, do so from the traffic side of the car, if the film is in the rear seat. If it is in the trunk, stand as close to the center of the road as possible while unloading. Carry only one can of film at a time. Step over the gutter opposite the place where the sidewalk dead-ends into the curb from a point as far out into the center of the road as possible. Do not ever walk on the grass at all, also do not step into the gutter at all. I will be watching these films, or these tests, or these dailies, in a darkened room. Think of what can be ejected from the surface of the celluloid as the film moves through the projector spools at such high speed. Walk to the bungalow keeping as near to the center of the sidewalk as possible. Do not sit the film cans down on the sidewalk or the street or anywhere else, except possibly on the porch of the bungalow area if the third man is not there. While waiting for the third man to arrive, do not lean against any portion of

the bungalow or the furniture on the porch, but remain there
standing quietly and await his arrival. When the third man
clears the door, step inside quickly carrying the can (single) of
film, just far enough to be inside. Do not move and do not
say anything and do not sit the film down until you receive
instructions where to sit it. If possible, stay two feet away from
the TV set, the wire on the floor and the walls. When leaving,
kick on the door and step outside quickly as soon as the third
man opens the door.

THE EMPEROR OF EMPIRIN

I T IS DEEP IN the night, and one floor below me Jack
Real sleeps the sleep of the dead, as they say. Or
the jetlagged, at least. I don't move. I can't move. I'm
exhausted from all my thinking and planning and
remembering. But no, there is nothing to worry about.
The medicine will see me through.

It is difficult speaking of failure. I feel I have been
fighting my way through some dense thicket out of
which, every now and again, I emerge into a clearing.

The medicine and the memos, these are my tools.
These are how I keep the world in place, or rather, the
forces at bay.

Because that was the last crash, Jack—the XF-11
I was telling you about. There weren't any more after
that. And these memos are the reason why. What the

crash meant was that I had not taken care of every little contingency. I hadn't covered all the possible angles. My plan was not detailed enough. My plans, I should say. And I had to start protecting myself from the things that could go wrong. I had to plan better. Because it was easy to forget. And I was always very comfortable writing lists. And then gradually the lists became...instructions. Because then the Mormons were in my life. And you cannot trust that everyone is as smart as you. You can't make that assumption.

The thing is, if I might elaborate for a moment, sometimes I just used to...get stuck. You see, Jack, there was a loop, and it was hard to get out of. It was like a wolf, always there, always waiting for you to make a mistake. I think you're following me. It would take you down and you were gone: the loop began, it fed on itself, it just kept eating and eating. And what people don't understand is that the medication keeps the loop at bay. Codeine allows, somehow, miraculously, the thoughts and the words to keep on coming out, in sequence, in the right order. That is the opportunity, that is the moment to get it down in the memo!

And then nothing can get out of control.

Sometimes, in those years before I got serious about the medication, sometimes there was a lot of terror. Because when you think of the thought, and the words to say it, that is fine. But when you think of the thought and the words to say it and then you say it, but then immediately you are not sure if you said it or merely thought it in preparation for saying it, this can get you into awful trouble. It's just a little short-circuit in the wiring. It's just a millisecond, that harmless moment before déjà vu takes effect, but if you get trapped on the *inside* of the loop then the milliseconds suddenly multiply like a virus. And then everything is out of control. You've got to stay *outside* that thing, Jack.

Back when this was happening, Noah Dietrich was getting awfully worried about me. I would call him up, say, to talk about moving the RKO stock options. So what I needed to say was: Noah, we need to talk about those options. So that's what I'd say. Maybe there was a moment in there where I'd think, Okay, did I say it? Is it out of the way? This is called the speech act.

But the next thing, there's Noah's insistent voice on the end of the line, interrupting me, Howard, Howard, Howard, HOWARD, slow down, slow down.

What? What?

Howard, do you know what you're doing?

We need to talk about those options. Yes.

Yes, I know. But you keep saying it. I just counted. Twenty-three times, Howard. You just said We need to talk about those options twenty-three times.

Well, it was shocking, of course. Because Noah, he doesn't play practical jokes. So I know it's the truth, even though *it doesn't feel like it happened.* Which can only mean *I am losing my mind.*

And this got worse and worse, this getting caught inside the loop. Because you need to make sure you get everything right, because you need to be in control, because you can't let things fall apart. You can't relax. But back around this time, I may have been overcompensating. I got trapped in a men's room, overcompensating, caught inside the loop. Washing a sauce stain off my shirt, but the water spread, so I kept on washing, washing the stain out, washing the water out, but the water kept spreading till I took off my shirt, then the whole shirt was wet. So I was trapped in there, with Jane Greer waiting patiently in the restaurant, and I couldn't tell her, had no way of letting her know, couldn't interrupt the sequence of events, one thing at a time. Wash it, and dry it, and get the shirt back on. Which was impossible, of course. The maitre d' broke the loop, pounding on the door. I'll be out in a minute. I had to sit back down with Jane, with my shirt wringing wet. It was very uncomfortable. Not to mention the shame. My life was limited, I know. But you have to be methodical, one foot in front of the other. Every step accounted for. I was drowning, Jack, I was drowning. Then the drugs came along, breathing into my blue lips their serene oxygen. Do you see what I mean? Everything I ever dreamed of, the peace of the oasis, the whiteness of the blossom, in Empirin, in Valium, in Librium, in Ritalin, Our Lady of the Amphetamine, Our Lord of Morphine raining down His gifts. I had a Condition which needed Medicating. It was nothing to be ashamed of.

And so now I attack the problem from two sides: there's the medication, and there are the memos. The first makes me all right inside myself, ensures that my thoughts and actions will all be correct. The second ensures that those working on my behalf act with neither ambiguity nor uncertainty. Then the whole world can get on famously with itself.

COUNT OLEG THE BRAVE

SOMETIMES THAT WOLF TOOK on human form. I was never one for violence, all that strutting manly business. Most men frankly dismayed me. At school I had scuffled with Stanley Rowley while the other boys, Dudley included, looked on and cheered. There were flailing arms and fists that may or may not have connected, but we wound down to stalemate in a heaving wrestle of headlock and throat-constricting adrenaline. Nor was I much of one for sport, which was really just violence with stricter rules. So when Oleg Cassini, a lowly fashion designer who should really and may well have been a fag, whooped me one night with a piece of two-by-four, it was an awful minute of powerlessness and fear.

Because I had been seeing his flame Gene Tierney, and he did not like it at all, with his greaseball macho pride, faintly ridiculous Rudolph Valentino darkness and a certain European arrogance. He treated me, an honest hard-working American, like a bumpkin, which merely made me more determined to continue fucking, on the sly but without overly comprehensive security, the lovely Gene, with her crooked teeth, tiny lisp and oh so licentious overbite. In order to irk him.

I had seen Gene in *Laura* and, like half of the country, had fallen in love with her. Setting up a date was of course no problem. Her romance with Count Oleg (what kind of stupid name is Oleg?) was at this stage only budding. I didn't see that as a problem either. It wasn't that I wanted what I couldn't have; I could have pretty much anything. It was the annoyance that other men would even bother to compete. I couldn't stand these greaseballs. Sinatra had the same stupid chip on his shoulder about me and Ava Gardner. As if I cared. The little wop shit (Sinatra, not Cassini) thought he could lord it over me. I'm a patient man. Twenty years later I bought a whole casino just to cancel his engagements. Anyway, it really made me mad that Gene could be quite happy to fuck me but that she didn't take my proposals of marriage seriously. (They weren't serious. I just wanted her to take them seriously.) In her Westwood apartment I offered her a diamond ring, a necklace of pearl. She seemed genuinely disturbed and said, Howard, this is lovely, but I can't take this. Out of sight, out of mind, no harm in trying, worth the effort, all's fair in love and war, what did it really matter? Fuck her. I consoled myself with Linda Darnell, moonshine on heat.

Some weeks later I took Gene's call.

Howard, I want you to hear this from me before you read it in the papers tomorrow. I'm going to marry Oleg.

I told her she was making a very grave mistake.

She said, Thank you for your kind thoughts, but Oleg is a more balanced man than you. He's simpler, Howard.

Well, I said, I wish him well with his balance and simplicity.

They got married. Needless to say I wasn't the best man. Later they had a child but it was born a retard. I tried to express some magnanimity by showering them with money for specialist treatment. Gene resisted and I insisted. For the good of the boy and his future, I said. I wanted to appear to prove I could rise above the rivalries of men. At the same time there was an element of wanting to make Oleg feel less than a man. I never pretended life was simple. There are many motives running parallel.

It's just that, while I didn't mind sleeping with any number of women at a time, I really felt it rubbed me the wrong way when a woman chose to spread herself around among the men. And what right had Oleg to partake in anything resembling a competition?

But passion cools off and marriages too, and the stress of bearing a retard certainly couldn't have helped. Plus ultimately every Hollywood actress is only as good as her currency in this week's scandal rag and last week's box office. Only as stable. They have an image of themselves that could hardly be said to come from within. In any case, the focus tends to be on the career. A year or so after the birth of the unfortunate child I was back between

Gene Tierney's lanky legs for a little while, and Oleg none too happy. At a dinner party at Jack Benny's he shouted me down in front of the other guests, Gene saying, Please, Oleg, please, not here. He called me a fraud, among other insults and insinuations. You leave my wife alone, he said. I'll whip you like a dog, he said.

Mr. Cassini, I said, you're talking ancient history. You're embarrassing yourself.

I'm gonna embarrass you, he sputtered. You're gonna have trouble picking your teeth up off the floor when both eyes are closed up!

At this point I left the proceedings. Almost immediately—I waited only a week—I made the point of making Gene Tierney an offer she could hardly refuse: promises of talks regarding a specious movie deal, and a weekend for two in Las Vegas. She took the bait. God only knows what she told Oleg she was doing.

Alone once again, she really relaxed. That weekend in Vegas I loved Gene Tierney as much as ever, as much as any other woman ever, I mean. She smelled so nice in her armpits, you could inhale so deeply, you could breathe it in like your life depended on it; oh, there were bouquets of hyacinth hidden inside her. She laughed so deeply at the roulette table, I was happy just to sit beside her, to bathe in the presence of uncomplicated joy. Greaseballs and retards may well have been light years away. I was happy to help her relax.

But when we came back to LA, it was all a little complex, and Gene went strange and cold on me, as if we barely knew each other. And I had to work very hard, and do another Vegas trip all over again, but this time she was stiffer. They had been married little more than eighteen months. That is the whole problem with marriage as I see it: it divides your loyalties between duty and desire. After that second trip, back in LA, I was trying to be discreet, I was taking out her luggage from the trunk, I was not in front of her house but hidden from view by a hedge in front of the house next door when out sprung Count Oleg the Brave, like a crazed Visigoth, wielding high in the air his lump of wood, only the stars behind it.

I screamed in terror.

I tried to throw Gene's suitcase at him, but it was too heavy and it skidded sideways from my hands.

He brought the weapon down across my shins, twice, *thud, thud.* I crumpled to the ground. I tried to crawl out of harm's way. Gene was screaming, Oleg! Oleg! I held my hands over my head. But the Count was savagely attacking my legs and lower torso. This is just a lesson! he kept saying, as he hit me, *oomph, oomph,* across my buttocks and thighs. I don't care who you are, you stay away from my wife!

I somehow made it to my car; perhaps Gene was restraining him. Lights were going on all over the neighborhood. He dented my bonnet with the two-by-four as I sped away. The trunk flapped open, mouthing, Goodbye Gene! A Tierney hatbox spilled out from it, disgorging its contents as I took the corner, two-wheeled and panicked.

Every day was an adventure, Jack! The past is so far away. Only the infinite is left. Looming away, as it does. I never liked violence, I never saw the point of it. My bruises were like a map of sorrow. For days there were continents drifting tectonically down my thighs. I walked with a limp for at least a week. I never fucked Gene Tierney again.

SELF·MEDICATION

YOU SEE, THE PROBLEM is, waking is insufferable.

BUT THERE WERE STILL MOMENTS

I WAS AWARE, OF course, of the great divide between simplicity and complexity. Sometimes that awareness was cluttered, like a thought half-realized on the edges of one's day-to-day turmoil. Other times it was simple and pure, and I simply sat, within myself, as if that perfect fit was all there was.

I was recovering from the big accident, when I'd broken apart in Beverly Hills. My body ached, even through the morphine. Jean Peters, the first face I had woken to in the hospital, in my suffering, in the glare of bright light, was a balm. There was a fit there, too, of sorts: me in my need, her in her need to be needed. I didn't get around to marrying her for a decade, Jack! She was the most patient creature. Back then she hadn't yet started to drive me crazy.

When she was shooting *Captain from Castile* in Mexico with Tyrone Power I would often fly down there to be with her. These were the days when leaving was good, flying was good, arriving was good. Not, admittedly, consecutive days; but there were times, there were moments scattered through my life when all was well, when goodness and not anxiety was the defining medium. When even being between Jean's legs was like a choice I had made and not an accident of compulsion that had befallen me. As if one descended through clouds to love at last, to Guadalajara and something reminiscent of...ease.

Cary Grant and I took a trip down there once. To talk to a man, intimately, was very different from talking to a woman. If nothing else there was the liberty of being able to be more honest. There was less tension because there was less of a feeling of even *having* to talk. Less of that sense of an obligation to cram the empty space. I was comfortable in silence with Cary. So I was going to Mexico to see Jean but first of all I had to go to New York for a TWA board meeting. I picked up Cary and we flew out of there and southwest. In Amarillo we refueled. Storms buffeted the DC-3. Cary mixed himself a cocktail at the bar. Myself, I was never a great one for drinking. We skirted the storm front and touched down in El Paso.

The evening sun beat hard on the steaming runway. Waiting for customs clearance into Mexico, we sat on the tarmac on folding chairs outside the tiny airport building, drinking chilled milk straight from the bottle. In the distant north the purple mass of cloud sparked and bulged with silent lightning. We sat, largely conversationless, largely content. TWA did not exist. All the money, all the women, were far away for just that moment. It was not the case that life was screaming past, not for me, not for Cary, not for anyone. But I drank that milk like it was life itself.

ONE COULD IMAGINE HER WETNESS

OH THE SIMPLICITY! I kissed Rita Hayworth beside a boatshed once, on the shores of Lake Tahoe. We had flown out there for dinner at McGreary's. We arrived late afternoon and went for a swim, the sunlight pale and crisp. It was almost unbearably cold. This was the first time between us: this was the delicious anticipation, when the whole world was filled with possibility, when one could imagine her wetness, the mucoid slippings and moorings of the night ahead, and not be far wrong. We were in the water for less than a minute. I was half-erect following her out, focusing on the glisten of the texture of the goose bumps on her thighs. Her bathing suit the color of vanilla ice cream and maybe even the taste.

After McGreary's we went for a walk along the lake, above which hovered a mist. Otherwise the entire sky was clear, and a full moon rained down silver on the pines and the jetty and Rita and me. One expected a coyote to howl. Often with women I had so little to talk about and would find myself yabbering on, or co-yabbering, as the case may be. But on Tahoe it seemed pointless to talk of business or the movies. We stood in silence, me just behind her and to the right, and when I slid my arms around her shoulders from behind, she turned and leaned her face up to mine.

We took a hotel. She had the sweetest smile. I booked in as Mr. H. Hawks. We never heard the coyotes but the night seemed filled with the hooting of owls. Rita Hayworth was as perfect as a woman comes, and gave and gave until a man felt not a man anymore, but a being brought to sobbing by the simple beneficence of love. She opened her legs and drew me on top of her. She said, First, just the tip. Just the tip at the entrance. Slowly, slowly, as slow as you can. I swear I pulsed and swelled in that ecstatic loading dock. And to push down against her and into her at last: vine of the vine and the grape crushed to spirit and the word made flesh. Time may well have been Nature's way of making sure not everything happened at once. But sex with Rita

Hayworth was Time's way of excusing itself from duty and the ticking of the clock.

A DELICATE OPERATION

I WILL NEED TO tell him about tiredness, of course, which eventually becomes a factor. I juggled too many painkillers and women. By the mid-fifties it was not so tiring juggling the drugs. But the women—well, I had a great sadness in my life, I felt very empty. In addition to this I was assailed, rightly or wrongly, by germs, or at least by a sense of the lurking of uncleanliness. Possibly also there was a sexual virus eating at my brain now these last ten or twenty years, a dose of the clap I'd caught from a starlet somewhere along the line, making me a little cranky. There was so much to be annoyed about. I signed up Yvonne Shubert and made Walter Kane, one of my security men, her minder, but at some point she took hold in my mind, also perhaps like a virus, and I became obsessed with the need to win her.

Would this be the thing? To make time stand still? And me, an old man by now! Fifty. The years had gone by so flippantly. When I looked in the mirror I did not look the same. Thus it was a delicate operation, seducing Yvonne. I was self-conscious about my wrinkles. In the screening room I fed them films, Yvonne and her mother, with Kane chaperoning. I slipped in late and sat in the dark up the back of the room and watched her, night after night. I had not yet met her. Her mother thought she was being "groomed" for a "career" and that this was the education. By day Yvonne took her dance and drama and voice classes, paid for by me. She was buoyed along by my promises of fame, the usual thing. By night I watched the play of light from the projector's beam on her jet-black hair. I watched her laugh. I took pleasure in imagining her excitement about this world of special treatment. The medicine made me so patient, I could study her for hours. I booked double features. I sensed her mother getting bored. After a few weeks her mother dropped away, feeling her daughter to be in safe hands. Walter Kane was about as unthreatening as a man could be, in that way. (On the other hand, as a Hughes security man, you wouldn't have wanted to cross him.)

At last, one night I emerged from the back of the screening room. Walter introduced us and then he too slipped away.

Her eyes were alert in the darkness, a fawn in the forest. We sat in the same row, several seats away, and watched the movie. It ended. The lights remained down. My jowls were drooping by now. I couldn't bear my life. I had to have her. I would win her with my voice. We talked and talked. She knew nothing. Her innocence was astonishing. But it was too much effort, my body turned sideways in that seat, the strain of presence, the weight of speech. I needed some distance.

Now, Miss Shubert, I said. I want to keep talking—do you?

Oh yes, Mr. Hughes—

Please call me Howard.

All right then. Howard.

And I'm enjoying talking, too. I'm enjoying getting to know you. But I'd feel more comfortable if you'd do this for me. Go into that second office, that second room along the corridor. Close the door. And wait there. And pick up the phone when it rings.

She acted as if there was nothing strange in my request. She glided down the dimly lit hall. I loved her more that moment. I went into the projection booth and called her extension. She picked up the phone. Now we could talk for hours. Now I could relax. I also found it comfortable to touch my genitals if necessary, but not in a dirty way.

We talked every night for eleven weeks. I had never experienced such a build-up. I had never taken anything so slowly. We talked of me and her, dreams past and present, and all the great films. I had to make sure that she loved me. I could not imagine a world without love. I could not imagine failure.

We talked long into the night.

I am old.

Oh, but Howard, you are young at heart to me.

Do you mean that? Do you really mean that?

We played out the farce, the money of it all, which was all there really was.

You are like a sister to me. You know, I never had a sister. But then again, you are very beautiful, too, and

that is not the way one thinks about one's sister. Your
skin is like...like silk.

Howard, you've hardly even seen my skin!

I've seen your photos. I've seen the publicity shots.
But I have to admit, I would die happy, were I to see just
a little more.

Oh, Mr. Hughes!

Because I think, Yvonne, that I am falling in love
with you.

Silence on those sterilized phones.

Do you think you love me, or might, Yvonne? Do
you think you could?

I think, she said. I think, she paused. I think I have
a kind of love.

Oh, Jack, it is cruel—to think I maneuvered her into
saying those words. And to think how the saying of those
words must have corroded her, just a little.

Still, in order to sleep with her I had to promise
I'd marry her. After that initial contact it all becomes
a matter of stalling and pampering as the months melt
and decay. But that first night, when it finally came,
when we finally touched, when we finally fucked, when
I fought, successfully, the fear of germs, to simply lie with
her, that first night was boon and balm. She gave herself
to me, or let's be realistic here, to my imagined millions.
For months and months I enjoyed every moment. There
was a little shuffling now and then because Jean Peters,
silly little Jean, also thought I was going to marry her—
and isn't it funny how she turned out to be the one

who was right? For a while also, somewhere around this time, I was plowing fields with Susan Hayward who now, thirty-seven years old and recently divorced, smelled only, in my presence at least, I swear to God, of desire and abandon. It clung to her dress, straining in its disarray, it rose from her pulsing groin till I could lick it, literally, off her neck. She never wanted more than to fuck, quickly and urgently, to fight her way through the drugs she was on. This was a difficult time for her. We never compared notes, but we clarified whatever befuddlement we may have been experiencing, through this burning interlocking of sinew and groin. Everything was all the better because it was going nowhere, nowhere. (Though Susan Hayward, like all the others, no doubt had her secret hopes.) But Yvonne Shubert was more straightforward, because when you add eighteen more years to the initial nineteen, things get a little complex, so Susan had those extra layers of trouble. Very attractive. For a very short while.

MULBERRY BUSH

NONETHELESS, ON NEW YEAR'S EVE in 1955 I couldn't work out exactly who to please and I went a little strange. I had spread myself too thin with promises. I had overcommitted myself. If you put yourself in my shoes you would understand: not one of us really likes to have others dislike us. I didn't wish to incur anybody's wrath. Or disappoint anybody. I was eager to please. I just found it hard to say no sometimes, Jack. I wanted the whole world to be happy. So I said things that sometimes...weren't true. On an individual level, I was Johnny Appleseed, I had happiness for everyone. And a rather random approach to scattering myself.

As November bled into December and the New Year loomed, I found that I had made New Year's Eve commitments to Susan Hayward and Yvonne Shubert and, interestingly enough, to Jean Peters, too, who I'd now been seeing, more or less irregularly, since the crash in '46. I loved them all in their own way! I had heard there are two types of people, the glass is half-empty or the glass is half-full. So I decided to march into this calamity of overbooking as if all the gods were smiling and the greatest good fortune was raining down. My glorious organizational skills were dusted off, awaiting the parading of their glittering magnificence. The Beverly Hills Hotel was to be their stage.

I put Silly Jean in the Crystal Room, best table in the house. Gardenias and a diamond brooch. For Susan it was the Polo Lounge, best table in the house. Gardenias and a diamond pendant. Yvonne in one of the bungalows out back, in the tropical garden down the manicured paths winding through lawns and camellia hedges, festooned with Christmas lights, four serving staff and my personal chef and music soft on the gramophone. Gardenias and a diamond necklace.

Bottles of Dom for all of them. And lots of my men, on double pay, coordinating my movements, walkie-talkies crackling, their own New Year's Eves gone missing.

Jean Peters first, rapturous in a white satin gown (was I supposed to be reading a message into that?), and we popped a bottle and chatted. I could feel the tingle of adrenaline in the back of my throat, the uncertainty about whether or how I could pull this off. I imagine there were beads of sweat across my brow. I felt slightly uncomfortable in my tuxedo. And then a man came with a message for an urgent phone call. And off I raced, attending to "business." Jean was as meek and forbearing as ever.

Susan Hayward's eyes were translucent and radiant with whatever medication she was on that evening. She was happy in her world. We came together so wonderfully and remained so wonderfully separate, so airtight, so watertight. I liked that. I stroked the sleeve of her strapless peach gown. I commented on its...God knows what I said. There are some things dispensed with in the halls of memory. The cleaners got to them years ago. But another man, another telephone call, and I was off again, leaving Happy Susan sipping her champagne and smiling at the cotton napkins and the bright sheen of the silverware.

In the bungalow Yvonne (gown of cream chiffon and silk brocade) was waiting patiently, her world unsullied as yet by collusion or need. I liked her lips so much, though not disembodied as such. Everything related to everything else. She was so happy there, waiting for me and in love, or pretending with satisfactory enthusiasm. I look back now, Jack, and all I see are all the things I've spoiled. It wasn't that I wasn't aware that the other humans were real, like me. It's simply that I wasn't aware of myself so much as being just another of the humans. We popped a bottle. I managed to stick around for the asparagus starter. (I would have to be careful. I would be eating three times.) There was a telephone call for me.

One whole circuit—I was off and running! I had no idea who I was even going to end up with that night. In the ultimate sense, I mean. There were times, back then, and even now, when I was confident enough with the workings of the unfolding of all things that I didn't have to control every single outcome from start to finish, but only the initial parameters. Looking back on New Year's Eve 1955, I'm not sure just how trapped I was. There are loops as well. Perhaps it was not the behavior of a fifty-year-old man.

I went through the asparagus facade again, with Jean. Another call. Business never stops, the cogs keep turning, the furnace needs restoking. She was annoyed, but as always did well to hide it. Oysters with Susan, that was more like it, still three mains to go. But after two circuits, doom set in, which is perhaps not unlike the history of the world itself. Not even two circuits: I hadn't yet got back to Miss Shubert a second time. Because Miss Hayward got smart, or suspicious at least. She went for a wander. I was back with Miss Peters, perusing the menu.

Miss Hayward stormed up to us. The other diners were watching already.

What the hell is going on? said Susan.

I hadn't planned for this. What on earth had I imagined? Perhaps only the difficulty of saying goodnight to two out of the three.

Well I'm in the Polo Lounge, Jean, said Susan, looking down at her. And you're here in the Dining Room. You work it out. I'd say that makes me date number one.

Howard? said Jean, looking at me with those hurt eyes. Hurt from Jean beside me, anger from Susan above. I didn't know which way to look. Certainly not to all the *other* eyes upon me.

Well, they both stormed out of there. It was certainly a rapid simplification of the evening's plans. Yvonne, Yvonne, Yvonne, Yvonne, Yvonne. And I wouldn't have to eat so much now.

We didn't dance alone that night and I didn't take her dancing across at the Polo Lounge. Wouldn't look good in the gossip columns, there'd be problems enough in that regard with the Hayward and Peters situation as it was. The table had been cleared, the staff dismissed, I was partaking of a rare third glass of champagne, the candles flickered low. And Yvonne was none the wiser about the other two. What I suddenly imagined was: going down low, direct route below the table, onto my knees (it was the position of worship in some religions), pushing that chiffon and silk up her breeze-streaked inner thighs (there are breezes everywhere, there are tremors not even a seismograph could trace) as the width of my shoulders forced a minimum spread in her knees. But Yvonne was very young, awash with those romantic dreams, head full of story books and fairytales no doubt. Not good to crush those. No point in scaring the wits out of her. I was fifty years old, very much a dirty old man. What I did instead was: took her hand, and kissed it, and said, To bed, my dear, to bed.

Or words to that effect.

I had seen that hand-kissing worked. It had worked for Errol Flynn.

AS IF FOREVER

I WONDER HOW JACK'S DOING with his sleep? I wish I could sleep. No, I don't. Not just now. I'm too full of...energy. So much to tell him. Half the night gone and half still to go. Somewhere out there in the distance that tranquil waterway, the Thames, leads of course to the uttermost ends of the earth. In here, nothing changes. Nothing enters from outside. The position of the lamp doesn't shift. The shadows remain exactly the same. The grainy texture of the light seems to have settled as if forever on the furthest corners of the room, so that the fox-hunting prints remain indistinct and ambiguous, and may in fact, I suddenly realize as I try to focus on them across the vast expanse of the room, be scenes from Greek mythology, Tithonus perhaps in his great agony, long abandoned by Aurora in a back room in Heaven, his useless arms and legs wasting away, his endless complaints endlessly unheard, his body desiccated to its cicada destiny, his beauty gone forever and only forever awaiting him. And Aurora, full of juice and glory, renewed every day at the dawn.

Along the wall beside me here are my bulging file boxes stacked five high. I love having my boxes of memos within arm's reach. They give me the sensation of substantiality. The medicine box when I want to fly; my memos when I want to return to earth. I don't plan to weigh Jack down with reading. I just want to give him an idea of what I need to do to keep things running smoothly. I'm not expecting sympathy. We're grown men, after all. But a small selection will give him insight. He will understand the operational economy of the memo system. He will understand my retreat from the public gaze. He will understand that I cannot afford to crowd my world with inessentials, as I inadvertently did for a while on that final night of 1955.

That is all I am trying to do with my life, through the memos: reduce the inefficiencies.

I knew how to streamline the wings of a jet, Jack!

III

But now I have ceased to believe in my surroundings; I
have withdrawn into myself, have shut my eyes, have not so
much as batted an eyelid. I have the feeling that this torrent of
visions is sweeping me away to a tranquil dream: so rivers cease
their turbulence in the embrace of the sea . . .

—de Saint-Exupéry, *Wind, Sand and Stars*

ROUND-THE-WORLD RECORD, 1938

So, WE LANDED IN France, Jack. And all the flashbulbs flashing. I drifted off a little from the round-the-world trip. When Jack wakes I must remember to stay on target.

Mr. Hughes will have two hours' rest. One could hardly call it sleep. I was pretty much immortal already.

In fact we stayed four hours at the airfield in Paris: a broken strut and buckled stabilizer needed repairing. Things were a little funny with old Hitler around this time; he had a certain anxiety about war preparations being photographed. The French newspapers were warning us not to cross German airspace. But Germany was the fastest route to Russia, and we were falling seriously behind. So we flew anyway. Not wanting to lose face, Field Marshal Goering ordered us to fly at a high ceiling. ("We hope that our flight may prove a contribution to the cause of friendship between nations," I had said in my speech at Floyd Bennett Field two days earlier, "and that through their outstanding fliers, for whom the common bond of aviation transcends national boundaries, this cause may be furthered.")

We buffeted through electrical storms for twelve hours; the great fronts squeezed us lower and lower to the ground. All night we were flanked by Luftwaffe fighter planes, tuned into our frequency and screeching *Verboten! Verboten!* We ignored them.

Toward dawn, somewhere over Poland, while the men all slept, I found myself thinking of death. One moment I was in the cockpit—seemingly a simple matter—and the next I was deeply immersed in the absolute clarity of the knowledge that I had everything, and yet nothing, and that this was the end of the world. The glow of the control panel was both profound and distressing. In the intimacy of an airplane adrift on the sky with my cohorts deep asleep I could have shouted *Hosanna!* I could have put the barrel of the flare gun inside my mouth and scattered my head into phosphorous and flame; eventually the Cyclone would have fallen from the sky.

The tricks night plays. At dawn we landed in Moscow for a quick refuel. We didn't stay long. We were trying to make up time, and besides, those Bolsheviks gave me the jeepers creepers. I couldn't think of anything good to say, so in my speech I spoke of how much I admired the airport design. Then we commenced the long haul to Omsk, Siberia, flying blind over great rain clouds, an infinitely bulbous dream of landscape. By now the time zones were blurring. My ears rang from the buzzing. It was cramped up there in that little metal room. But the amphetamines put a sparkle on the control panel, and everyone was focused on their tasks.

All day we trundled and droned high above the Steppes.

At some point a great sorrow overcame me, or perhaps it was just the sadness continuing from the night before. At first I felt it as two bands of pain across my middle back. I shifted in my seat and indeed stood up for a moment to stretch, but when I looked out all around me once again, the sadness merely resumed its position. It felt in fact like exhaustion. Undeniably the mood was brought on by that faint sense one imbibes, at ten thousand feet, of the curve of the earth. From there one contemplates the potentially debilitating, despair-inducing and claustrophobic notion that it (the planet) is *not actually so huge after all*...and yet, may the gods weep, it is endless. Hours and hours of the rolling Russian Steppes, rolling underneath, changeless, lead one to feel, or infer, a certain weight of sadness which must be going on, of its own momentum, down below. I am talking about the tawdry sadness of human lives. Odd to think all these things and keep one eye on the instrument panel as well. Every once in a while one sees a tiny town. It is quite oppressive really, the thought of it. The glowing gold of Russia's summer wheat fields. Down there the peasants must be swamped in existence as in an inferno. From there this sky I fly through must appear implacable and pitiless, this plane a distant and determined bird, a speck of movement on the great blue static.

And then the bad weather and the mountains moved in.

The Lockheed strained and boomed and rattled as if its very hollowness were an echo chamber of fragility. As if every bolt and rivet had a life of its own and as if for every bolt and rivet the only music, the only destiny, was the blunting of thread and the tearing of metal. I imagined us suddenly exploding in the sky, the plane simply divesting itself of its metal, and my crew and I, unable to reach for our parachutes, flailing our graceless paths earthwards and downwards. The descent into Omsk was terrifying: the wings iced over, we bumped and lurched, our tiny ship was heavier than sleep. But somehow we landed safely on that raggedy godforsaken airstrip. Omsk, the ugliest outpost I have ever seen, a sorry excuse for a town, a repository of mud in the Siberian void, manned by imbeciles the likes of whom are not to be found in the United States.

WEDDING BELLS BURIED IN THE CALIFORNIA STATUTES

IF I TELL JACK the story of New Year's Eve back in '55 then I'll have to tell him about marrying Jean. Jack, I'll say, now the good thing was that on this particular night, at least, Jean had only Susan Hayward to project her worries onto. Jean knew about (and hated) Yvonne Shubert; she just didn't happen to know Yvonne's whereabouts that New Year's Eve. The next day it was easy to patch things up with Jean—I just upped the volume on the marriage promises. Indeed, I had been planning marriage for some time, not because I had any faith whatsoever in the institution—it meant nothing to me other than claustrophobia and entrapment—but because my mind had not always been great for about ten years now, not wholly consistent in its piecing together of the world, let's say, and I was sure I could sense the occasional rumbling from my men: would a day ever arise when it was necessary to commit Mr. Hughes? I had secretly asked my attorney, Greg Bautzer, to investigate the California statutes, and buried deep in there he came across the provision that the decision to commit to an insane asylum rests solidly enough, in the eyes of the law, with the husband or wife. And why would Jean ever commit me, knowing it might take her further away from her inheritance?

So I married Jean a year or two after that rather complex night. Another saga in itself. Jean was safe, easy. I never really liked sleeping with her. It had been business as usual with Yvonne for some time; I was, it may be clear by now, Jack, ever the restless type. But I could feel that particular...*energy*...fading. I was in my mid-fifties now. To be frank, I didn't know what I wanted. As for Jean, the press didn't even find out about the marriage until two months after the event. So for a while I thought I'd gotten off scot-free on that count. But one night I arrived to visit Yvonne, and she screamed and raged, and threw the newspaper at me. It was a story, of course, about my recent marriage. Fortunately the press is so wonderfully corrupt, and she'd seen at first hand how the gossip columns simply made things up, that it was rather easy to convince her that of course it was all lies. I had to admit to her that I was still *seeing* Jean, as a friend, but only because one doesn't just shut someone out of one's life, does one? One has to let them down slowly. And I promised Yvonne we would marry very soon.

When will that be? she said.

Just as soon as all the circumstances are right, I said. Just as soon as everything is in place.

She was ever so happy to hear that.

I decided it was the new phase of my life. No more nonsense! A new decade was coming. The sixties were like a gleaming vista stretching before me, endless space, room to breathe. My plan was to get everything sorted out and organized. Clean. I could consolidate everything and be a normal man, too. I was sorry to have told white lies to Yvonne, and sorry to have hurt her feelings. Jean Peters, as part of my new plan, was the simplest, most non-problematic person I could imagine; marriage seemed like a good idea. She fitted into the scheme of things, and my vision of the future. But for goodness' sake, there was no point in rubbing Yvonne's nose in it!

THE STREAMING OF THE LIGHT

A ND EVERYTHING WENT SWIMMINGLY for a while. Jean was quite the homemaker. I was making more dosh per *minute* from Hughes Tool and Hughes Aircraft than the average American made in a *year*. I didn't know what to do with myself. I was not so much the Don Juan anymore. At last, I hear you say, Jack! Not so much the extrovert. Because a new thing was developing: I really liked the sensation of being still, in an enclosed space, with the curtains drawn. It took away the pressure for a while.

I keep saying, For a while. That's the gist of the problem right there. There are a limited number of for-a-whiles in your life, and then they, and it, are gone.

For a while they gave me Ritalin tablets and for a while on Ritalin I felt really good. I was rarely in the cockpit but I sure knew how to fly. This was around '61, when I was having big problems trying to hold TWA together. On certain days my stress levels would rise. The nervous anxiety embodied itself in the feeling that I was about to be overwhelmed. That I would, quite simply, quite spontaneously, collapse. The doctors were worried I might implode and thought Ritalin would help me focus on all the memos and deal permutations sure to emerge as the whole TWA buyback unfolded. It had been a long time since I'd had the thought that I might lose everything. My consciousness was made heavy by exhaustion. By now codeine and morphine and Valium and Seconal and Librium were like trusted friends. You have to be careful when a new friend is introduced into the mix. It can upset the balance. But I thought we all got along just famously.

Ritalin. The last time I'd had speed that good, goddamn, I was making *Hell's Angels*, running a million over budget (this was 1928, Jack) and it, the speed, shouldered some of the weight for me. It was the solution to problems of budget and focus and overload, and it helped me maintain control over a bucking project, since control, ultimately, is all there is. The problem was, this darned stuff is so good you take more (why wouldn't you, if it works so well?) and nobody tells you that eventually it'll tilt your axis. There were portals opening from my brain to the universe, there was such purity in the light and the shape of clouds, my breathing was magnificent. There was a crispness to existence. You feel that all engines will run forever.

It is all just a glory. There is no sense of cause and effect. Ritalin doesn't rush right through you in that ecstasy of urgency the way an injection does. But some hours later you find yourself beatifically propelled into the Onrush of Life and the Clarity of Things and the Purpose of Purposes. And there is just no stopping you. And the sense that not only is life sublimely good but that you can, methodically, efficiently, with speed but not haste, get all your tasks done, is a strong thick *smell* before it's anything else, anything felt, heard, thought, abstracted, processed.

And it all streamed out of me, like light. Memo after memo, I ruled my world.

And for a while you don't know it's the drugs, the new friends working things out among themselves.

Note to self: ask the Mormons about Ritalin. It might be good for the flying. Does wonders for that clarity, I seem to remember. Perhaps Jack would like to try some, too.

Speaking of Jack, when the hell will he wake up? I wonder what time it is. Perhaps I should try to get some sleep myself soon. Then the morning will come faster. In the morning I'll be as fresh as a daisy. Where was I? Ah, the Ritalin. Back in '61, I'll tell Jack, I tried to live with Jean (Peters, not Harlow) for a while, as man and wife, in the house at Cardiff-by-the-Sea. It almost worked, for several weeks the signs were good. Oh, she was a breath of fresh air, that little sparrow. That annoying tweetie bird.

Howard darling, can I get you something to drink?

We almost made it, we almost got to live that life. Perhaps all I really lacked was the capacity for social niceties.

That little tweetie bird. Flinging open the blinds, plumping up the bed. My own airline was suing me for mismanagement! For five hundred million in damages! I needed the Ritalin to work out my strategies. There were forces out to get me! The other business, the codeine, all that was just the underlay, the fabric of existence. I had to keep the wolves at bay. And Jean was so irredeemably *up*. And I was sinking and sinking, after the initial rush of the first few weeks, after the energy and excitement of *new perspectives* had worn off. She thought the salt air was so *great*. Wasn't the view of the rolling hills so *great*? Wasn't the green so *intense*? Wasn't the air so *wonderfully crisp*? Wasn't it *marvelous*, Howard? Didn't she realize how contagion was all around us, how cleverly it traveled through the air? So I ordered the blinds taped shut again, and banished her to another bedroom. The problem was not the dust, which is inevitable; it was the disturbing of dust. So I had to ban the cleaners, too.

Memo, 1961: Jean's cat is missing

I want someone who is an expert in the ways of animals of this type and who would know where to look and how to look and how to go about this. I mean, for example, directly, dogs get a cat treed up a tree and the cat just stays there, afraid to come down, and the dogs rush around in the vicinity somewhere. If we can find some evidence...the cat's body, or somebody who heard the episode...Now, it just seems to me that if Bill gave a goddamn in hell about my predicament down here he would have obtained from somewhere, from some place–I don't know where from–from Los Angeles or some place, he would have gotten some expert in the ways of animals, cats in particular, and had him come down here and then put about eight or ten of Maheu's men at his disposal and they would have conducted an intelligent search based upon being instructed by somebody who knows the habit and ways of an animal of this kind. But, instead of that, so far as I have been able to make out, not one thing has been done . . .

Okay, I am not going to run this organization this way anymore, and now Bill Gay goes cruising around today, having a good time, where nothing is done about looking for this cat down here. Not one goddamned thing except having a few of our guards cruise around in their cars. Maheu is in Los Angeles. You could have had him send a team of men down here. You could have gotten some experts who knew about cats and know where to look. There are many, many things that could have been done during the entire period of today to try and locate this animal or find out what happened to it today. I am goddamned sure that if some police case depended upon the determination of knowledge of what happened to this animal today, by God in Heaven they would have had a team of men scouting the countryside and located the cat or some shred of evidence of what happened to it.

This is not the jungle; this is not the Everglades; this is not New York City with the dense population. It is thinly populated and it is no problem at all to question the people here and have them questioned by somebody and get at the truth and not permit somebody to conceal the truth just because they are afraid of being sued or something like that. Proper questions by people skilled in questioning could have been had. The animal could have been searched for by a team of people skilled in the ways of animals of this type. I know one thing; if a zoo had lost some valuable animal in this area, there would have been twenty-five or thirty men scouring the countryside, men skilled in the habits and ways of an animal of this kind, and they would have found it by now.

If there was a dangerous animal escaped from some zoo or circus like a goddamned wildcat or leopard or some animal, you can be goddamned sure they would have found it by now. I consider the loss of this particular animal and the consequences it has had to my wife to be just as important, and in the light of my resources and ability to pursue a matter of this kind, I feel that there is absolutely no reason why a search should not have been instigated for this animal equal in any way to what would have happened if some damned train had broken down here and some leopard or panther or what-not had escaped. There is absolutely no reason why a man of my resources and having the resources and organization that I have got, there is no goddamned reason in the world why efforts to locate this animal should not have been made equal in every way to what would have occurred if some dangerous animal had escaped in this area.

In this situation here you don't think Bill has done anything wrong, going off today to pursue his social activities, whatever it may be, while this situation of complete tragedy occurs down here and my home is likely to be broken completely asunder? You don't think that at all? You think that it is my business and my worry and if Bill wants to go to his social affairs that is okay and I am expecting too much.

I never meant anything more sincerely than I mean this.

HIGHER TRUTHS OF THE DESERT

J ACK WILL UNDERSTAND WHY I had to get away from California and Jean the tweetie bird. Because finally, in the Desert Inn, I became invisible. Because eventually what had happened was, I made up my mind that I did not want to see anyone again. I mean business, I mean meetings. I mean even Jean. It didn't quite work out with Jean, of course. We certainly gave it our best shot for a good few years—but it was all so exhausting. Just being alive, just trying to concentrate. Frankly, I just didn't *care* what color the drapes were. Is dark a color, my dear?

It was the new phase of my life. *This* time. For certain. No more nonsense. I'm not quite sure how the years rolled on. But when I moved to the desert in 1966 to begin my New Life, it was as a monk that I went, to my high cave, my aerie, the top two floors of the Desert Inn in Vegas, with my acolytes, my Latter Day Saints, my men of good cheer, my minions, my Mormons; and I left sweet Jean behind in California: where the shopping was good.

I saw myself as pure being in the pure geometry of the desert.

In Las Vegas we blacked out the windows and made ourselves at home. (By day the glare of that desert place would set the brain to throbbing. At night I could barely stand the *thought* of all that neon, let alone the sight.) The habit continues to this day. I'm light-sensitive. Jack can see that. And I needed to rest.

I had become so exhausted after so many years of avoiding court appearances regarding *TWA v. Hughes* that I sold my entire TWA holding, and in May '66 I received a check for $546,549,171. So I was a little cashed-up in Nevada.

In my simple tiny room I experienced such a sense of vastness. I wanted for nothing. Simply nothing. I had my bed, my Barcalounger, my television, my projector, my screen, and my medicine kit.

I had broken every record, I had flown around the world, I had slept with all the girls. Now I just wanted to breathe for a while, gently, unobtrusively.

I sat in the dark. The films were delivered and taken away, delivered and taken away. I watched the girls up on the screen. I remembered blow jobs, fine dinners, flashbulbs, this one's lipstick, that one's slender neck, negligees draped across the chaise longue, drives in the Hamptons. Sometimes I could barely concentrate on the storylines, so cascading were the memories. My little room was a theater.

All the girls, gone forever. When I got sick of the movies I would turn on the television. One day on KLAS I saw Yvonne De Carlo in a program called *The Munsters*. I'd forgotten all about De Carlo. She'd been a beautiful girl in '46, and we'd spent at least several lovely weeks together. There was that faraway day when she'd worn a pleated dress of heavy silk, under which I had buried my head as I held on to her thighs and she had stood, giggling, No...! Howard, no! It is a good position in which to begin to get worked up but the actual physics are not good in that one can't easily get one's tongue in there unless the woman crouches an inch or two and bows her legs a little like a cowboy, a position she then can't sustain for too long. And you get a crick neck. But Yvonne De Carlo was game. The dress swayed around me in the semi-dark, every pleat like a synchronized bowstring. There was the rustling of fortune in my ears. I peeled away her underwear. Her buttocks were cold and firm beneath my hands. I breathed her in and hugged my face into her. We tumbled onto the bed. This was Vancouver in 1946. Her hometown; I'd followed her to

Yvonne De Carlo Week. Once I focused on getting hold of something I really found it hard to just let the issue go. Watching her twenty years later only served to confirm that even Yvonne had drifted irrevocably, tragically, from the center, from the center of things.

I loved watching movies at the Desert Inn. But after only a very short time Moe Dallitz, the manager, was regretting taking us in, since the Mormons and I didn't gamble. Even though we paid our rent and room service, Moe considered two entire floors an extravagance, that being two whole floors that might otherwise house, feed and fuck any number of high rollers. He commenced eviction proceedings. He didn't know what hit him.

To solve the little problem, to get him out of my hair, I bought the damn hotel, in March '67, for thirteen million. And sacked Moe Dallitz, of course.

So. Then I had the taste for it. All this was a kind of momentum. My thrills were multifold. I know, I know, I said I had gone there to rest. But my thrills were multifold! I had flown all around the world, but real estate was to become my new expanding horizon. You only had to pick up the phone. After the Desert Inn, I bought the Sands for twenty-three million. Then I bought The Castaways in October for 3.3 million, The Frontier in December for twenty-three, The Silver Slipper for 5.4 in April '68, then The Landmark for seventeen, and Harold's Club in Reno for ten.

It was play money. The IRS thought they were closing in; they always thought that. The Vegas licensing people started paying an awful lot of attention to me. But money is the city's most respected commodity. And with Maheu my security man and the Mormons running interference, one always had the feeling one could, to some extent, switch off. Or at least, in a high desert cave, focus on the higher truths.

Oh, and I bought the local TV station, KLAS, for $3.6 million, Jack, because I may have had an empire to run, but I'd gone to Nevada to rest and to drift, as I said, and the late-night programming left a lot to be desired. I wanted to have some say in that myself.

THE CLEAN MEN

I HAD THE ENTIRE top two floors of the Desert Inn, yet one simple room sufficed for my domain. I liked that sense of security, of a full floor of buffer zone beneath me. I had Mormons on shifts, manning phones, guarding hallways and elevators. The same set-up I have here, in fact. The same set-up I have everywhere I go.

You might be wondering, Jack, why this obsession with the Mormons. It's really very simple. How I hired them in the first place was that I came to understand that meticulous is good. It was back in '47, I was retreating from Hughes Aircraft and Hughes Tool, from the day-to-day running of it all, the money was multiplying, the Senate hearings had wearied me, I wanted to be less visible, and after the XF-11 accident and my terrible injuries, I wanted to conserve my energies. I asked Nadine Henley, one of my secretaries, to find me a personal assistant, someone who could look after all matters, who could stand between me and the world outside. Meticulous is good, I said to her. And she had found Bill Gay, who had been preparing files for us for the hearings, and who, she said, was upright. Upright is good. He happened to belong to the Church of Jesus Christ of Latter Day Saints, Jack, the Mormons. That's all there was to it; it began, just like that. You want to rely on someone. You want to know that it all gets done. Someone does a good job. They don't drink. They don't smoke. You want a good job done round the clock. You ask about their friends. They all turn out to be Latter Day Saints. They're methodical and loyal; it helps that they're such clean people, too. So you start hiring. There is so much to do and so much to take care of. Just being alive, just trying to concentrate, it is all so difficult sometimes.

Eventually these men were my right arm, my left arm, my soul, my conscience. But what I actually needed, beyond all that, was an alter ego. This is where Bob Maheu came in. Bob had a solid background in intelligence, was connected in D.C., was a strong man and could get things done. He'd been involved in trying to get rid of Castro, a communist and a wop, when I had a drilling concern on an island on the Cay Sal Bank that I'd leased from a young Texan cowboy called George Bush, who owned Zapata Oil. Maheu had thought they could launch the Castro hit from the Cay Sal Bank. I never found out what happened there; I liked to keep my distance from the CIA. But of course, the last time I noticed, Castro was still alive.

In fact, I first hired Maheu simply to run surveillance on Ava Gardner while she was going through her divorce with Sinatra. That was just a fun thing to do. A test-run for Maheu. Of course, Ava was a very nice woman and I saw at the time the possibility of reigniting things; surveillance was therefore a given.

He passed this first simple task with flying colors. Frankly, I think he felt it was a little beneath his dignity, but he never complained, and his reports were always thorough. Eventually, Maheu did all my work and dirty work, became my primary representative and number one problem-solver. He dealt with whatever came up. So in a sense he was the most important man in Nevada.

But that's funny, about Sinatra, because there's a connection there with the Sands. I was telling you I bought the Sands on my little spree. Now, Sinatra was under contract there at the time, and running up too much credit on the casino floor. You see, there was a history between Sinatra and me. You may already know that, Jack. One-sided, but a history nonetheless. The skinny wop had been sore at me, and had bad-mouthed me, for twenty years. From his perspective, he'd once lost Ava Gardner to me. I think it meant something to him, Jack, as if it tied us together in some kind of pathetic rivalry. This is twenty years earlier, for God's sake! Some people can't let go of things! Truth is, Sinatra meant very little to me. He was just an entertainer. He moved in worlds I owned. I didn't think of him from one decade to the next. I never really knew the man, never met him as far as I can recall, no more than a handshake perhaps in a crowded nightclub, but from what I knew of him I couldn't for the life of me understand what Gardner might have seen in him. Ah, the mysteries of women.

So, I've just bought the Sands, and Sinatra's running up too much credit on the floor. And the question filtered up to me, just how much can we spring him for, and filtering back down was my answer, given with great pleasure: Frank Sinatra has reached his official credit limit. Well, he caused no end of ruckus. He demanded to speak to me. He felt he'd been publicly humiliated. He ripped the phone lines out of the hotel switchboard and then made the mistake of overturning a table on my casino manager, Carl Cohen, a solid man, who promptly knocked poor Frankie down, separating him from a couple of teeth. The incident was good for a laugh.

They were fun times, Jack, me up there in the penthouse directing traffic. In a neighboring casino, mind you. I was asking for quarter-hourly updates! I was on such a roll, I could almost feel the energy of that clash, of mad drunk Sinatra coming back for revenge, riding a golf buggy through the plate glass windows, screaming, Let me talk to the bastard! Let me talk to the bastard! Lemme get my hands on him!

BRONZE BELL TRAVELING
THROUGH SPACE

N o, I couldn't see what Gardner saw in him. Let alone why she would marry him. Because Sinatra was a greaseball. And Ava Gardner was a very classy lady. Back in the forties when we hit our stride together she was on her way up at MGM and recently separated from that insecure braggart Mickey Rooney. I liked her mostly because she seemed so uninterested in me; somehow this rendered the lovemaking even more full of sparks. I'd been so used to women agreeing to my proposals with open arms; after that the problem was always how to placate them while putting in place the eternal postponement. So Ava Gardner, all North Carolina dirt-farmer lust, all take-you-or-leave-you, was a novelty.

She stood up for herself. Case in point, perhaps I'll tell Jack about the early days, when we had something of a messy episode. My surveillance had revealed that Ava would still occasionally fuck Rooney, a runt compared to me, and I was somehow offended—or one night at least, when I first found out, offended may not be the word, enraged would be better. So I stormed into her home. She didn't know I had a key, but of course I had a key—I'd put her into the apartment. I crept along the corridors. I quietly turned the key in the lock. I stood in her foyer and listened for noise. Nothing. I burst into her bedroom. She was alone, asleep. She woke and shrieked. It took her a confused moment to work out what was happening. My adrenaline had nowhere to go.

Where is he? I shouted, fists clenched, though already in those first few seconds I was realizing it was a forlorn question.

I had rather hoped I'd make a scene and knock a quivering, naked Mickey Rooney to the ground. Instead, it was only Ava in a nightdress, sprung to life, shouting at me, pummeling me with her fists.

You horrible, horrible man! You're pathetic, she said. How dare you, how dare you! she screamed.

And something snapped and I shook her, or at least tried to make her stop hitting me, and then I slapped her, hard. Okay, perhaps I hit her. More than once perhaps. But fast and sharp. I didn't mean much by it.

The look on her face. I could see the sting. Her eyes filled with shocked tears. Then her chest suddenly swelled. There was an ornamental bronze bell on her bedside table. She reached for it and swung wide and hard and brained me. I saw it sail toward me, as if slowly, this heavy bell traveling through space on the full reach and arc of her swinging arm. I did nothing. I didn't flinch. Crunch. I felt teeth crack, I felt something shift in my jaw. My body catapulted rapidly sideways then, until my eyes were intimate with the carpet and I could see the dusty shoeboxes under her bed. I tasted blood and perhaps blacked out. It was a tremendous blow. I'm quite sure all her kindness resurfaced. I carry with me

172 • Luke Davies

still the vague memory of a face towel and the caress of
warm water.

You silly man. You silly, silly man, I heard, opening
my eyes as from a dream. Oh Howard, I heard, why do
you bring this on yourself?

Let's all relax, I gurgled.

That's your problem right there, she said. You just
can't let be.

I lost two teeth to Ava, just as Frank Sinatra would to
Carl Cohen twenty-five years later, so this represented no
doubt a kind of balancing of the forces of the universe.
She had split my head and broken my jaw. Apparently
my men carried me to the car, to treatment and safety.
Apparently I had gurgled to her to fetch them, parked in
the dark across the road. We flew, my men and I, in one
of my Lockheed Constellations, to the hospital, to San
Francisco, because there was absolutely nowhere to hide
in the Los Angeles hospital system.

The whole episode was a terrible misunderstanding,
an awful moment. I regret very much hitting her; I see
the pealing of that bronze bell on my battered skull as
a just desert. A week later, back in Los Angeles, she
apologized for hurting me and I apologized for arriving
without prior arrangement. Ava, I said, it's just that I
can't stand the thought of you seeing someone else. It's
just that I care for you so much!

That's all well and good, Howard, she said. So why
don't we just make an arrangement that neither of us is
to see anyone else?

Well, she had me there, the old devil! I had to laugh, which believe me is not at all easy with your jaw wired up.

She fed me soup for a week or two, spoonful by loving spoonful. She nursed me back to health! It was like a practice run for the following year, when it was mostly Ava who looked after me in hospital, after I crashed so extravagantly that day in Lake Mead. I haven't told you about that yet, Jack. That's the thing about Lake Mead, it's hard to get in the proper sequence. You leave it behind only to have it rising up to meet you. The cold-water tang in the back of your throat.

Anyway, she spoonfed me back to health and we were in each other's good graces again. I laid off the surveillance. Or perhaps she made me promise that I hand back the key. And perhaps I promised her that I'd already thrown it out. I never tried my luck with an unexpected visit again, but we did have some good times for another year or two. I had well and truly expended my Ava energy by the time Sinatra came sniffing around her.

Extravagance. I think it means more than enough.

Memo, 1967: Malarial with anxiety

They're planning to build the new Holiday Inn right smack in front of the Sands. To make it much worse, they are planning to make it a showboat sitting in a huge lake of water. A showboat with a pond of stagnant infested water.

If they are considering using water from Lake Mead, the effluent in the water would smell to high heaven. Jesus! When I think of that lake of sewage disposal on the front lawn of the

Sands. Ugh! It may even smell up our Sands Golf Course. You can't recycle water. It is not so much the technical purity or impurity, it is the revolting, vomitous unattractiveness of the whole thing. It is sort of like serving an expensive New York cut steak in one of our showrooms and having the waiter bringing the steak in to a customer on a beautiful plate, but, instead of the usual parsley and half a slice of lemon and the usual trimmings to make the steak attractive—instead of this, there is a small pile of soft shit right next to the steak. Now, maybe technically the shit does not touch the steak, but how much do you think the patron is going to enjoy eating that steak? I think he would lose his appetite very fast.

In any case, whatever the source of the water, there would be the additional problem of mosquitoes. They would not be able to have water running in and out, so it would become stagnant and an ideal place to breed mosquitoes. Bob, I am quite malarial with the anxiety of it. How can we quash this thing?

Everyone seems to want to build a hotel here in Las Vegas. The philosophy of the community seems to be: lend a helping hand to everyone who wants to build a new hotel or casino, the more the merrier!

Please remember, Bob, that it was this philosophy—that there is no bottom to the barrel—it was this philosophy that led to the 1929 stock market crash and seven of the worst years this country ever faced.

It was this same philosophy that led to the construction of a miniature golf course on every corner in Los Angeles, and the horrible, tragic crash of this industry—taking with it all the little people involved.

YOU GET THE THING YOU WANT, BUT . . .

I WILL NEED TO tell him, more than almost anything, about frustration. You get the thing you want, but when you get it, it is not what you thought it would be. Disappointment always follows anticipation. I've tried to capture that moment again and again. But there is no present, no exact here. Leaning over a bridge, you drop a leaf into a raging river, and it's already, instantly, carried away by the current: already the past, you see. With Empirin Compound, as with anything else, I am striving for the keys to the...to the bridge to the...to another side, to the newer thing. In narcosis, near blackout, there's a moment when you're almost there. You teeter on the brink, you are almost in the present. And you wake up later, cranky. Out of the nod, all ill at ease. Where was that thing? Where's it gone? Why wasn't I there? It's like a mountain without a peak. Damn. Damn.

Whatever the question, the answer is always More. This is called chasing the tail that feeds you.

Sleep is something else, of course. And I do not know where I have gone each night. Only that it feels, in the light of those translucent flakes of memory silently falling through the now-still air, that it was a sweaty place. That the tendency of cotton sheets will always be toward yellow. That morning is awful. (Or I mean to

say, *waking* is awful, since it's often afternoon.) And only
the medicine will get one back on track. There are only
compositions of consciousness. Oh apples of my eye. Oh
overblossomed tree.

Actually, Jack, it was in the Unreal City that this
habit of not sleeping, deeply, the whole night through,
became entrenched. In Las Vegas there are no clocks;
time never really passes.

You get the thing you want, but hardly. Hardly have
you breathed your way into the next thought than the
last thought fills you with yearning and is gone.

To say nothing of all this constriction.

NAKED IN THE EPOCH OF THE CLOTHES

I'VE NOT BEEN WEARING clothes a lot these past fifteen
years because they are such a hindrance, really, when you
look at it, when you think about it, rationally, deeply. And
on the spectrum of priorities, there's a lot of organizing to
get through in terms of getting clothes on and off; time
and energy better freed up for more important matters
such as writing memos or running empires! Clothes are a
complexity barely worth thinking about.

Germs are the issue here, too, of course. Clothes are
so replete with folds and crevices. It's like giving those
things a home, a festering ground. You might as well be

sticking your hand down toilet bowls. Licking sidewalks. Rolling in the back alleys of restaurants. It is a teeming world of dangers. It is best to paint the windows black, several layers thick. As a bare minimum, in emergencies or temporary circumstances, thick curtains and masking tape suffice. Because here in London the proprietors were not happy with the paint idea, and I'm in no mood for buying the whole hotel. But what rides in even on sunlight can destroy us.

You see, sunlight activates the particles of dust. That's why you can see motes dancing in sunbeams. So a darkened room would mean reduced mote activity, and that means reduced chance of infection. There it is, everything operates according to a sublime logic. There are patterns of interference everywhere, ready to menace us, and there is a divine path opening out so smooth and clean that even sunlight passes straight through it. There is destruction and disease; then there is the electricity of ease. By this I mean there is an actual electrical charge carried through the Empirin, there is a colluding of molecules down the needle of the syringe that transmute into the platelets and cells of the blood. They are clean. In there, deep in the blood, there's not a germ for miles around. But one must always be careful. The logical extension of all my theories is that electric lamps, properly placed in a room, unmoved, the globes being of moderate strength, are less liable to agitate the dust and the microbes than sunlight. There are worlds of death and strands of virus whirling on flakes of matter tinier than pinpricks. That is why my Latter Day Saints must help me in the quest for cleanliness.

In fact, I remember when clothes first started annoying me, in the thirties when I was seeing Ginger Rogers, whose advances and retreats were inordinately frustrating—it was not a goddamned fencing match. Ginger, I loved her perhaps the most. Ginger, or Kate, or Jane Greer, perhaps even Ava Gardner, oh, and Billie Dove much earlier. When I think about it there were a few, but Ginger, I certainly loved her a lot.

At the same time I was discovering the world of the East Coast debutante balls, easy pickings from the socially ambitious in Newport and New York during the Ginger off-periods. The debutramps were happy girls in a bright new world. A few times off Newport I had rented luxury yachts, since the offer of a speedboat ride out to a floating palace for a glass of champagne on a moonlit deck seemed somehow to these teenage socialites less frightening than the journey inland via limousine to my hotel suite.

So I'd fallen happily, luckily, upon a method.

Then, of course, I wanted to make the method bigger and better and safer. So I sailed to Scotland and bought the *Rover*, and refitted it and renamed it the *Southern Cross*. I may have mentioned that already. Much effort was expended in the master bedroom. And yet there were times, with the gap so narrowed between desire and achievement, between compulsion and compulsion-acted-on, that I should have felt happier. Instead, I felt merely unclean.

I got what I wanted; it was never enough. There wasn't enough scrubbing a shower could engender that could make me right again. Tiny unseen creatures, billions of them per cubic inch, which were even then—decades ago, Jack—beginning to invade my world.

Because I had learned the hard way, you see. I'd seen the blisters on my hands before I'd noticed that my penis was leaking. I no longer even remember the name of the starlet. Dr. Mason gave me penicillin and said, No sex for six weeks. Also it's contagious, so don't shake hands until it clears up. I've not shaken hands in the thirty years since, Jack.

A fever set in. My cock burned with ulcers. I lay in bed for a week, dosed up on penicillin and "combative chemicals." I moved in and out of delirious dreams. The chemicals and the confinement made me seethe with a murderous rage.

I was being eaten alive. I was about to be forced to curtail my activities. It was controllable by medication but not curable. If left unchecked it could eventually affect the mind. I would be wise to eat foods heavy in iron and to maintain a balanced diet. With luck the episodes would not be greatly recurrent. Would be intermittent. Would perhaps, if I were truly lucky, never return.

In bed those long strange days, syphilis and fever coursing through me, I thought it would be good to turn over a new leaf. To rid myself of all this impure past. So you can see how the debutantes were appealing.

On those lissome expanses of skin, so unblemished, so firm, one could imagine, if only at the level of microscopic topologies, could imagine for a moment, for an evening, a joyfully inviting sterility, arctic expanses of danger-free flesh, infinities of purity, a world erased of disease. And so my *actual* adventures, the ocean nights, the debutramps themselves, were swashbucklingly ejaculatory, oh milky way, oh milk-white skin.

I promised so much. I meant every word I said: give or take. I was immersed in my enthusiasm. I was a devoted listener. I wanted to give them all my attention, all my will.

And all my sap. It must have been a limited supply. Because I do feel rather weary these days!

But I've gotten off track. I was talking about when clothes became a problem, not the debutantes. I'm trying to focus my memory but it keeps bursting out on its own. I'd better get it right for Jack. The closer morning comes, the more excited I get. Where was I? My emptiness expanded with all those easy girls. The wind was getting in. Back in Los Angeles, Ginger Rogers behind me, the debutante season over, I stared blankly around my room. Suddenly it occurred to me that we keep clothes for years—a lot of time for things to grow in the dark spaces of wardrobes, a lot of time for festering—and maybe we've got it all wrong. Even the cross-threading of a woolen suit is filled with the very chasms made by the cross-threads themselves, and every chasm a hidey-hole for an unseen horror. A tweed suit can double its weight in dust. A suit bag means nothing but more darkness, more humidity. Mere hay fever would be a benign outcome. There is so much in wait for you, Jack.

I felt alive with insight. At this moment my attachment to clothes became less important than my desire to cleanse my body, my house and my soul. A turning point.

I tore through the house like a man possessed, pulling the closets apart. I threw the clothes in piles in the courtyard, categorized according to type: sweaters, linen suits, woolen suits, cardigans, socks, underwear. Life was filled with purpose once more. I called Noah. He never asked questions. He followed my instructions, organizing the men with protective clothing, including industrial rubber gloves. They piled the clothes into canvas postal bags. I padlocked the bags and kept the key. The bags were driven to industrial kilns. The men returned the charred padlocks for my inspection. Only then was I satisfied the threat was gone.

I purchased underwear and socks. A dark suit and a light suit, off the rack. Two pairs of chinos, shirts, tennis shoes: this was all I needed from now on. Howard made lighter by adversity. Howard ready to flee at any moment.

Everything was cleaner in the air. The higher you soared into the stratosphere, the less the thickness of the physical world, the less the cloying of germs and evil things. Up there, in a plane, mostly alone, my lungs expanded with a great pure joy.

Around this time I took to taking off. And I don't just mean taking off my clothes—I made a kind of pun, I hope Jack laughs at that!—I mean, first I'd disappear from home and then I'd leave the very earth. I worried everyone terribly—Noah would tear his hair out—but I needed to be invisible. When all the events down here became too complex, I would drive out to Inglewood Air Field and simply Go. I rode the air currents as others hopped freight trains. I spread my maps across my knees. I noted wind speeds, pitch and yaw. My notebooks filled with theories. Undulated altocumulus thinned at the horizon. How can I ever have given it up, Jack? Of course, the medicines, properly assembled, properly taken, can give one a sense of being borne aloft—and without the complexity of leaving one's bed. (Though bed has its own risks, as I've learned.) What matters is that I plan to fly tomorrow. I'll see that curve of the earth once more.

I commanded from such heights, Jack. Back then, the sky was my friend. America was a giant, growing enormous beneath me. I had a share of that, a solid slice of haunch.

Memo, 1959: On retrieving my hearing-aid cord from the cabinet

First, use six or eight thicknesses of Kleenex pulled one at a time from the slot in touching the doorknob to open the door to the bathroom. The door is to be left open so there will be no need to touch anything when leaving the bathroom. The same sheaf of Kleenex may be employed to turn on the spigots so as to

*obtain a good force of warm water. This Kleenex is to then be
disposed of. A sheaf of six to eight Kleenexes is then to be used
to open the cabinet containing the soap, and a fresh bar of soap
that has never been opened is to be used. All Kleenex used up
to this point are to be disposed of. The hands are to be washed
with extreme care, far more thoroughly than they have ever been
washed before, taking great pains that the hands do not touch
the sides of the bowl, the spigots, or anything in the process.
Great care should also be exercised when setting the soap down
on the soap dish or whatever it is set on to assure that the hands
do not come in contact with anything. A sheaf of fifteen to
twenty fresh Kleenexes are next to be used to turn off the spigots
and the Kleenex is then to be thrown away. (It is understood
that while each Kleenex tissue as it is normally pulled from a
box consists of a double thickness actually, when one Kleenex
is referred to, one of these double Kleenexes is meant.) The
door to the cabinet is to be opened using a minimum of fifteen
Kleenexes. (Great care is to be exercised in opening and closing
the doors. They are not to be slammed or swung hastily so as to
raise any dust, and yet exceeding care is to be exercised against
letting insects in.) Nothing inside the cabinet is to be touched—
the inside of the doors, the top of the cabinet, the sides—no other
objects inside the cabinet are to be touched in any way with
the exception of the envelope to be removed. The envelope or
package containing the cord is to be removed using a minimum
of fifteen Kleenexes. If it is necessary to use both hands, then
fifteen Kleenexes are to be used for each hand. (It is to be
understood that these fifteen Kleenexes are to be sterile on both
sides of each tissue with the exception of the very outermost*

edge of the tissue, where the fingers first touched it. Only the center of the tissue should come in contact with the object being picked up.) If something is on top of the package to be removed, a sterile instrument, say, a set of tongs newly purchased and freshly boiled*, is to be used to lift it off.

[* Refer to separate instructions for purchasing and boiling of tongs.]

THE SHEET BLEW ALL AROUND HER LIKE A SAIL

I HUNCH FORWARD, CONCENTRATING intently, my body completely mobilized, completely attentive, like a cat about to pounce on a snake, as I inject myself in the left arm. I pull out the syringe and put it down on the table. I know this instrument now almost as well as the instrument panel, with which I will become familiar again tomorrow, but one thing at a time. I dab a corner of the sheet onto the droplet of blood on the inside of my elbow. I close my eyes, holding the sheet to my arm, and moan once, long and soft. I pull myself up higher against the pillows.

Nevada. Nevada. All that eroded desolation, all that demon-ridden expanse. I was talking about Nevada, if I recall.

After an injection, after the first prickly rush of the codeine subsides, ten percent converts to morphine in the body.

A naked woman flowed across the lawn. She took the bedsheets from the clothesline. The sheet blew all around her like a sail. Where was I? The things that visit me when I close my eyes.

I was thinking about Nevada, if I recall.

Las Vegas was pure money with no product, the grand and glorious skeleton of capitalism; nothing was manufactured there but hope. Or rather, hope becoming desire, desire becoming yearning, yearning becoming this desperate, this desperate...I remember the spangled patterns, the Stardust, the Sands, Caesar's Palace, the beautiful lights. But in fact I could not see. The windows were black. I was somehow lost in all that light. When I bought KLAS in '68, because of that midnight-to-dawn programming issue, I started running the old Randolph Scott films. What a lovely man was Randolph! Then, deep in the heart of night, I felt connected to the day, and the desert, to Randolph, so righteous, so certain, so steadfast, so pure, blazing away at the bad guys. The Vegas way dovetailed nicely with the Howard Hughes way. People are alert and active at two in the morning. My hotels and casinos made large amounts of money. And I didn't have to pay state taxes as long as it was my principal place of residence.

But when *Sunrise Semester* came on at 6:30 every morning, I would feel very flat, as if another night had passed, and all its safety had dissolved, and I hadn't quite got hold of it, got the measure of it. And I couldn't go on programming Randolph Scott films forever. Even I knew that.

But it wasn't nearly as bad as London, Jack—the TV *shuts down* at midnight here! There is nothing on now until nine in the morning! And what is on is rarely good. These Brits are an odd lot. When you come I will quote to you from the *Times* TV guide. There. Look at this. If I wait until 8:55 we can see *Open University–Reading Development*, or *Open-Air Eucharist in Trafalgar Square*. Or *Funky Phantom* at 11:05. What the Sam Hell is *Funky Phantom?* You can see why I travel everywhere with my projector.

What's worse, there are only three channels! *Three!*

NIXONBURGER

I HAVE NOTICED, IN this other section of the paper, the non-TV-guide section, the front page in fact, *The Times,* June 9, 1973—which may be today's date but is more than likely yesterday's already, time marching as it does brutally on, it seeming now to be exceedingly likely that we are well, well past midnight, and possibly nearer dawn—here on the front page beside me on the bed I have noticed, and been greatly amused by, an article, "Haldeman admissions cause new embarrassment to President."

The damnedest thing. The damnedest thing.

What to make of those hearings, Jack? I'll say, tossing him the folded paper, perhaps. It all seems rather a mess old Nixon has gotten himself into.

"Mr. H.R. (Bob) Haldeman," he'll read, "closest man to President Nixon until Watergate accusations forced his resignation from the White House on April 30, has for the first time admitted he might have heard about the plotting before the break-in at Democratic Party headquarters..."

We will sit and talk, as men do, about power, about how to understand it. It is all, of course, just a dreadful cockfight. It is not nearly so dignified as you might think, Jack. They're calling him Tricky Dick. I had to laugh, the first time I saw that!

Somehow I fear—though fear is rather too strong a word, I fear!—that all of Tricky Dick's present woes lead back, though thankfully in a largely invisible path, to me.

What happened was in fact very simple. Dick Nixon came to me in '56 and asked if I might please lend a hand and bail out his brother. It didn't make sense. I would have thought that Dick owed me; I'd been a regular contributor, after all. But when he became vice-president, the balance apparently changed.

Donald Nixon, the idiot brother, owned Nixon's, Inc.—too grand a title, in fact, for three restaurants and a supermarket which bled money hand over fist. Donny had been savaged by the press when he tried to get the Young Republicans to cough up cash in a public stock offer, the problem being that it was perceived he'd somehow misused big brother's name in grifting the money. That particular kerfuffle all went nowhere.

Now with Dicky as VP I received some polite enquiries, all seventh hand of course. It doesn't matter how many removes it actually was. The fact is it was Dick Nixon coming to me and asking could I help his brother with a little problem: Nixon's, Inc. was going under, fast, and it seemed that nothing but an immediate cash injection would ward off imminent bankruptcy. I was always willing to help out a politician in need, and I understood the desire to keep a strong family name as untarnished as possible. The upshot of all this being that Noah transferred $250,000 from one of our Canadian divisions, through an accountant in a Hughes Tool subsidiary who handled the paperwork, to Momma Hannah Nixon, who dropped the "loan" down to Don, though the central problem there is, you throw truckloads of money at a fool and they still remain a fool. Bad business, on paper.

It was not the kind of loan I'd normally engage in; and I didn't engage in loaning. But Dick was fresh in office, under Dwight D., and with such a huge winning margin it paid to be friendly. Generosity was the point. If one had the wherewithal to secure certainty in any of its guises or to increase the odds of outcomes, if one could make the future safer, better known, then one's duty was to follow down that path. Dick Nixon per se was nothing to me; his bones were a highway.

The point is, no male called Nixon was to be responsible if the loan defaulted. And Dick himself was the ultimate cleanskin, of course. We secured a place in Whittier as collateral, held under Hannah's name. Donny had once run a gift shop on the site. Now it was a gas station, leased to Union Oil. By the waters of Babylon that fossil fuel did flow.

How indeed can we sing our song, in oh such a very strange land? Donny, of course, squandered the two hundred and fifty thousand about as quickly as is humanly possible, and in February came crying to us, through seven removes yet again, What am I to do, oh woe is me. I got Noah to set up a committee, informal of course, to see if we could save the Nixonburger chain. I wasn't, you may not be surprised to hear, Jack, interested in saving the Nixonburger itself; I just wanted Brother Dick in as much compromise as possible. Little Brother Donny said words to the effect of, Trust me, there is a bright future, a big future involved in an ever-expanding network of franchises delivering to a growing customer base hamburgers of unwavering quality quickly and in a clean environment. Whoever gets in early, Donny assured us, will come to know untold riches. All this relayed to me by Noah.

I said to Noah, Expanding my ass. Expanding delusional fantasy. The fact is the man owns three restaurants which are going under as we speak. I said, See what you can do to ward off the creditors. And get Bob Maheu to call the vice-president; let Dick Nixon know, loud and clear, what we're doing for his family, for the continuance of its good name. Well, Maheu spoke to a Nixon aide. He was a very eloquent man, our Bob, despite his shortcomings.

The message got through. On the First of March the IRS handed down its decision: the Howard Hughes Medical Institute was now a tax-exempt charitable organization. That's why it's the colossus it now is, Jack. All this helped me immeasurably in avoiding a few tax issues and some problems relating to Hughes Aircraft and a number of spurious, or rather, annoying, claims of mismanagement. Deus ex machina be praised. I tender all these as unrelated facts. By the end of 1957 Nixon's, Inc. had collapsed and Nixonburgers, such a grand and glorious dream, with it. Donny got a job in middle management with Carnation Milk.

How's the Milkman, I would say to Noah. We had a good laugh over that.

Eventually the Milkman filed for bankruptcy. I never saw the two hundred and fifty grand, never expected to, didn't lose any sleep. For a while my gas station in Whittier chugged along just fine.

Memo to Bob Maheu, June 6, 1968

2:00 a.m.

Bob—have been watching all day and night on Channel 8 the Bobby Kennedy news. I hate to be quick on the draw, but I see here an opportunity that may not happen again in a lifetime. I don't aspire to be president, but I do want political strength.

I have wanted this for a long time, but somehow it has always evaded me. I mean the kind of an organization where we would never have to worry about a jerky little thing like this antitrust problem—not in 100 years.

And I mean the kind of set-up that, if we wanted to, could put Gov. Laxalt in the White House in 1972 or '76.

Anyway, it seems to me that the very people we need have just fallen smack into our hands. Also, if we approach them quickly and skillfully, they should be as anxious to find a haven with us as we are to obtain them...

So, in consideration of my own nervous system, would you please move like lightning on this deal—first, to report to me whom you think we want, of Kennedy's people, and secondly to contact such people with absolutely no delay the minute I confirm your recommendation. I repeat, the absolutely imperative nature of this mission requires the very ultimate in skill. If it is not so handled, and if this project should leak out, I am sure that I will be absolutely crucified by the press.

However, I have confidence that you can handle this deal, and I think the potential, in manpower and in a political machine all built and operating, I think these potentials are just inestimable, and worth the risk—provided you move fast. Please move at once.

9:00 a.m.

All right, I need to clarify this further. I want us to hire Bob Kennedy's entire organization—with certain exceptions, of course, I am not sure we want Salinger and a few others. However, here is an entire integrated group, used to getting things done over all obstacles. They are used to having that Kennedy money behind them and we can equal that. The group was trained by John Kennedy and his backers, and then moved over to RFK when John died.

It is a natural for us. I am not looking for political favors from them. I expect you to pick our candidate and soon. I don't want an alliance with the Kennedy group, I want to put them on the payroll.

PLANETS FILLED WITH MEN

I MUST ASK JACK whether he ever tried a Nixonburger. Because he's missed his opportunity now!

Where was I? I was working out how to tell him how this "Watergate" business fit in. Because back then the Nixonburger loan cost Nixon the '60 presidency, in that the IRS tax break I was granted while Nixon was VP, after we'd helped out his brother, saved me millions, and in that this news somehow became public in the '60 election race and helped ruin Nixon's chances. JFK the conquering hero, all hail. Not a thing I could do about Dick Nixon's 1960 woes; it was nothing to do with me. Some crusading East Coast journalists stirred the whole thing up.

Years later, separate issue, after RFK was killed by Sirhan Sirhan, it struck me how close RFK had been to becoming president. The Kennedys had been a thorn in my side for decades. I'd been as big a contributor to them as to Nixon, of course, but they were a particularly hard nut to crack, and sometimes I felt I was pissing my money up against a wall. At least with Nixon, you knew the man had a price, and you pretty much knew what it was.

So RFK was dead now. A terrible business. We must put a candidate in the White House who knows the facts of life, I said to Maheu. It did not seem too much, I thought, to hope to elect a president who would not only be deeply indebted to us but who would recognize his indebtedness. But I was ever at the mercy of the tidal forces, of life itself, pulling events this way and that.

Maheu eventually brought us Larry O'Brien from the Kennedy camp. We put him on a retainer of fifteen thousand dollars a week to act as my consultant, not that I ever met him, of course. He was a seasoned warrior, a real old salt, who went back to the JFK campaigns. We called him The Navigator. What's important always is to find the right place, and the right people, and then go ahead and buy what we want! The plan was to use his knowledge or at the very least compromise his integrity. (What did he think was going on for fifteen grand a week?) No, I'm joking. But word did come back to us via other conduits that Nixon was appalled by our snaffling O'Brien. Oh, we trembled in our boots.

I could see Nixon's point, though. O'Brien did know a lot about getting people elected. And back then, five long years ago, I'll admit I was nurturing the idea—I've given it up now, and London is so pleasantly far away—of placing someone in the White House. Of course it was an added bonus, too, that O'Brien knew a lot about federal antitrust law, and I was juggling all sorts of tax issues in this era, as you know. All this scared Nixon so badly that he always wanted to get rid of O'Brien. As if Larry's sole purpose on the planet was to bring Nixon to his knees. That was Nixon's problem: he thought the whole world revolved around him. The reality was, we were merely shifting Larry O'Brien into private enterprise. Or rather, we decided it was time to begin viewing politics as being an efficiently functioning sub-branch of big business.

But Nixon's paranoia was at fever pitch. This is the point I'm trying to get to, Jack. Eventually he ordered his burglars to break into O'Brien's office in the Watergate Building, and bug phones, ransack files and search for dirt on the relationship between me and dear Larry, who I never even met or spoke to, as I said. The capacity of the government to spy on its citizens was a breach of the contract of trust we entered into by voting in a democracy; my god, the contract of trust we entered into by being born in the United States of America. My own paranoia was garden-variety in comparison to Nixon's, and I believe I had a more valid claim to it, extending as it did back to '47 and the Senate investigation into my deals with the military for the *Hercules* flying boat and the Constellation. What am I saying? In fact, by '47 the FBI had been tailing my every move for four years—listening in on my phone conversations, even checking my sheets in hotels. You had to take it all with a grain of salt.

Nixon could have learned a lesson from all this. But he was obsessed, he was irrational. He sent out his burglars in the middle of the night and got more than he bargained for. And now even the Brits are reading about it in the London *Times*.

It tires me to talk about all this now, Jack. It seems so long ago. Myself, I don't care for personal charisma. Politicians come and go; back then I just wanted to cover not only the bases but the possible permutations thereof. I'd come too far to let my guard drop, as small men do—and heaven knows the planet is filled enough with them.

Another surprising thought, of course, when you think of planets filled with men, is that the entirety of everybody who has ever lived on this earth is still on it, or, more to the point, under it. When I think too much of that, this need for any one of us to get the upper hand on any other one seems mildly absurd. But I guess these days I'm more relaxed.

Then again I might say to Jack, Sometimes my lower hand simply doesn't know what my upper hand is doing!

THE EARLY BIRD

B UT MY EMPIRE ALWAYS knows. I think of it as "electrospace." In '65 we put the *Early Bird* in orbit, twenty-three thousand miles straight up: the world's first communications satellite. Hughes Electronics, thank you very much. My dream was a world in which everything was instantaneous—phone calls, television, ecstasy. We called it the Geosynchronous ComSat. Everything else flowed from that. From high in space my signals

spread, packets of energy, photons and bleeps. *Howard...
Howard...Howard...*everything trailed and echoed around
the globe.

And other globes, too: on the Ocean of Storms, on
the surface of the moon, the Hughes *Surveyor 1* landed,
in 1966. We sent the first photos back to earth. I was
everywhere at once. My satellites kept going up. We
photographed the communists; they couldn't hide.
Missile guidance systems: mine. Early-warning radar:
mine. Antitank missiles: mine. Range, bearing and height
data: a high-speed Hughes computer. Television coast to
coast: carried to you on a Hughes cable system. The laser:
Hughes Research Laboratory invented that, in 1961. I was
everything, Jack, I was everywhere, for a while.

Even the Hughes Aircraft Company, which eventually
I let run itself, did good things, or so I am told. Globes
within globes, networks beyond networks. The smallest
globe was the drop of solution protruding from the tip of
the needle. There was even a world in there.

THE NATURE OF ACCIDENTS

OH, THERE WERE SO many worlds. Some were easier
to manage than others. Certainly there were some
unhappy endings. I never finished telling you, Jack, about
pretty Yvonne Shubert. She certainly did some growing
up and wising up in the couple of years that followed

that overcommitted New Year's Eve, 1955, when I still had my sea legs—and a taste for it all. It was the end of an era. I wasn't to know it at the time, but she ended up being the last of the young ones—well, other than silly Jean Peters, but I'm not counting wives. It wasn't all pretty, I'm the first to admit it now.

Yvonne knew my men kept tabs on her movements, though I don't imagine she would have known, at least not in the early days, that her phones were bugged. She practiced counter-surveillance and occasionally practiced it successfully, eluding some of my best men, getting herself out for nights on the town. I suppose now, lying in state, years away and galaxies away, I can understand. I was young once, too. I had kept her so isolated from her peers, that other choir of giggling girls, heads full of *Photoplay* and *Hollywood*. Away from the attentions of all those young and gormless, penniless men that young women seem so attracted to. I had kept her from a kind of growing up. She snuck out and searched for it in all the wrong places. Maybe there was something else she wanted, too: the body of a young buck. And I'm loath to admit it, but his stamina, too. Who knows? I was fifty, fifty-one, fifty-two. I was heading toward sixty! It is all such a frightening... It is all so fucking frightening.

She snuck out and searched for it and found it. What can you do? I should have wished her all the best. I should have stood aside. I should have been decidedly European. I should have known my time had come, was coming. I should have found for her, at last, a role in a film, however small. I should not have strung her along, her or anyone else. I would have liked to have discovered how I fared on my own merits. But without the things that made me up I was nothing, I was no one. Without the money, without the fame. I just needed to curl up, I only wanted to curl up, to curl up in their arms, to bury my head in their soft breasts, and possibly, eventually, if all was safe, to weep. I just wanted, like all of us do, for my hair to be stroked.

And Yvonne, perhaps, wanted only to grow, at something resembling the normal rate.

I am assailed by headaches. It is no way to live.

I am struggling to retell all their stories. I must give them their due. It is a paltry way to remember them. It is better than nothing. For this and all my other sins I am truly sorry, Jack.

She snuck out and searched for it and found it. She found a young man called Johnny Rand, an ex-marine and a big-talker who thought he was a gangster. He was, in fact, a fool. All her conversations were bugged, of course. So we knew she liked him. We knew they talked and schemed. We knew she knew she was under surveillance. They talked about it in their bugged phone calls. He told her she was a prisoner. He spoke of looking after her, of harming me if necessary. She said, Be careful, I was very powerful, be careful even saying that. Howard could hurt you more than you could hurt him. Howard could hurt you more than you could know.

I have a gun, he said.

We knew they had plans to shake off my men. And they almost did. They changed cars three times. And where did they end up? At a firing range in Long Beach, where he wanted to test a gun he'd bought, and teach her how to shoot.

And get this: he killed himself, in front of her. Such a strange coincidence. It was the darnedest thing.

An accident at the shooting range. I am not making this up, Jack. His gun misfired; he turned it round to check the barrel; he shot himself in the head.

Now I had told Maheu to look after this chap. To deal with him. If Maheu did it, I am proud of him. I'm not saying he did it; coroner said it was an accident. I'm just saying if Maheu somehow organized it, I am proud of him.

Yvonne was hysterical, wound up in hospital. She'd had a bad run with hospitals. A couple of months earlier she'd found out she was pregnant. I knew I was the father; my operatives had accounted for her every movement for a couple of years now. After the operation, she went a little funny. Turned up in hysterics at my bungalow once or twice; it was out of order, but what can you do? She had been through some experiences, she was only seventeen. It's after that she started getting stroppy and more reckless. She rubbed Johnny Rand in my face. She didn't care what we knew.

In any case, Maheu justice or universal justice, the situation sorted itself out.

She was really the last of the women; it's been me and the drugs and the darkness ever since.

It's been such a grand old passage of the years!

BLUEPRINT FOR CHANGE

B UT ALL THAT MAY be changing soon; the drugs and the darkness, I mean.

I may have mentioned to you, Jack, that Cary Grant has been in London this week, and leaving messages with my men. How simple things once were; in another time I would have picked up the phone and said, Hello there, Cary! Just like that. Let's meet at the Hyde Park Corner. Let's meet at the Trafalgar Monument! Let's take a walk.

Because I'd very much like to see him. And I want him to see me, but not quite in this state. The vanity of an old man, Jack. Get some pink back in my cheeks, is all I'm talking about.

What would I need to do? Let's think about this. Well, I'd need to slowly reduce off the Empirin. I'm sure I can do that. I'll only have every second injection. That sounds achievable. That's what I'll do. Every time it's time for an injection, I won't have it, until it's time for the next one. Let me work out the mathematics of it. There's something exponentially decreasing in this. I could be stopped a lot faster than I think. Then I can catch up with everyone, for old times' sake. Not just Cary, but Randolph Scott as well—but no, Randolph is dead, I think—in any case everyone who's still alive. Perhaps Randolph is alive after all. My god, I have little idea of who's dead. Sometimes I see it on the news. When Ginger Rogers died I didn't cry, but I dreamed that night of her radiant cunt. Anyway, all the living can come over, including all the girls, heading toward their middle ages now, or else already old like me, heading to that apotheosis common to us all, the desiccation of species.

Yes, exponentially decreasing. I'm sure this can be done! Okay, let's not get ahead of ourselves. One step, one little step at a time. Every second injection henceforth no longer exists. It is only the potentiality of injection. How much discomfort can I bear? Well, it's not as if I'm a weak man. At Fessenden School I was a wrestler, and I was substitute tight end. Over my shoulder I watched the football spiral toward me from out of the sky, perfection of arcing, my only touchdown, one touchdown per lifetime is enough. The twenty yard line becomes the ten, the ten the five, such glory looms. All these disguises of zero, of which the goal line is merely another. I was approaching zero knowledge. I was fourteen years old. No dream was impossible. A little discomfort is nothing. I've known loss of consciousness at thirty thousand feet. Been sleep-deprived for days on end, around the globe and otherwise. Broken bones and ruptured spleens. Frozen near to death in cockpits everywhere. Burned into my clothes beside the wreckage of my plane. Weathered goddamned Egyptian mosquito plagues at Camp Teedyuskung, and held out, despite knowing that my mother was panicked and fretting in a hotel nearby (ready to swoop me out of that place), despite knowing that the mosquito plague was the perfect excuse, despite knowing the grand treats she would shower upon me before our return to Houston, holding out simply because I *knew I could do this* and because I *needed my mother to leave me alone*, holding out because being away from her was not nearly as bad as she'd had me believe it would be and, goddammit, Camp Teedyuskung was the greatest fun I'd ever experienced. And there was nothing wrong with mud! How much discomfort can I bear? How much have you got?

Well, of course, I'm not going to go crazy here— no point pushing the limits to where it hurts—but discomfort, sure. Bring it on. It'll be no worse than the mosquitoes. I'll simply reduce the Empirin, gradually. Missing every second injection might sound like a lot but it's not—I'll keep that going for a couple of weeks. That's what I mean by gradually. Then after a couple of weeks, I'll start missing every second one again, according to the new schedule. That's what I mean by exponential decrease.

And surely every second injection (the abstract, the negation) will not be missed, because every *other* second injection (the real, the experienced) will come as a great reward!

I really think I can do this thing, Jack!

And maybe I can cope with more discomfort than I think. It would be hard to know, since the Empirin is a painkiller and I am the first to admit it might therefore have *masked* some effects, some sensations of discomfort over recent years. So something even more astounding may await me! That I could stop. That I could go outside again. That the world might not assail me with its... intentions. What a breathtaking idea.

I'm so thrilled with it. When should I begin? No point in not beginning now. All right. The plan. I'll only have every second injection. Just let me get this right again: every time it's time for an injection, I won't have it, until it's time for the next one. It is so diabolically simple! So. So then. So is there an injection due around now? I guess so. So perhaps I should have this one, and then not have the next one. That sounds fair enough. Or what about—better still—I'll *not have* this one, and *have* the next one? That's tougher, but if I'm going to be serious about this I'm going to have to be tough. I've already worked it out. Some discomfort will be involved. But I have reservoirs of willpower. I built the world's largest flying ship, I flew around the globe faster than anyone else, I bought studios, bought companies, bought elections. I could outmaneuver anyone. So I can do this.

So that's the way I'll do it. Good.

No injection just for now.

I'll just lie back and think about things for a while.

A smooth, uninterrupted row of thinking. That sounds nice. And chat with you, Jack.

So what will it be? What can I think about?

Cary Grant, for example! Once we were all one big family. In 1946 we were all in love with life, we were sitting on top of the world. I had just taken delivery of the new Lockheed Constellations for TWA, and I flew us all to a party in New York—Cary, Tyrone Power, Virginia Mayo, Randolph Scott and Walter Pidgeon and Linda Darnell and others, but most of all, that day, that week, that month, sweet Gene Tierney, whose presence in the plane made my head swim with anticipation. This will be a difficult flight, I had whispered to her at the airfield in Los Angeles. Difficult not to touch you. We have to behave among our friends.

Well then, behave, she said, smiling demurely like the cat that licked the cream.

That night at the Ambassador I came out from the bathroom. Gene lay naked on the bed, a dozen chocolate hearts wrapped in red tinfoil spread over her body. Happy Valentine's Day, she said. Though the chocolate was a secondary feast.

Okay. So far so good. It's easy to think. It all just flows along. I lie here and everything just comes to me, all wealth, all memory, all events real and imagined. Am I thinking out loud? I don't want the Mormons to eavesdrop on what I plan to tell Jack.

It is so easy to think. It all just flows along. It is the easiest thing in the world. And it doesn't need Empirin to prod it along. And see, I didn't have my next injection, and so now my *next* one is a real one. Which is much better than doing it the other way around. The only question that remains is, *when* to do my next one. Well, let's see. I'm not at all used to clock-watching. But I figure it must be...soon. Probably *now* would be a bit too soon. After all it's only... what, half an hour? Who knows how long it's been since I thought of this plan. I'm exhausted from all this thinking. Maybe hours. I will have to enlist the Mormons' help in getting the timing right with my new plan. We can develop a program, a timetable. That would mean I could get it all more precise, and wean myself off it more quickly. With their help I'll know exactly when *not* to have the injection I was about to have, and when to have the one that follows, after the appropriate time lapse. And, after a while, when to have *less* of the one that follows, of the every-second-one, and, more importantly, just *how much less*. It gets complex, so you can see how the Mormons fit in.

And eventually—no more Empirin!

Except for specific physical pain, of course, should it arise. And no more Valium—except for specific sleeplessness, should it arise. And morphine would only be a *very rare event*. I'll be fully weaned, more or less. What Cary would think of me then! How proud he would be. I'll be a new man. A new Howard Hughes. It's never too late.

I can barely remember the days before the painkillers. I can remember all the events, every little thing that happened, but not so much how I was feeling. I seem to remember an awful lot of anxiety, though. I'm not sure if that's a feeling or an experience. But in the mere remembering, a little anxiety comes back into me now. Which is not a good thing. Since I'm currently in the period of the lead-up to the every-second-one. No point creating additional anxiety. I'm embarking on a new plan here, and every new plan contains elements of the unknown, and hence whatever one can do to keep things smooth, well surely that can only be a good thing. So the thing to do now would be not to focus on any anxiety, past or present, which might increase the load of the past.

Of course, the sheer effort of not thinking about the issue of the missed—the forgone—interim injection, or indeed of the upcoming every-second-one, could in itself be an anxiety-inducing event. So I'll think good thoughts instead. Try to think of Cary Grant, of how we'll laugh over all the good old times. (Talking to you, Jack, when you wake and come to see me, will be a practice run for this type of thing, for the new Howard, for the new Howard just like the old Howard, out on the town and full of life.)

Yes indeed. The less I think about timing and the upcoming injection, the more it will be a pleasant surprise when it arrives out of the blue. Not literally out of the blue—I'd still know it's coming, sooner or later. I just mean that if I haven't been thinking of it then I haven't been expending unnecessary energy on it and I haven't courted the possibility of entering into anxiety, which really is, when all is said and done, a thing that eats you up.

He would come here—no, I've got a better idea, don't have him come here, get out and meet him. I would meet him...let's keep it simple...let's say downstairs in the lobby. I would stroll out of here, take the lift down, stroll across the lobby. Cary would rise to greet me. I would be wearing a comfortable suit, no tie, perhaps tennis shoes. No point dressing up, we were always the best of friends. I would have worked all day, checking stock prices from New York on the teletext, putting in a few calls, buy and sell, dictating a few memos to the Mormons if necessary, or no, writing them myself, I'd be feeling energetic. I would have shaved and showered and brushed my hair. We would clasp hands, hug perhaps. Cary would have a cocktail; for me, a lemonade.

There would be so many things to talk about. I wouldn't be living life from the bed anymore. I wouldn't have a care in the world.

Ah, Jack. Ah, Jack. Ah, Jack. Wake up. Please come and visit me. There are so many things that hum. The refrigerator, the television. The air-conditioning system.

IV

Let us grant that there is an exhilarating dynamism in our condition, but this does not prevail, and it is not the norm of our existence. Trauma is far closer to our days and nights: fears of lovelessness, deprivation, madness, and the anticipation of our deaths.

—Bloom, *Omens of Millennium*

ROUND-THE-WORLD RECORD, 1938

IN 1938, WHERE WAS I, we flew from Omsk to Yakutsk, ten hours of incessant vibration and drone. Gradually the Steppes gave way to the tundra. One tends to go into oneself. It is tiring, trying to shout over the noise.

In Siberia (above it, I should say), when the rain clouds we flew above for seven hours parted, there was revealed to me then sunlight glinting on lakes in the tundra, the lakes flashing one after the other like a rolling semaphore, the barren expanses like a clanging and a wailing in my heart. Sadness? I'd gone far beyond that here. No thoughts in any case of putting a flare gun into my mouth. The end would be soon enough for every one of us, no point in hurrying. As the low sun lit the land, I sensed the coldness of every long shadow. I tasted the tang in that water that would freeze the chest. I knew myself to be closer to knowing the planetary despair of life's essential uninhabitability, of all the astonishing emptiness between atoms, than to feeling sadness, just because to be a peasant, a wheat farmer, a commie, or all three, is equally as absurd as anything else.

All this trip we were buffeted by winds.

The yokels in Yakutsk were beyond belief. They knew of the International Date Line: how in one part of the world it might be Monday, and in another, Tuesday. Through an interpreter we learned they were perplexed by the Lockheed's name, *New York World's Fair, 1939*. Was there also a line that divided 1938 from 1939? In any case, I was the harbinger of the future.

Twelve hours from Yakutsk to Fairbanks, Alaska. Halfway across the top of the world, near dusk, I saw both moon and sun suspended in the sky—one to port, one to starboard—globes of perfect stillness. No stretch to call this the nicest moment (non-sexual) in my life. I sent another cablegram to Hepburn: *This is an extraordinary beauty. Still safe, HH.* Across the Bering Strait and into Alaska we fought freezing headwinds. I pissed into a jar and cradled it between my thighs for warmth. So there is another ten minutes of my life accounted for.

At Fairbanks we were refueling and Dick was doing his standard airframe checks. We had filled much of the lining of the plane with ping-pong balls—our theory was that if we crash-landed smoothly on water, we might float longer. Dick was tired, possibly even delirious by now, and opened the wrong hatch. It was a fierce, blustery day out on the airfield. A tornado spout of ping-pong balls erupted from the plane. For an instant Dick was like a man on fire flapping at the flames, the little white globes swirling all around him, Dick the stunned center of a white dust dervish, jumping backward away from the hatch in his panic. Thousands and thousands of ping-pong balls cascaded onto the runway. They scattered in all directions, bouncing and skittering, pulses and tides of them advancing and retreating on the tarmac, looping in slow motion and spreading, thinner and thinner, off into the whiteness, where they simply disappeared. God knows, they're probably still out there today, swirling like the snows.

From Fairbanks it was an easy run to Minneapolis. By now the press was in a frenzy. From Minneapolis we might as well have been gliding into New York.

At 2:37 p.m. on July 14, 1938, we touched down again at Floyd Bennett Field. We had flown around the world in three days, nineteen hours, seventeen minutes. We had opened new possibilities for the future of travel. Twenty-five thousand people were waiting to see us home. Twenty-five thousand people crowded around the plane on the tarmac. The reporters were fighting for a piece of me. "The whole country is captivated by this heroic young man and how he has not let himself be spoiled by inherited wealth," said Lowell Thomas. Pleading tiredness, I slipped away from the official welcome to go see Kate in her townhouse near Washington Square. But the press were all camped out there waiting. I went back to my suite at the Drake Hotel and called her on the phone instead. She came around and fucked me into sleep. One can get very tired but one is never too tired for that. It was a very warm place, to fall into her arms. You are my special Howard, she said, nibbling at my ear. You are my hero. My muscles still hummed from the endless vibration. And all the strain dropped off.

COULD I CUT THE ENGINES

I HAD ALWAYS LIKED THE clarity of the higher altitudes. I had liked to rise above Los Angeles. The air was very clean. I liked to fly north over the San Gabriel Mountains, or across the high deserts to Palm Springs. I loved the constant presence of the sun. I loved the vibrating of the fuselage.

One dark night in 1937 I had ventured far out over the water. High above the dark Pacific, out on a long aimless loop from Los Angeles, through space, through my thoughts, I switched off the control-panel lights. In a blackness I had never known I felt the fear that freedom brings.

Suddenly, I was aware of the ceaseless drone of the giant Lockheed engines. The brutal magic of the stainless steel that pushed me through the brittle air. For many hours this deafening comfort had lodged in the back of my mind. Now, with light cut, my senses clung to noise. It seemed an intruder in the blackness, the blood through my temples noise enough.

Could I cut the engines? Did I have the courage? Could I cut the engines and would they start again? To crash in the ocean. To sink down there where the giant manta rays glide, profoundly untroubled. A death without form and location, unnoticed by all who watched my every move. The one who is known by everybody in the world: that is fame. To be in a place that is neither true south, nor true north, but true nowhere: that is the trick. For death to be uncertain.

So I cut the engines.

Not silence but something close as the engines wound down. And the soothing rush of wind on steel, high in the air in the middle of the night. I put my hand in front of my face. I could see nothing. Looked all around me, to the roof, to my feet, to where the windshield was. Nothing. I saw more light when I closed my eyes than in all that open space.

I said, I am Howard. Howard. How-ard. Howard Hughes.

I could hear the words come out of my mouth, my own clear voice for the first time since take-off.

I could not tell if in any way I could feel the descent of the plane. Not yet. I hoped my sense of time stayed true. Eight thousand feet, strong tailwind: I calculated I could give myself one hundred seconds of darkness and silence, allowing a huge margin of safety.

A kind of blood rush. A kind of unconsciousness. The blackness crushes you. You feel it in the thighs. You feel so hot. It's the cunt of the goddess of night. The plane descending. The blackness descending. Squeezing your tiny thighs. My tiny thighs. The thighs of Howard Hughes, so frail beneath the haunches of the night. The haunches of the night descending on my cock.

I needed to come. I wanted to come in that black silence of descent.

I switched on the engines and control lights. The cockpit glowed. The engines shuddered and took. Climbing toward twelve thousand feet, I licked my right hand and began to masturbate. The normal images. Women I'd known. Jean Harlow going down on me. A mass of blonde hair, a silver sequined gown. Elma Rane at junior high in Houston, the girl beyond attainment. How I longed to stroke her knees, untie the ribbons in her rigid hair.

Several times in the climb I came close to coming. Then I'd stop for a moment to let it subside. Or open my eyes to check the instrument panel. For seven thousand feet I drifted in and out of this languorous state as the plane strained and hauled through the air.

Then for the second time, I cut the engines and lights. Instantly the bright fantasies of submissive women disappeared. The plane began to angle downwards. Dark gales howled inside my head, whose boundaries expanded wider than the cockpit and wider than the Pacific. Down there my body and my legs and my cock connected to my right hand.

I dreamed—did I dream?—that a giant, a goddess, had straddled me, was fucking me. I am most worthy I said. Fuck me fuck me. My head rolled back. That fierce wind, the wind of sex. More saliva. A huge woman. The rolls of fat. Her thighs. My thighs. The fatness of the night.

She had a face, but it was galaxies away. It did not matter. I buried my expanded head in her breasts. I was no longer this small tin thing crawling through

the air like an ant across a football field. I began to
moan. The cosmic push of her belly on mine was the
deep satisfaction that death must be. The smell of the
goddess: diesel and grease. I could fuck you forever oh
goddess of diesel and grease. I could fuck you forever.

I slipped into the final stage, the long slide into
coming when you're powerless to stop. I was beside
myself with a pleasure that years later would be matched
only by morphine. Crystal patterns broke and reformed
in front of my eyes. With my left hand I pushed the
joystick forward. The plane dived steeply. I spread my
legs. Inside my boots my toes arched backwards. My
spine pressed hard into the seat. In near-vertical descent
the plane reached terminal velocity. The ocean was
down there in the darkness, heading straight toward me.
I had no way of knowing how much time was left. My
hand was hot, the only hand in the world. No, goddess,
the only goddess. My hand a vehicle of the goddess.
Instrument of the will of the goddess of sex and death.
Or was that night and day? I could not think straight,
pinned to my seat and facing the roiling Pacific at lethal
speed. If I was to die it was important that I came first. I
imagined the ocean smashing my eyeballs back through
their sockets. My head awash with death and salt.

But the goddess lets us have our cake and eat it, too.
I came. She pushed down hard upon me. I felt her pelvis
grind on mine. I tilted my head and frowned. My left
hand splayed in front of me, palm open, as if saying, to
everything in the world, Wait. Wait. Wait for what? I was

in the middle of it, suddenly hot on the web of my hand
between my thumb and index finger, hot on my belly
and my undershirt.

I tried to gain my breath. The metal screeched. My
temples throbbed. I heard the wind louder and louder.
Terminal velocity. Where was I? Jesus! I pulled the joystick
back, straining at first. The plane pulled into a curve
as if it was set on a toboggan run. I flicked the ignition
switch. The engines cut back in, stuttered, then roared.
Gradually the Lockheed pulled level. It might have been
that nothing had happened, nothing at all for thousands
of feet in the infinite night. I switched on the lights and
felt the deep sadness that so often came after coming.

I was dangerously low: eleven hundred feet. I took
it slowly back up to eight thousand feet, wiping myself
with a rag, lumbering toward Los Angeles and the dawn.

Memo, 1961: Summer

*The weather man says this is a record heatwave. Some
of you will be aware I am preoccupied with purchasing five
Electras from the Lockheed plant in Burbank. But I feel we
need to protect them from germs. I am worried that the sun will
beat too fiercely down on the fuselages, which could make them
an incubator for germs. So I want one of you to get onto Jack
Real and see that he gets them towed inside an air-conditioned,
germ-free hangar.*

*Pass this message on to Jack—Jack, all I can say is to ask
you as urgently and as humbly as I know how—I ask you and
implore you, Jack, not to be satisfied with doing it as well or as*

perfectly or as smoothly or as gently as you have in the past, but please today just simply bust a gut striving as you never tried to do anything before in your life not merely to equal the best operation you have achieved in the past, but instead improve upon it and today conduct the most careful, the slowest, most perfect, most gentle, the smoothest towing operation ever, ever conducted before and with each acceleration and deceleration so infinitely gradual that it would take a microscope to measure it. Men, I want you to treat this task with the precision with which you deliver my magazines to me, when you move the cart an inch at a time, and do not breathe, so the air and the dust are not disturbed.

In stillness all the microbes are inert. It's been proven by Science. Please don't let me down on this.

PROCEDURAL PHILOSOPHY FOR THE LANGUAGE OF POWER

EVERYTHING I SAY IN the memos is only the language of power stripped of all its frills. I have ridden the wave of a certain power, of money, and speed, for nigh on three quarters of a century. And I don't plan to forgo any of that just yet. When I was born, the Wright Brothers had only two years earlier lifted above those tussocky dunes for those elated seconds. Now there are Hughes satellites circling the planet. The planet!

And yet I get so jittery, Jack, and sometimes I wonder if it's worth it, all this vigilance. On July 20, 1969, a man landed on the moon. I could not stop crying. One does one's best to be a patriot. I've had my sorry backside hauled before Senate enquiries for no good reason, because I wanted America to be the best, because I cut corners, or not so much cut corners, but there are ways of getting things done, of defying the protocols. It was all jet propulsion. We were the gifted ones. And yet certain members of our duly elected government have the audacity, under the cover of integrity, of righteousness, to question my motives, my methods. That was the forties, the fifties, before I became invisible.

Nobody kicks around this country without acquiring a reputation, good or bad. I'm supposed to be capricious, a playboy, eccentric, but I don't believe I have the reputation of a liar. Nobody has questioned my word. I think my reputation in that respect meets what most Texans consider important. If anyone thinks that the Communist Party is the same as the Democratic or Republican Party, I can answer it this way: we are not fighting any Democrats or Republicans in Vietnam! *Fortune* magazine called me the spook of American capitalism, a moniker I'm happy to wear. I was loath to give anything up, loath to admit error, but everything I did, I did for the greater good, from the aerospace industry to the cinema, from oil wells to airfields, from casinos to the star system, from the design of Jane Russell's bra to that of a bomber. Now everybody wants a piece of me, there are investigations flaring like fireworks, all of it is nonsense, the CIA connections, the *Glomar Explorer*, the tax evasion, the political interference, bribery, conspiracy to defraud the United States, false tax return, perjury, false statements, the FBI, the land deals. What did I do wrong? I'm a great American. I built a backbone to this country. I bought Trans World Airlines, a piddling concern that Lindbergh had started in the thirties, and over the next fifteen years I turned it into a giant corporation and opened up the very future of passenger aviation. I built the Lockheed Constellation. Jack, you were there, you worked with me, you know this. I changed the world. I'm there any time they need me. I built the *Glomar Explorer*, a huge beautiful fraud of a ship (ocean-floor research!) to raise a scuttled Russian sub from the northwest Pacific, because knowledge is everything, everything, and the CIA paid me. There is nothing anywhere but information.

That is why I had surveillance done on the women. It wasn't anything more sinister than that.

You always want what you cannot have; perhaps it has been like an illness for me. Perhaps I have not been well, for a long time, perhaps. A slight wooziness in the head. I told you last night how Billie Dove left me, back in '31. I never told you *why*. What the hell was I worried about? It's all done now.

She said, Howard, I am not your damned prisoner and you are not my damned jailer.

Well of course not, Billie, well of course not.

Then why do you have me followed every minute of the day and night?

Billie, I don't—

Don't even try to pretend!

It's for your safety. I don't want any harm to befall you.

She had packed and gone within a week.

I never felt I was controlling them, not one of them. I had to keep all my options open. Because you need to breathe. And it is important to know that everybody likes you.

That is why the surveillance planes were no different: we were just making sure that the country was all right. That is why my reconnaissance plane, the XF-11, was going to be so beautiful. Oh Jack, it is terrible to think of, so beautiful, the XF-11, in which later I would so spectacularly disintegrate. Did I tell you yet about my disintegration? Because the XF-11 was merely a pulse, flush-riveted, a vehicle of light. So something went very wrong. We were going to photograph the entire world, so that we could know where everything was kept, could know the proper place of all things. Instead I wound up in burning tatters on a street in Beverly Hills, with my dream in fragments all around me.

Two decades further along, that's all the Hughes Surveyor Satellite was: an attempt to gather knowledge. A loyal American, Jack! I didn't care about the money. I cared about this great nation.

Memo to Bob Maheu, 1966: Helicopters

Did you see CBS News at 11:00 p.m. just completed? If not, please get a summary of the portion devoted to helicopters in Vietnam. *More helicopters are being used than was ever contemplated and more helicopters are being lost than was estimated. CBS went on to say, over and over again, that this is a helicopter war. The first of its kind in history.*

Why hasn't someone made this clearer to me?

Bob, for you to have your White House relationship while at the same time our Aircraft Division sits empty-handed with the best helicopter design in the world—the whole situation is just the damnedest enigma I ever heard of.

Can't you do something about it?

MALEVOLENCE OF MICROBES

J ACK, THE LAST COUPLE of years, some newspapers are implying I am being drugged beyond acceptable levels of basic painkilling necessity. And this is, as you can see with your own eyes, entirely untrue and indeed scurrilous. Nobody drugs me. I am aware of what I need. I try to practice moderation and the amount of medication I take is in fact a response to the levels of pain I constantly encounter. Not just that, mind you; difficulty with the other humans also. Or else how would I have attended to the memos all these years? Left to its own, the empire would wind down to stasis, not a single rotor blade would spin, not a contract would be sought, or signed. Each new memo brings with it a new set of anxieties. Each anxiety invites a settling of the nerves, a medicinal solution. That's not to say the new Cary Grant reduction plan won't go well. It will have teething problems, like any new venture. But it is going very well, thank you.

Indeed I feel few would understand the acuteness of the pain I suffer and have suffered fairly constantly since 1946. If I was not so unfortunate as to have this level of pain in my life, I believe I might not have needed to take such drastic measures of seclusion, of putting such layers between myself and the world out there. It's not so much that I'm addicted—I know I can stop if necessity dictates, in fact the reduction plan is about to be put into action as we speak, and I will let the Mormons know about it very soon—more that I feel I need to maintain a certain level of focus. The more I take, the clearer it all gets. If I've got enough in me, everything is flat, perfect. I am striving for nothing less than the perfection of forms. It is imperative to trust nobody—present company excluded, Jack—as even physical presence can invite calamity, catastrophe, the chaos of germs and the sheer malevolence of microbes. To say nothing of psychic disturbances. Therefore I pay Latter Day Saints to be, essentially, invisible. I have not looked closely at a vase full of flowers in more than twenty-two years. All that pollen, ghastly. Yet inside of me whole fields of poppies sway, and along a quiet hedgerow the gorse glows yellower than butter and smells of coconut oil, and Axel my sleek brown pointer bounds ahead delirious with joy, and disappears and reappears through the hedges. Now *there* was loyalty. He flushes out a giant hare that almost bowls me over. In that moment in which Axel follows and brushes right past me his muscles bulge and his intent is absolutely, resolutely pure. (I will never know a summer's day like that again.) That is the purity of which I speak, the invisible form of the world. I am sullied and assailed by life's more ignoble duties, daily, hourly, on an endless loop, but I will not be bowed or bloodied. I will face every challenge every memo every obstacle *in sequence* and *as appropriate*. I will give to each matter its allotment of time. I will run this empire smoothly. I am doing this for all of us, the Mormons, the arms of empire, even Jack Real. I am trying to hold this together. I am handicapped by the pain but the medication helps me regain ground, achieve balance. In this way, dammit, can't you see the medication is nothing, no more than a spirit level in the house of forms that is my life each day? Dammit, those file boxes need some cleaning up now. Have I been sitting up? Did I rifle through them like that? They look like the neglected refuse of a long-departed, highly disorganized accountant, all that yellow legal paper spilling out over the floor. Better get the men onto it. Where was I? One day I'll get back to the way things were. In any case, I am not some strange recluse, as the papers like to think. I am as perfectly capable as the next man of walking out of this hotel and strolling through the park. Is there a park nearby? This place is called Inn on the Park, so I suppose so. If I was so fortunate that my concerns were worldlier, more domestic, I might well do exactly that. It is not for lack of ability. I am not in any way crippled. I have...responsibilities. I have a structure I am trying to maintain. I am the owner and creator and controller of a network so vast it is beyond the know-how of most men to move within it, to operate it, to organize its every nuance and fluctuation. I am, in short, *stuck here*. It's not something of my choosing.

But what is flying, if not my choice? You see, I'm breaking out, tomorrow—or no, of course, it's already today—with Jack Real, with you, Jack.

And yet one is always there again, where one begins. And in the end I retreated so far that any step beyond this room is rather gigantic. Not to say impossible. I mean, that's not to say it's impossible. If one wants to become what one wants to become one must start with what one is. Or has become. Perhaps I am sick, but if everything would just fall into place then I'm sure I can get better. Meanwhile, my voice gets thinner and thinner. I'm going to fly. I'm going to sit in the cockpit once again. Who devised this hideous speed of time? Who said it should go so fast? I am, very literally, *suddenly* sixty-seven. I didn't plan it like that. Things just kept happening without any breaks, events cascaded one on top of the other, no gaps, no room for sleep, for rest, for peace. And then at forty-one you discover morphine. This is all so long ago. And God says eat, eat all the fruit you like. Break all the rules, because money is kinetic energy, the potentiality of the congealed, and it is for you to make it liquid. Release it, release it. It drowns you in libation.

And yet you neither drown nor take on gills, but like Poseidon slumber in the deep. And all of the ocean is yours; even the heartbeats of the whales. And your life under water replaces the life that used to happen in the air. In any case, all is imagined and experienced as nothing more than combinations of oxygen and hydrogen in their different manifestations; flying and floating become one and the same thing. And all you are missing is fucking. I pushed Gene Tierney's knees high up beside her ears, her mouth was open half in pleasure half in surprise, and we both looked down at my cock moving in and out of her. When our eyes met, I felt almost shy. She said, Don't come, don't come. Her flesh was soft in the hollows either side of her labia. It was all oceans to me. I thought that if we lived only once, then I had loved, loved deeply, loved this, been overcome by love. But perhaps we are born many times, and I have been greedy this particular time. Perhaps I merely needed to relax.

What is contained in memory is made in any case infinite by the morphine. Please do not look down upon me as if I've found some lesser way to experience reality. I am trying to cram it all in. Some methods merely take preference. It is not particularly easy to do things any way other than the actual way that unfolds. Better the devil I know. My fear speaks to me with the authority of a god. There is just so much out there to fear, Jack, even if you are the wealthiest man in the world, *more so* if you are the wealthiest man in the world. It begins with the microbes, the germs, the tiny worlds of danger in the dust. It ends God-knows-where. I am very far away, all right, I'll admit that much. But, dammit, in the morning I will be ready for action. I will take them all on!

Memo, 1961: Backflow of germs

Now. As you know, Bob Gross, who ran Lockheed, died yesterday, eaten up by cancer. His wife has asked me to be an honorary pallbearer at his funeral. This is patently not possible. But send flowers, telegrams, messages of condolence. Really go the limit on this.

However:

We have to go to great lengths to prevent the backflow of germs. Everything involved in this entire Gross operation, whether it be flowers, telegram, no matter what the hell it is, I want the absolute maximum greatest precaution and even greater precaution than we have ever taken before to close off all return paths. In other words, to make the operation truly, literally, absolutely irreversible. This will mean if we are going to use our florist for the flowers then the delivery will have to be made by some messenger service whom we will never use again, who will not be sending us literature, a bill, who will not be writing to us or sending or mailing us anything, who will not be calling upon us to try and solicit business, and furthermore, who will not do anything like this with our florist, for soliciting or business, sending literature to our florist, not sending bills or invoices to our florist, and not to be used again by our florist in any way. As for the message, it can simply go by telegram.

Mrs. Gross will undoubtedly write a message of thanks for the flowers. Bill, can you send me a very complete memo setting forth the scheme for the receipt of this message?

I want the necessary instructions given to achieve a block-off of all return avenues and to make the situation concerning the flowers and the telegram and anything else of that nature which may be required—to make any such transmission completely irreversible so there is absolutely not the slightest possibility of any backflow or return transmissions or anything of that kind even of the most indirect nature such as I have described herein.

STEAM RISING OFF ME

I IT IS ALL A catastrophe. And all a glory. What am I hoping to remember, and what am I trying to forget? It's difficult to keep it all straight. Because everything cycles around again. She viewed my stool before I flushed. The anxiety. The long bath. The thorough soaping. The harsh shock of the towel-drying. The running of her fingers through my hair. And every night the inspecting of the testicles. I would stand pink and steaming from the bath. She would take each testicle, one at a time, in her delicate fingers, looking for lumps. She would take her time, just like a doctor, and very gently, almost imperceptibly, feel her way around each testicle: the most careful, the slowest, most perfect inspection ever.

She had a special little wooden chair for it, Jack, a kind of milkmaid's stool. Perhaps I told you this before. And I stood, night after night, steam rising off me, willing it to be over. Then she would pat me down with talc and help me into my pajamas. She slept in the same bed with me until I was six years old, in the same room until I was eleven. Downstairs in the kitchen, her vigilance was the last defense against the amoeba-swarming vegetables.

Why did she think that death was out to get me? How did she convince me that she was right?

I have long since fallen, Jack. I landed here in this world of love and sleep. It is all a catastrophe.

I'd better break with the Cary Grant reduction plan, and have another shot. Did I think that already? We'll start the Cary plan tomorrow, when everything is fresh.

The memos don't come from a perfect place. They are more a response to a world gone wrong. I used to see them as blueprints of the inside of me, of my soul. Manifestations of my focus, which I know you admire so greatly. They were meant to protect me. But perhaps they can't tell the whole story. Which is why it is so good to see you, Jack.

THE FIRST AND THE LAST

WHEN JACK COMES I will say, Did you have a good nap? I'm sure I did. I will tell him the most important events, in appropriate sequence, and even the unhappy endings. I feel so much better myself. It was good to talk about Lake Mead. Did I talk about it already? To think about talking about it, anyway. It is so easy to forget where I was.

I saw Yvonne Shubert for the last time a few years after that New Year's Eve. My fifty-third birthday: Christmas Eve in 1958. I had not seen her for some time; she had flown the coop after the shooting accident in which Johnny Rand killed himself. I had taken a turn for the worse, I mean the world was just that much harder to deal with, I mean retreat was more necessary, I had upped the medications, I just needed to lie away from everything for a year or so, and the lawsuits with TWA were looming. Yet my thoughts turned to Yvonne's purity, to what I had sullied; to chances I had missed. I tried to contact her again. She had changed. She had moved on! She had no interest in seeing me. At first she didn't return my calls. She was reluctant. She resisted. I was offended. After all I had done for her. At last I got her on the other end of the line. She told me I was not the man she had thought I was. How disappointed in me she was. How untruthful I had been. How duplicitous. I was shocked and hurt. I wanted to see her, just to put things right. The truth is, given her resistance, I wanted her back again.

So I convinced her to come and visit me. She said, All right, but just this once, to say goodbye properly. I thought I could change her mind when she arrived. I thought we could be like we once were.

Perhaps I did have problems by now. Because perhaps I'd forgotten to dress, perhaps by now I was starting to take less care of myself. It was all relative. In heaven they don't wear clothes. It was a matter of priorities. In the grand scheme, how important was cutting one's hair?

I was trouserless. I was underwearless. I was wearing a shirt. It was unbuttoned. I am trying to paint you a picture. We had been naked together many times before. So why did she now take offence? I couldn't say. I can't speak for her. I don't have access. I was lying on the bed. She took me by surprise. I was quite medicated. I mean, I *knew* she was coming. It's just that, I didn't know what state I'd be in. But they let her into the room and she positively shrieked.

Oh, Howard. Cover yourself!

Perhaps I was being provocative. It's all a little hazy now, what is it, Jack, nearly two decades ago—how does that happen? So I pulled the sheet up to my chest.

Yvonne, I said.

That's better, she said.

Well now that Johnny's dead, we've cleared the air.

And she walked straight up to me and slapped me once, a real stinger.

How can you be so cruel! she screamed.

I took her wrist and rose up, buoyed by codeine and a sudden surge of anger. I slapped her. She slapped me back again. This was too much! I felt suddenly very old and entirely impotent. I was frightened and filled with adrenaline. She was young and beautiful, she was gloriously strong. I was old, thin of lip, weak of heart, slow of vein, shipwrecked of soul. And I knew in an instant: I could not keep up anymore.

I only wanted to talk to her. She was pummeling me. She was incoherent. I fled from that bed. I retreated into the bathroom and locked the door. I could feel my heart screeching. I could hear my breath, the hysterical wheezing of my fear.

Now Yvonne—now Yvonne, I stuttered. Now Yvonne—

But she was gone already. The door slammed. And then there was only Bill Gay's voice at the bathroom door.

Mr. Hughes? Mr. Hughes? Everything all right in there?

And I composed myself. Because for what did dignity count, if not in its presence on the battlefield, if not in our dealings with the minions, the Mormons, the men of good cheer?

She was the last of all the women. Perhaps I will have told Jack that already. Perhaps it will be clear. The very last. I had expended all my energy. I had scattered myself far and wide. What a beautiful century it had been. Aside from this sense that something was missing, that I'd done something terribly wrong, or rather, had not been present to do something terribly right, for which, Jack, I apologize to you, here and now, or whenever the hell you arrive from downstairs, on behalf of everyone.

That's not quite right. No, you need to accept my apology, on behalf of everyone. That's more like it.

Forgive me. Forgive me. In 1923 a redhead prostitute, she must have been no more than seventeen, came to me in my room at the Vista del Arroyo. That grand shock, the ecstatic strangeness of her disrobing, created perhaps a template for all of the future. Fifty years have glowed red! That girl was dumb as dogshit and I loved her for that night. And Yvonne Shubert was the last.

Well, except for silly Jean Peters, as I said. But who's counting the wives?

I COULD NOT WORK OUT THE SEQUENCE OF EVENTS

SURELY HE'LL BE AWAKE soon. Because I certainly feel that I could begin now, what with morning approaching and all. I feel that it's been a very productive rehearsal period, and that second time around, when I get the words out, it will all come out right, everything in its position, each memory dropping softly into place, and I will have nothing to fear, from beast or person or thing. The words will flow out. Each penthouse fortress I have lived in is an echo of the original cave and I am no different from anyone else in that all I ever wanted was protection from the cold.

Lake Mead was deep and dark, a bowl of cobalt from three thousand feet. I always loved approaching airfields, that sense of space unfolded into a gash, that lack of obstacles. But landing a seaplane on water was entirely different. One felt one was moving, if things did not go well, from one transparent medium into another only slightly more dense. And things did not go well for me on May 16, 1943 as we took her down on that part of the lake known as the Vegas Gulch. We were testing my Sikorsky amphibian, it was a high-pressure day, we were under scrutiny from the Civil Aeronautics Agency—they'd sent two flyers up with me—my engineers Dick Felt and Gene Blandford were there, too, and the cockpit seemed too crowded, like my tender brain that day, I needed a coffee, I had been up all night with Ava Gardner at the Desert Inn in Vegas, things were not so right with the world, this was the wind-up, the clockwork coiling before my long retreat from the, from the, the what is it, the multihued complexities of life. It was a lovely cloudless day. I had landed the Sikorsky on the lake so many times as we ran through all the modifications, it should have been a formality. But I was so distracted by the blood in my brain and a sense of impending suffocation that I didn't notice the ground crew hadn't loaded the tail ballast. Because we were all so rushed, not just specifically that day but the whole of the century has moved awfully fast for me. I hate it when those talks get serious with women. I hate it when they (the women, not the talks) gently lead you to see the inconsistency of your position(s). I hate it when they (the women *and* the talks) make you feel flatness, nothing but flatness.

Ava Gardner was like some Eastern deity, forbearing of my uncertainties, patient with all my quirks. She never pressured, never created dramas, other than the Drama of the Bronze Bell. She gave me all the room I needed. (What went always unspoken was that this meant room for other women.) It may be why I saw her for longer than most of the others. But in her infinite kindness, deep in the night in that artificial city in the desert in Nevada, she led me somehow effortlessly to the self-imposed question, What is wrong with me? It is just an awful blackness to be there. It is worse than the worst gold digger trying her tricks and plying her skills, all things you can deal with, all things tradeable for sex. It is nowhere near that. It is Ava saying, Howard, you are so troubled, I can hardly bear to be near you for too long. It is realizing that Ava *actually liked my company*— but only for a while. That she actually liked me. Yikes. Because God knows I hated to be alone with myself.

What on earth is the matter with you, she said, propped up on her elbow, looking down on me in bed.

Ava, it's just the CAA. You know what I think about these government men.

She sighed and lay back down and turned away. I know you're not answering the question, she said.

We can take this somewhere, Howard, she said. We really can. We can *take* it somewhere.

I felt a bad headache coming on. My sweet, I said. I'll do the test-flight. Then when I come back tonight, we can talk about where we can take it.

But, of course, my whole life was a test-flight. And where had it taken me, exactly? With the women, I mean. So I was dark and troubled on that bright day. Because I knew that either we would have that conversation, and I would consequently lose all practical interest in her; or we wouldn't have it, because I would avoid it, and she would lose interest in me. So Lake Mead was to be a turning point day, even without the accident. Not to mention these government officials, I felt them in the cockpit like little dogs yapping and nipping at my heels, their thoughts of me unkind, their own intentions black. Yes, yes, maybe I was a little angry, a lesson I should have learned, for all our sakes, after the '28 crash during the *Hell's Angels* shoot, maybe I was descending just a little too fast, but maybe I merely wanted the flight to be over, to get back to the Desert Inn, to pull the blinds and be with Ava, for the succor, for the comfort, forget all that exhausting talk. Merely to lie, to nestle inside or beside her. And sleep.

Instead, I was tired and I was angry, not necessarily in that order, and the circumstances were unforgiving. The lake was like black marble. Not a ripple on the water. I came in hard and steep and tried to level and adjust. The pontoons touched the surface. Eighty, seventy-five, seventy miles an hour. I braked the great propellers gently. Or perhaps not gently enough. We flipped forward abruptly to the waiting surface. A flash of darkness. The windshield shattered inward. A rush of water. We seemed to catapult. The sky arced by. The screech of metal tearing. We hit the water again. Behind me a man screamed. I clung to the controls, my seatbelt somehow holding me in place. We cartwheeled again, weightless but into impending doom. We flipped. Metal stripped backwards from the plane. The left wing snapped around in front of us. Then the cabin broke open as the giant propeller sliced right through the nose and headed straight for me. Here it comes again, I thought. But then the propeller Catherine-wheeled into our little space and sliced into Dick Felt's head, instead; I saw brain come away. A blade caught Ceco Cline beneath the arm; he lifted up as if pinioned to a paddlewheel, arched backward through the cabin, and slammed down into the lake where the cabin floor had been. Then the blade was not there. The plane sank all around us. The water churned. I could not see for the blood in my eyes. I could not work out the sequence of events. I could not work out how to take my hands off the controls and unlatch my seatbelt. The water rose to my shins. I could not clear my head for the screams of Van Rosenberg. Dick's brains bubbled in the chaos. What had I done? I'd killed them all! Van Rosenberg unlatched me and pushed me out through the side window, which was now facing upward as the plane began to disappear. I stepped into the water.

I had fucked it up again.

We struggled as the weight of our clothes pulled us down. The plane was nothing now but the burps and bubbles it surrendered from its descent. I could barely breathe for the cold. Van Rosenberg clung to Blandford who held up Dick Felt who moaned and gurgled, coughing water in his delirium. The plane was gone, Ceco Cline gone. There was nothing now but the shore so far away. If I were to die I wanted to lie with Ava one more time. Then a rescue boat came churning into my vision to deliver us from evil.

I can still see the grain of the planking on the deck of the boat where, pale and numb and on all fours like a dog, I heaved up a bellyful of that cold Lake Mead water.

The others went to hospital. Dick Felt died. I sat in the airport office with my engineer, Glen Odekirk. He bandaged the gash on my head. After a while I noticed how much blood was on my wet clothes. Some of it must have been Dick's. Perhaps I became hysterical. The main thing was I had to buy a change of clothes from the first store we could find. The other main thing was to get back to Ava. But I wouldn't be able to stay there long. My plans had all been shattered on the lake. When I left Las Vegas and Ava that morning there existed in the world the possibility that something inside me may have changed forever: that I might have settled down, that one specific woman might have been as good as any other, that it was all just a matter of making a decision, that you couldn't keep searching forever, that suddenly all the other women in the world would have represented nothing, no need, no compulsion, to me, and that Ava would hold me in her arms. And suddenly all my tension would leave, like the birds flying off from the tree.

But the crash was a way of putting me in my place. I
had to control the damage. I had to get back to Los Angeles.
Talk to Dick Felt's widow. Deal with the Cline family. Pay
the money. Pay the money. The enquiry would have to say
mechanical failure. But never pilot error. Pay the money. I
had to wash the blood away. Read the signs. Cool it with Ava.
Switch yet again to Faith Domergue. Simpler parameters.

There was so much money, and so much sky, but it
was hard getting the balances and sequences just right.

THE PHYSICAL BODY

A FUNNY THING HAPPENED RECENTLY, Jack. Just a few
weeks ago, and apropos of nothing. I became aware
that for many years what I've been lacking is any kind
of...well, physical body. I'm entirely abstract, stretched
on hooks through space. The codeine widens everything.
Even one's understanding. Even the understanding that
the codeine widens everything.

NICARAGUA, DECEMBER 23, 1972

A LL THESE YEARS, JACK, I thought that death would
be the punishment for my sins. Managua made me

reconsider. You might be wondering what we were even doing there; it was our last place of residence before we high-tailed it here to London, six months ago. My tax-free status in Vancouver had only lasted until September '72, so after that we packed up camp and went to Nicaragua, a place more open-armed than Canada, more flexible in its attitudes on how to welcome...how to welcome and treat its distinguished visitors. I didn't entirely like the constant upheavals of our travels, but I had to do it for the sake of my money, which had feelings, too, after all. (It didn't like the idea of being separated from me too permanently! Ha ha!) I liked that President Somoza had sent an official police escort when we first arrived, because Managua was such an ugly ruin of a city that you wanted the trip from the airport to the hotel to be as quick as possible. Automotive air-conditioning: now *there's* a wonderful invention. Somoza's police escort: now *there* was some gentlemanly conduct. The Intercontinental loomed into view, enormous and stepped like a Mayan temple. We moved into the penthouse, the Mormons and me.

It was a gray city on the edge of a sulfurous lake that smelled of five decades of raw sewage, a jerry-built shambles of adobe and raw plaster, stretching for mile after gray-dust mile. Even the electricity lines seemed to sag in the heat. Scalloped lines of black volcanoes glowered on the horizon. By day Managua suffocated in an auburn cloak of petrochemical fog; you could stare straight at the sun and not squint. At night it sweltered beneath a yellow moon. But nobody had told us that the whole city trembled at the delicate intersection· of three adjoining tectonic faults. Nobody told us that Nicaraguan reality was so porous.

I was watching *Goldfinger* on the Barcalounger in the darkened penthouse of the Managua Intercontinental when the earthquake hit. The first sign was that the image went out of focus, and I was ready to shout for a Mormon to come and adjust the damned machine when the second shock cut in, and then everything cascaded and blurred. I was as brave as a Boy Scout that night! The screen shuddered. The wall lurched wildly back and forth. The light fitting flailed like a metronome. The bed stuttered awkwardly toward the bathroom door. I thought in those first instants that someone in the next room was moving furniture too roughly. Someone who was going to pay dearly for this outrage. I noted the sudden sound of breaking glass. The room kept shaking. A Mormon drunkenly crouched toward me. But since when do Mormons drink? A speaker fell from its stand. *Goldfinger* jumped from its spool and snaked across the room. And then the·very building roared.

And I knew in a flash and with great clarity that I was experiencing an earthquake, and there was no one to blame, I was simply the victim of geology, and I would have to be brave.

The movement died. The room was in disarray. The spools on the projector loudly whirred. Four Mormons were fussing around me.

Don't panic, I said, it's only an earthquake. If you make it through the first jolt you're okay.

Mr. Hughes, no injuries? Everything all right?

I could set the example. I was wonderfully calm. I was a leader again. I was responding to the unexpected.

Then a low growl entered the room, and the walls vibrated. The men spread their legs and arms in alarm. It was greatly amusing to see them out of their depths while I remained horizontal and free of all worry. Good men, good men all of them. All these years we've spent together, it's a shame we've never really gotten to know one another. The humming died away. Then once again the walls began to shudder, and I felt the ticking of doubt. I reached to the bedside table for my little medication box. I held it to my chest. All this took place in less than a minute but it was a very long minute indeed.

In the next twenty minutes there were thirteen aftershocks. The phones were down. There were sirens beginning to cry out all over the city. At first I wanted to stay in the hotel and continue in my role as Fearless Leader. The worst was surely over. But the light outside the window grew more orange, until the whole sky started to glow, and the Mormons told me there were fires spreading across the city. Perhaps indeed we needed to reappraise the situation. It had been a long time since we hadn't had a contingency plan. Earthquake? My good Lord. But clutching the medicine I felt fine, a self-sufficient man, ready to travel at the drop of a hat, speaking of which, where was my fedora? The Mormons would know.

They couldn't find my clothes quickly; by now it had been some time since I'd last been dressed. Finally they outfitted me in a pair of boxer shorts, a bathrobe and sandals. They wrapped me in a woolen blanket and strapped me to a stretcher, just me and my box of medicine. One, two, three, lift! They carried me down the fire escape, down nine flights of stairs. The bends were tight. I tossed in my stretcher as if at sea.

When we burst into the open air I felt scared. We had no protocols to follow. The stench of burning filled my throat. I resisted the urge to retch. Dark-skinned people ran through the night. I craned my neck up from the stretcher. A three-story building a block away seemed to be leaning impossibly over the street. At the instant I focused on its strange architecture, it relaxed, and began to collapse in an extraordinarily leisurely fashion. Bricks spat from it like baseballs. My cordon of men fumbled with the stretcher and the back door of the limousine. Dust billowed outwards from the still-settling rubble of the lately deceased building.

I was extremely anxious by now, being manhandled at improper speeds into the Mercedes. There were many sights and sounds to process. There was a lot of information simply yearning to slow down. I was not at all used to such rapid stampeding of the rhythms of my life. We were in the open and exposed, in a single limousine, in a city without rules or traffic lights, and all the phone lines down. I began to take stock of our situation. I knew I would have no chance finding a vein

in a moving car without proper interior lighting, so I felt
descending upon me a kind of sullen glumness, tinged
with a sharp edge of anxiety.

But then our way was blocked by a freshly abandoned
bus, and I began to pant, and my heart raced greatly.
More dark people rapped on the window, one of
them holding his bloodied broken arm before us. The
Mormons handled the reversing superbly.

Whole blocks were now in flames. We were not
driving anywhere; we were just driving fast, until we
arrived somewhere less devastated. There were more
buildings collapsed. There were bodies in the street. Our
windshield was covered in dust. The windshield wipers
merely smeared it worse.

Sweat ran into my eyes. My head spun. The Mercedes
was nothing but a Very Small Room.

Take me back to the hotel! I screamed, my voice
hoarse. It's this dust that will kill us! Please, take me back!

Sir, we can't go back. We need to head out of the
city. Away from the fires and the buildings.

Then hurry up!

Because all our safety measures had been breached.
There were microbial spores no doubt coming through
the air-conditioning vents. There was calamity all around
us. I could not afford to take a chance with germs.

The wider earth, these powerful forces, were not
to be trusted. I remembered back to that terrible time
in 1968, when the Atomic Energy Commission ran its
underground nuclear tests in the Nevada desert, and

I tried so hard to get them stopped, and even Nixon couldn't, or wouldn't, help. On April 26, 1968, I had cowered under the bed for two hours. I'm sure I even felt the blast. Everybody knows that bacteria and spores are released in underground nuclear tests. On July 10, 1968, yet another underground test, I stayed in the bathroom all day, washing my face and arms with rubbing alcohol and paper towels. That atomic fallout was invisible! Who was to say it was not the same with an earthquake, that rapid realigning of the plates? And who was to say this nightmare in Nicaragua was not the beginning of a war? None of us knew anything. Communications were gone to hell. Even my satellites, circling high above me, meant nothing here. Nobody knew where we were!

A Mormon injected me straight into my shoulder. I was never a great fan of intramuscular as opposed to intravenous injections, but then again December 23, 1972 was not an ordinary night.

We drove for shelter to Ambassador Turner Shelton's house, but once there learned there had been some structural damage. I refused to go inside: think of all that gently cascading plaster. So Shelton organized access for us to go to President Somoza's summer estate in the hills outside of town. I liked being back on the road. It was good to move forward. I was thinking straight again. We sped through the smoke and the ruins to the Somoza villa.

As we reached the foothills the air cleared, the dust thinned. The orange glow pulsed behind our shoulders.

The hills before us were dark and pure. We rose up out of the tectonic pit.

The Somoza estate was a Spanish-style villa that reminded me of Los Angeles in the twenties. I remembered the Vista del Arroyo, when we lay on warm concrete by the pool, my cousin Kitty Calloway and I, and the hummingbird sucked from the stamens and ravaged the jasmine. I had thought back then that it was impossible to become old. Now half a century had passed, and in the hills outside Managua there were fruit bats screeching in the fig trees. I was filled with dread.

Somoza was out of the country; lesser lackeys took care of us. I refused to go into the house. There were too many unknowns. But I did take up their offer and transfer from the Mercedes into the presidential limousine, which was certainly more spacious. A Mormon turned it around and parked it for me at the top of the driveway. Then he left me to sit and gather my composure, the engine purring, the air-conditioning running, with my medicine box by my side. From high up there I watched the city burn as dawn rose to meet my sixty-seventh birthday. I prepared an injection just to celebrate alone, and this time, with slightly calmer hands, I could find a vein at my own pace. My men would tell me later that seven thousand people were dead. Six hundred square blocks of the downtown were leveled. The city was an ash-heap. We had to get out of there. I needed extra Valium and Librium that day, just to keep my adrenaline in check. Soon after dawn we sped back down the hills, back into the swirling smoke, through the outskirts of the city and on to the airport. I was fervently wishing that the future would come: tomorrow, or the next day, somewhere safe. All these years, I thought my punishment was to die, Jack. Perhaps in fact it was to live this long. In Managua I felt sorry for the dark people, with the dust and soot everywhere, and the buildings burning. But if this is what my life had become, it would frankly be better to die.

Or ascend, as the case may be. Our chartered jet took off at 7:00 a.m. We flew to Fort Lauderdale. A lifetime ago I had disappeared there, too, when I was the wandering man on the beach, mad and happy for ninety days with nothing but the seagulls and the dunes. But we were merely refueling, and with the tax issues, in fact, we had to get out of there in a hurry. We were thinking on the run. It was like the glory days again! We would go and live in London for a while.

Then we were temporarily impounded on the tarmac in Florida. Flight clearance was refused. The IRS demanded I disembark. We sat in a stalemate for nine hours while the press gathered in the terminal and negotiations continued. In actual fact there was something of a phone-around. The phones were running hot, if not us. And I remembered Nixonburgers, of course. My men contacted the president's men. Finally the IRS was told to back off. Instead they insisted on a compromise: that an Internal Revenue agent board the plane, to interview me—in person!—to *sight* me, like a document—to verify that I was actually alive.

It was an awful dilemma. I had to be present; my presence was required. Perhaps my hair was a little lank, my beard unkempt. I was very much used to the Mormons. But I did not like strangers.

I took extra medicine to calm my nerves.

I sat in shadow, beneath a blanket at the far back corner of the cabin.

He came on board, a nervous man with a briefcase.

Mr. Howard Robard Hughes?

That's me.

Sir, I'm sorry for the inconvenience.

And so you should be.

Sir, I just need you to sign this document, stating that I've sighted you.

I took the pen and scribbled. No, my fingernails were not as long as everybody said. I knew about nail clippers! I wasn't an animal.

And then we flew to London. And here we are. Isn't life just splendid? I cannot believe it was only six months ago.

The earthquake was a message: get off the earth. Just as a horse bucks a rider from its back. And we came here to this beautiful Inn on the Park. And took the top two floors. I needed only to settle down for a while, get the blood flow back to "galactically slow." And I called Jack to London. I called you here to London, I will say. And I gained my breath. And I found my strength. And I knew that we would talk into the night—because you know I've come to believe, Jack, that communication is everything.

Memo on memos, 1973

A good letter should be immediately understandable...a good letter should be immediately understandable...a good letter should be immediately understandable...a good letter should be immediately understandable.

Think your material over in order to determine its limits... think your material over in order to determine its limits...think your material over in order to determine its limits...think your material over in order to determine its limits.

A dash, or two, shall be used to denote words preceding, or following, a quotation. Two dashes shall be used to denote the deletion of words when a group of words are quoted and one dash shall suffice when only one word is quoted. In either case, there shall be a space between the quotation mark, the dash, or dashes, and the quoted word, or vice versa: i.e.,–and will best assure–.

The word "shall" shall be used throughout instead of "will" in the third person singular and plural, making all sentences in the imperative rather than the indicative.

The infinitive shall not be used to express a major thought, except as an auxiliary to a main verb.

No changes or marks shall be made on the original pencil version.

The numbering system set forth in the notes shall not be a criterion for any future numbering systems.

INN ON THE PARK,
LONDON, JUNE 10, 1973

. . . MORNING . . .

V

My honey must flow off in the great rains,
as all the parts thereto do thereto belong
ha, and we are pitched toward the last love,
the last dream, the last song.
                              —Berryman, *The Dream Songs*

THE DAY AFTER MY return, a million and a half people lined the streets for the ticker-tape parade, from City Hall to Battery Park. The world spilled down upon me in an open limousine, a blizzard of confetti; how happy I felt, how bewildered by the goodwill of others. Standing ten-deep on the sidewalks, the crowd was hysterical with admiration. They leaned out their windows from the high canyon walls of the office buildings. The air was dense with scraps of paper, all gaily fluttering Hughesward. As I waved my fedora at the well-wishers I was remembering only Katharine Hepburn, how I had woken in the night, the night before, when she'd come around to my suite at the Drake Hotel, and I'd watched her smiling and twitching in her sleep. I was thirty-two years old, Jack. My goodness.

That evening after the parade I went to the reception, with Katie on my arm. There were many speeches and I was rather bored and later I would have to do it all again—parades and dinners and speeches—in Washington and Los Angeles, and Houston, of course, where the hometown boy truly made good.

"Coming from Texas," I said at the Houston banquet, "peculiarly fits a person for flying around the world. There's nothing you can see anywhere that you can't see in Texas, and after you've flown across Texas two or three times, the distance around the world doesn't seem so great. We didn't see any mountains on our trip that were any steeper than the mountains of west Texas. We didn't see any plains broader than the plains of central Texas. And we didn't see any swamps that were any wetter than the swamps of Houston."

They laughed at that one.

Then it was all done. I had mastered the planet. I landed in this world of shattered forms, broken shadows, anxious dreams. After all the ticker tape washed down the gutters, I felt the sensation of emptiness. Perhaps, then, it was time to settle down, perhaps that would take away the emptiness. So a week or two after my astonishing feat I proposed to Katharine—would she marry me?

She was silent and said, I will tell you tomorrow. She sighed and said, It is not a question I take lightly. I thought this was the magnificent unfolding of events, the etiquette, the propriety. I looked forward to the dawn.

She was pensive at dinner, though she smiled for the photographers. I tried to cheer her up. I was feeling light. I was feeling the future bear me aloft. I didn't talk about marriage, though. I let her find her way. She attacked her ice-cream sundae as lustily as any other time, and I took this to be a good sign.

We didn't stay together that night. I need to think, she said. I took it as yet another good sign when she blew me a kiss, smiling from the back of the limousine.

In the morning the same limousine picked her up and brought her around to the Drake, where my suite was festooned with flowers, and a simple breakfast of bread rolls and English jam and freshly steaming coffee was spread on a yellow gingham tablecloth.

She walked into the room, ushering in, as always, that joyful energy, and she said, How lovely.

But she sat, and pressed her fingertips together, as if in prayer, as if unable to move forward with the ritual of the sugar and cream lest it put her in some trance from which she might not wake.

She said, Howard.

She pursed her lips, drew in deeply through her nose, and sighed.

No, she said. No.

She said, No, Jack!

Howard, she said. My sweet darling.

I think we've become more friends than lovers, she said.

She could have fooled me. We had made love only the night before last, and I had proposed in the aftermath.

I said nothing. I had been removing my napkin from the silver napkin ring, and suddenly the action seemed suspended as if it would never now be completed, as if I were looking down at an oil painting of a hand and a napkin ring on a yellow tablecloth.

She said, Howard, this is a very difficult decision. But I think we are not really heading in that direction.

She said, Please don't be offended by this, but I think perhaps your mind is elsewhere.

I felt nothing; I felt myself falling, as if through empty space.

I thought, I'll show you what elsewhere means. Elsewhere is every woman lining up.

Then again, perhaps that's what she meant, Jack! But I think she was actually talking about my planes.

She suggested I was not the marrying type. (She must have liked the marrying type, since she stuck by that goddamned cocksucker Spencer Tracy all those years while he refused to divorce his wife.)

We've had a good run of things, she said, but our lives are so widely divergent—I don't know if she said widely or wildly, Jack, to be honest—and it might be good to have a break. Just see where things land in a month or two.

Or a year or two, I said.

She was already fading from my presence as she spoke the words. All that wild abandon, fading. It was as good as gone. I didn't care. Sure, she could be my friend, but I didn't focus on my friends. Why was it always so hard, all this talk? It was simpler just to act. The reason there is Yes and No is that at some point you have to make a decision. Goddamn. Goddamn. There was nowhere to turn. All the things on the inside were a problem, all the thoughts. And all the things on the outside were a problem, too: how to communicate. Or rather, how to bother. Only the medicine has ever made it right.

I was an all-or-nothing kind of person, Jack. I just couldn't stand the thought that someone might not be thinking of me every second of the day.

There were simpler fillies than Hepburn prancing through the fields: all beribboned mane, all sinew and swishing tail, all wide-eyed and tetchy and pawing at the earth. All those goddamned elsewheres. Excuse my language, Jack.

Of course, I didn't realize it at the time. But whatever it was that I needed so badly, it was clearly not there in the arms of the women. Yessiree. But that's called retrospective wisdom, as we all know. I saw her to the door. We briefly hugged. I was rejected, Jack. It is as simple as that. I thought I could have whatever I wanted. Kate came along and thought otherwise. Well, it's another ten minutes of my life accounted for; that's a good way of looking at it, yes?

Nevertheless, it was hard to shake my sense of disorientation. I had circumnavigated the globe, sustained by the anticipation of reunion. *She* wasn't supposed to be going anywhere! It was physically unpleasant, the shock of it. It began as a burning sensation between my shoulderblades. I had thought she would say Yes, but what she said wrenched me in the opposite direction. There was no warning. Just the sense that I had blinked, and opened my eyes to an entirely foreign world.

When I closed the door I turned around and sat down on the bed. I was never one for wailing. The room, of course, had suddenly become strange: not unfriendly, but of an alien disposition. The walls shimmered with otherness. At first I felt very alone, but after a while I felt neutral, and then numb. Then I gazed for a long time at dust motes suspended in a shaft of sunlight, and a great peace descended, which is different, surely, from numbness, if I am remembering it correctly. Then I cried.

I will have to tell you, more than almost anything, about how nothing ever happens in the way we like to dream it will.

NO MORE SLEEPS

I FLEW AROUND THE world, once. And I'm going to fly again: today, if I'm not very much mistaken! Today we go off into the sky together. But we must be vigilant. Outside, they will be everywhere: too many people, too many viruses, and the press, waiting in ambush.

A limousine will leave first. Behind its tinted windows will sit a skinny old man, of indistinct features, hired for the occasion. He has been instructed to sink into his scarf and slant the fedora hat down over his face. The press will follow the limousine on a tour of London.

I will then leave with you, Jack, and a couple of the Mormons in a nondescript car. We will drive to Fenwick Airfield. To the Hawker.

All this...migration into newness: I'm beside myself, I can't think straight. It's been so many years. The Mormons are merely men of the earth. They don't understand a single thing. But Jack Real is a prince.

And I'm a god, I'm the God of Air.

In Texas as a boy I had known solitude in the woods with my tin toys. Then I grew into that god. Airplanes allowed me to take my solitude into the air, into space. At night I tried to masturbate, but often could not focus on the image that would make me come. This was in the cockpit, mind you!

I'm talking not just of the rush of the wind, but of speed itself. I've flown in open biplanes; I've flown in the H-1, a simple streak of steel. In twenty-seven years the new century will begin, the blink of an eye. But I'm talking of something entirely different.

Twenty-seven years back in the other direction, in 1946, in the XF-11, lazily smashing through trees in the streets of Beverly Hills, I was struck by the unreality of that view unfolding. When the windshield shatters you realize how fast you are going. Then I caught fire.

Then, with the medicine, I became eternally renewed, I am my own garden, the sun bears down, a single leaf divides the false and true, such fineness is at work in the world, I am blossoming, I am branching. I understood everything when I understood that the reason there is Something rather than Nothing is that Nothing is unstable. Despite all the zeroes to which all things gravitate.

On the ground I'm a little disorganized and my thoughts tend to wander. But in the plane I'll be a plane.

Jack, I was the greatest aviator the world had ever known. This is going to work. I am going to fly. God knows I may even stick to that regime, taper off the drugs, starting tomorrow, and fly as regularly as I please. As far as I want. I've made three thousand four hundred and seventy-three flights in my life so far. In the first five months of 1943 alone I took off and landed the Sikorsky amphibian two hundred and thirty-one times on Lake Mead, though the last one was not so good, what with death and destruction and drowning all around me, and Dick Felt dead and Ceco Cline sliced up and drowned.

But overall, my ratio of successes to disasters is exemplary.

I am getting a little worked up. I feel like a child, but in a good way. I need the medicine box one more time before we get this thing begun. Let's call it cocktail time: the Ritalin will blend with the Valium (anxiety) and Empirin (pain) to create just the right level of alertness for the flight. This is not to detract in any way from the new Cary Grant reduction plan, which is imminent. This is merely to deal with what needs to be dealt with today. So I open the box. And, because it's a Very Special Day, I treat myself to a Brand New Syringe.

Where was I? That's better. I'm going to fly, again. I'm so clean even the atoms can't get hold of me.

I was telling you the secret of the memos, Jack. But I have another secret now. I'm writing less and less of them these days. I have a feeling they may not be so important after all. In the grand scheme, if you know what I mean. I'm beginning to relax.

Where was I? That's better. That's really something. I feel I've got the balances just right. I imagined somewhere perfect. I imagined a place I had once been, before this atmosphere blew in on the winds, before this oppression descended on the earth like a fog. I imagined the clarity of a garden, one bright morning. My breathing was very steady. Money had not been invented. I mean, acquisition, hunger. The frogs dropped softly on the lily pads. My breathing was very steady.

I *remembered* this place, Jack. I was sure I had been there once.

I was dreaming I was watching television. Perhaps I injected some Empirin or morphine. I can live on oxygen alone. I was remembering somewhere perfect, where the frogs dropped softly on the lily pads, where my breathing was steady and crisp. In that place I was very happy. Where was I now? I was getting the sequences in order. At last I have remembered everything.

* * *

WHEN I WAS A boy there was only life, and all the air thick with butterflies. *Life!* The maid was in the kitchen. I could smell the cookies baking. It was summer in Texas. I was everything there was.

The bottom rung of the oil derrick was a monkey bar. I hung from my legs with Dudley Sharp while our fathers stood talking with the surveyors. Our arms dangled, tingling. The ground rocked back and forth. The horizon swayed in the distance, upside down.

Once upon a time I gallivanted with William Randolph Hearst, Jr. and the starlets who jostled and clustered. His father kept a zoo at the ranch at San Simeon. It was like the beginning of the world. On crisp Californian nights when the fog rolled in from the sea and Jean Harlow abandoned herself to pleasure, or to mine at least, our lovemaking was punctuated by the roaring of lions.

I flew into the dawn with Katharine Hepburn, to New York, great city of the century. From far off it rose like a castle on the plain, its impregnable towers in grand silhouette; it is still there today, growing larger and lovelier.

I walked arm in arm with Jane Greer along Ocean Park. She held my hand. We rode the fairground rides. I pitched the baseball. My face was smeared with candy floss. She laughed at me and dabbed my cheek. And kissed me somewhat tenderly.

Twenty-seven years ago, lazily smashing through trees in the streets of Beverly Hills, I caught fire. Then I knew I was through with the other humans for a while. To pass through those last seconds before impact in such elongated terror. Who would not be unhinged? I've seen the streets of Hollywood in ways unique to me alone. Finally I felt still and serene as trees, telegraph poles, houses, roads, stood up one after the other to smack me in the nose.

It all seems so silly now, Jack. I had trouble with bucking joysticks, on occasion. Let's just put it that way. And the ground rose up to greet me. Hello, Howard. *Smack!*

And that is how I met the medication.

In the stillness after that plane crash I knew already it was creeping toward me, the irrationality, the intolerance, the endless migraines, the memory lapses, the constipation bouts, the enemas, the rotting teeth, the abscesses. I sat on the toilet for hours at a time, decades perhaps. Everything is an obstacle to freedom.

For a long time I have been everywhere and nowhere, yesterday and tomorrow, since all points of reference to day and night, up and down, have been done away with, in all these hotel rooms, for all these years. But in the Hawker Siddeley I will fight my way through space itself. For a long time I have locked into narrow rooms my lifelong hopes. But now it is time to set them free. For a long time I have been a fragment of what was once a fullness. Today I will become complete again.

There are many events gestating in the womb of time and one by one they will all be delivered, I have heard. I am waking from my long intoxication.

I will fly at last. I will unfold my wings. I will unpack my head. I will step back outside. One day I may even make love again. But one thing at a time. Let's not get ahead of ourselves.

Everything moves closer. I'm ready. I'm ready.

It's 7:19 a.m. You'll be up soon, Jack, which is a good thing, obviously, because things won't stay balanced forever. I'm all ready. I'm all fine-tuned. The light streams through me. Any second now I'm going to get up, without any Mormon help. I won't be lying down when you come in. Any second now, I'll walk across the room with stately grace, delighting in the strangeness of being vertical. I'll very carefully peel away some of the masking tape that holds in place the heavy curtains blocking the windows. I'll peek through the slit I have made. Perhaps a red double-decker bus will be trundling slowly by on the street below! Perhaps there'll be a Sunday morning sparseness to the traffic down there. I'll stand and look out upon the flow, at the vast city spreading away, at the light hardening, and I'll think about how this also has been one of the dark places of the earth.

Then I'm going to take a shower—a shower, Jack!—because this is a special occasion. I'll emerge smelling of soap, dressed in a linen suit, with my hair Brylcreemed back.

You'll say, You look like Fred Astaire.

And here I am indeed, I'll say, bowing low.

We'll sit like young dandies at the breakfast table, at which a silver tea service will have been laid out on a damask tablecloth. You'll pour the coffee, Jack. I will eat a slice of toast and marmalade and sip from a glass of orange juice.

And then we'll speak! But will you be talking, too, Jack? I can't remember exactly how this works. I'm sure it will come back to me.

I'll say: Hughes Electronics leads the way in avionics!

You'll say: Lockheed, the leader in speed!

It is a long time since I've chuckled.

It's 9:33 a.m. One of the Mormons has informed me that you are finally awake—that you'll be up here within the half-hour. So this is it! It is time to branch out, or else what would I say to myself: that in the end I did nothing? It's time to act. It's time, in fact, to think that thought is not the thing. It's just me and the medicine here, and soon, my dear friend Jack Real. The end of a long night or the beginning of a new day, depending on one's perspective.

I'm all ready. I'm all finetuned. The light streams through me. Enough of this rehearsal. I need to switch my head off. All right then, I'm turning the TV on, to pass the time till you're showered and dressed. I'm watching *Open University–Electromagnetics and Electronics*. It is either that or *Service from Park Avenue Methodist Church, Northampton*. Lord, the junk they put on. If I thought I was staying long enough I would certainly think about buying a TV station here. It is as if the British don't take television seriously! Ah, but I'm in no mood to get upset about it. Besides, I've always had a fascination with electronics. *Open University* it is, then.

My attention span seems to have lessened these days. I watch scenes rather than entire movies, segments rather than entire programs. But everything is more like a poem that way. Electromagnetically speaking.

I've got the balances just right. Therefore we should go soon. While the going is good.

I've been waiting such a very long time. No more sleeps!

How extraordinary, I must have nodded off for a few minutes. But I have not been forgotten. I wake up with Jack Real at my side! The Mormons are all a-dither.

As for me, I'm croaky rather than cranky. In fact, I'm almost happy. In the end, we are both too excited to eat. But Jack is my best friend, now: what need do we have for words? The showering, the getting dressed, these things I have fretted about all week—as it turns out, they are done in an instant.

There is no more planning. It is upon us. Everything is moving to a point. At any place on the surface of the globe, we are always rolling east.

The Mormons are in scurry mode. Their walkie-talkies crackle. I drink a glass of water.

Time, gentlemen. Jack takes my arm in his. I feel dashing and elegant in my linen suit. We walk slowly out of the room, followed by Mormons. They radio down for the decoy team to leave. In the basement we clamber into the second Daimler. I lay my head in Jack's lap. A Mormon covers me with a blanket. Jack's strong hand rests calmly on my shoulder. We drive out into the day.

I am comfortable. And the Valium has definitely helped. You need it for field excursions. I've got all the balances just right.

What I've been trying to say is: today is the day. I am going to fly. There are no more tomorrows to think about. It's the only life I've got. Ah, my lovemaking was punctuated by the roaring of lions.

After a while the Mormon says, It's okay, sir, you can sit up now.

My head reels with the glory and strangeness of London. There is so much activity. There are so many people, merely leading their lives! The sun shines down on the factories and the pubs. We move into the countryside. The green fields glow. The farmer drives the tractor. How will I ever forget how lovely this is? We cross a stone bridge. The butterflies hover. I am not afraid of germs anymore. It is only pollen, it is only pollen, it is nothing that can hurt me. Though we'll keep the windows up.

Jack Real points out the hangars in the distance: Fenwick Airfield.

What I wanted to say was this. That the world's magnificence has been enriched by a new beauty: the beauty of speed.

I suppose I should have been more like other men. I was not nearly as interested in people as I might have been. I'm leaving you a rather melancholy picture, but in the depths of my heart I'm happy. I have spoken frankly. Forgive me.

We pull up on the tarmac. They help me from the car and up the steps. I am sitting in the cockpit. A kind of terror, suffused with a delicious sinking feeling. The engines throb into life. My balls vibrate. I am approaching zero knowledge. The control panel is merely another part of me. Then I take off all my clothes. The pilot, I mean the co-pilot, tries not to look surprised. In a cockpit one is naked before God.

POSTSCRIPT

O N JUNE 10, 1973, a naked Howard Hughes sat behind the controls of a plane in flight for the first time in more than thirteen years. Jack Real accompanied him on the flight. Hughes flew all afternoon, and three more times over the next month.

On August 9, at the Inn on the Park, Hughes fell in the bathroom and broke his hip. Doctors inserted a steel pin at The London Clinic.

He never left his bed again without being carried. It was the beginning of the final decline. In December, Hughes and his entourage left London for the Bahamas—a tax-avoidance move—on a jet borrowed from the arms dealer Adnan Khashoggi. By early '74 he was no longer paying serious attention to his business concerns and memos. He watched movies over and over, or stared at the ceiling, rambling incoherently. Two years passed.

By early '76, for tax reasons yet again, the entourage had moved to Acapulco. By April, Hughes could no longer even inject himself. By April 4, he had lapsed into a coma.

Howard Hughes died on April 5, 1976, at 1:27 p.m., in an oxygen tent in a pressurized airplane cabin, eleven thousand feet over Texas and twenty minutes out from Houston, his birthplace, where a team was waiting to treat him at the Methodist Hospital.

Howard Hughes autopsy X-ray, Houston Methodist Hospital, April 6, 1976. The thin sharp lines in the biceps area are broken-off hypodermic needles.

(Copyright © Wide World Photos, New York.)

SOME BIOGRAPHICAL DETAILS

—Howard Robard Hughes born December 24, 1905, Houston, Texas.

—1908, Howard Hughes' father patents the drill bit that will be the source of the Hughes' money.

—Summer 1916 and 1917, Howard sent to summer camp at Camp Teedyuskung in the Pocono Mountains in northeast Pennsylvania; the second time with childhood friend Dudley C. Sharp.

—1919, attends South End Junior High in Houston, for less than a year.

—1920, attends the Fessenden School in West Newton, Massachusetts.

—1920, flies for the first time, in a Curtiss Seaplane, over New London, Connecticut.

—1921, attends the Thacher School in Ojai, California.

—March 1922, mother dies suddenly, aged thirty-nine.

—September 1922, returns to Thacher but pulls out before Christmas, lured to Los Angeles by his lonely father.

—January 1924, father dies suddenly.

—May 1924, Hughes buys out relatives and gains one hundred percent control of Hughes Tool Company.

—June 1925, Hughes marries Ella Rice in Houston.

—October 1925, leaves Houston to live in Los Angeles.

—November 1925, hires Noah Dietrich as accountant
and financial adviser.

—October 1927, shooting commences on *Hell's Angels*,
Hughes' first film.

—January 1928, first plane crash, while shooting *Hell's Angels*.

—March 1929, Ella walks out of marriage. Hughes
seeing Billie Dove. May 30, Hughes and Ella divorce.

—1932, founds Hughes Aircraft.

—September 1935, sets new land speed record in
H-1 prototype. Runs out of fuel on seventh pass and
crashes (very minor).

—January 14, 1936, sets transcontinental speed
record, flying from Los Angeles to Newark in nine
hours and twenty-seven minutes.

—November 15, 1936, Hughes has his third (minor)
crash when caught in a tailwind while attempting to
land a seaplane at North Beach Airport on Long Island.

—August 1937, Katharine Hepburn moves into
Hughes' Muirfield mansion.

—July 10–14, 1938, sets round-the-world record in
Lockheed Cyclone.

—May 1939, first acquires stock in Transcontinental and
Western Airlines, later Trans World Airlines (TWA).

—1940, shoots *The Outlaw* with Jane Russell.

—1942, enters flying boat contract to aid war effort. Hughes calls the plane the *Hercules*; the press dub it the *Spruce Goose*.

—May 1943, Hughes has his fourth crash, on Lake Mead, Nevada, during a test-flight of the Sikorsky S-43, leaving two dead, and Hughes and two others injured.

—Late 1944, Hughes suffers his first nervous breakdown.

—July 7, 1946, Hughes crashes for the fifth time, in suburban Beverly Hills, during a solo test-flight of the XF-11. Hughes suffers catastrophic injuries, marking the beginning of his painkiller addiction.

—August 1947, Hughes testifies before the Senate War Investigating Committee about irregularities in Hughes Aircraft WWII defense contract work.

—November 1947, flies the *Hercules* at Long Beach, its one and only flight.

—May 1948, acquires RKO Pictures.

—Early 1950s, Hughes suffers a second nervous breakdown. Germ phobia, obsessive-compulsive disorder and ongoing drug use by now becoming a permanent factor in his life.

—1956, orders first jets for TWA: thirty-three Boeing 707s.

—December 1956, Hughes Tool Company loans two hundred and fifty thousand dollars to Donald Nixon, Vice-President Richard Nixon's brother.

—January 1957, Hughes marries Jean Peters, an actress, but doesn't move in with her.

—May 1957, Hughes fires Noah Dietrich after a thirty-two-year partnership.

—Late 1950s, ex-FBI man Bob Maheu comes into the Hughes organization as Hughes' public face of action. Though they never meet in person, Maheu will be Hughes' right-hand man for more than a decade.

—December 1960, loses control of TWA; moves in briefly with Jean Peters.

—1961, TWA files antitrust complaint against Hughes.

—1963, Hughes loses TWA judgment.

—1966, sells his TWA stock for five hundred and forty-six million.

—November 1966, arrives in Las Vegas, and holes up for four years on the top two floors of the Desert Inn.

—November 1970, flees Las Vegas for the Bahamas, beginning the exodus of tax dodging that will last until the end.

—December 1970, Hughes fires Bob Maheu.

—June 1971, Hughes and Jean Peters officially divorced.

—December 1972, flees earthquake in Managua, Nicaragua.

—June 10, 1973, flies for the first time in more than fifteen years, in London.

—August 9, 1973, Hughes breaks hip; never walks again.

—Howard Hughes dies, April 5, 1976.

ACKNOWLEDGMENTS

WHILE THIS IS A work of fiction, I have used the actual events of Hughes' life as a framework. There are many, many books about Hughes; I have mined information from, and am grateful to, biographies by Donald L. Barlett & James B. Steele (*Empire: The Life, Legend and Madness of Howard Hughes*), Peter Harry Brown & Pat H. Broeske (*Howard Hughes: His Life and Madness*), Michael Drosnin (*Citizen Hughes*), Albert Benjamin Gerber (*Bashful Billionaire: The Story of Howard Hughes*), Richard Hack (*Hughes: The Private Diaries, Memos and Letters; The Definitive Biography of the First American Billionaire*), Charles Higham (*Howard Hughes: The Secret Life*), and James Phelan (*Howard Hughes: The Hidden Years*). The memo extracts in this book are largely verbatim transcripts of actual Hughes memos, as quoted in the various biographies.

With thanks to Alice Truax: a fine editor.